PENGUIN BOOKS

Seducing Ingrid Bergman

Chris Greenhalgh is the prize-winning author of three volumes of poetry and a novel. He wrote the screenplay for *Coco Chanel & Igor Stravinsky*, which occupied the prestigious closing slot at the 2009 Cannes Film Festival. He lives with his wife and two sons in Sevenoaks.

www.chris-greenhalgh.com

D0469756

Seducing Ingrid Bergman

CHRIS GREENHALGH

PENGUIN BOOKS

PENGUIN BOOKS

Published by the Penguin Group
Penguin Books Ltd, 80 Strand, London WC2R ORL, England
Penguin Group (USA) Inc., 375 Hudson Street, New York, New York 10014, USA
Penguin Group (Canada), 90 Eglinton Avenue East, Suite 700, Toronto, Ontario, Canada M4P 2Y3
(a division of Pearson Penguin Canada Inc.)
Penguin Ireland, 25 St Stephen's Green, Dublin 2, Ireland (a division of Penguin Books Ltd)
Penguin Group (Australia), 707 Collins Street, Melbourne, Victoria 3008, Australia
(a division of Pearson Australia Group Pty Ltd)
Penguin Books India Pvt Ltd, 11 Community Centre,
Panchsheel Park, New Delhi – 110 017, India
Penguin Group (NZ), 67 Apollo Drive, Rosedale, Auckland 0632, New Zealand
(a division of Pearson New Zealand Ltd)
Penguin Books (South Africa) (Pty) Ltd, Block D, Rosebank Office Park,
181 Jan Smuts Avenue, Parktown North, Gauteng 2193, South Africa

Penguin Books Ltd, Registered Offices: 80 Strand, London WC2R ORL, England

www.penguin.com

First published 2012
003

Set in 12/14.75 pt Dante MT Std
Typeset by Jouve (UK), Milton Keynes
Printed in Great Britain by Clays Ltd, St Ives plc

A CIP catalogue record for this book is available from the British Library

ISBN: 978-0-670-92211-6

www.greenpenguin.co.uk

Penguin Books is committed to a sustainable
future for our business, our readers and our planet.
This book is made from Forest Stewardship
Council™ certified paper.

ALWAYS LEARNING   **PEARSON**

For Ruth, Saul and Ethan

Not without reason (for he had a fierce gypsy
charm as well as the scent of danger), she fell madly in love
with Capa. And he was the real thing.

David Thomson, *Ingrid Bergman*

I

A moment of trust. The green light flashes. There's no time to think, and I don't need to jump – the blast from the propellers just sucks me out of the hatch. Straightaway I'm falling with a splayed flailing of arms and legs, the roar of the transport lost in the swirling clouds above me.

I have a shovel in my backpack, a camera strapped to each of my legs and a flask in my breast pocket. Buffeted by cross-winds, my jacket puffs up. My cheeks feel as if they've been slapped and my hands smart from the cold. The air feels squeezed out of my lungs.

I'm hurled upside down, tumbled like a bird in a storm. My bowels turn watery. The contents of my stomach slide into my mouth – a nauseous mixture of coffee and whisky and scrambled eggs. My eyes prickle with tears. I manage to right myself. I count one thousand, two thousand, three thousand, and pull the cord. The parachute shuffles out of its pack and unfurls in an instant, blossoming into a silken basilica over my head. The plummeting sensation ends, and I'm conscious of a sudden weightlessness, swaying, my hands fastened to the straps.

A bent-winged gull hangs motionless, not caring that this is Germany or that we have crossed the Rhine. And for an instant it seems as if I'm not falling at all. Instead, I feel buoyed up, held steady by forces unseen. Purged of fear and boosted by a new energy, I seem – yes – I seem to be flying, flung upwards like a dove.

The ground spreads out like a map below: rectangles of newly ploughed land neatly organized in furrows, a few farmhouses and outbuildings, the fuzzy stuff of trees. I unstrap my Contax and take a few shots. No time for tricks, I just keep clicking. All around me, the men of the 17th Airborne Division twirl like sycamore seeds, their heads rubbing up against the webbing of their helmets and their last letters home. I feel a few drops of what I presume must be rain. But it's not rain. Vapour condenses on the canopy and drips down onto my bare hands and face. The sensation is cold, my fingers numb. I'm careful not to let any moisture smear the lens.

Within seconds, everything changes. Bullets zing like hornets past my head. One punches a hole in my chute. I hear the snap of it against the fabric. I press my helmet down towards my chest, try to make myself small. I keep the Contax close to my face, still clicking. A chill spreads damply across my back.

It seems to take an age to reach the ground, though in reality it must be less than a minute. I think about a lot of things in quick succession – about the women I have loved and lost, about my mother having escaped the Fascists in Budapest, and about the fact that I am desperate to pee.

The paratroopers glide in slow diagonals. Most seem fine, but one is not so lucky. I can see from the trajectory that he's headed straight for the powerlines. He must see it, too, as he drifts with dreamlike slowness, unable to change tack, prey to the direction of the wind. I want to shout out but there's no way he can hear me, and nothing he can do. His body looks tiny. His legs wriggle in an attempt to veer off course, his arms yank at the straps, and at the last his mouth opens in a soundless cry as if this might lift him the extra few inches he needs to clear the wires. There's a terrible inevitability about his path. He slides right into the dark lines, his parachute crumpling over the wires. He writhes frantically for several seconds, but strung like a puppet he proves an easy kill for the machine gunners. And he's not the only one. Several others swing, stricken, fifty feet up in the leafless trees, their bodies dangling from their canopies, shrivelled pieces of fruit.

Is there a lonelier way to die?

Before I know it, the landscape enlarges, and there's a high whistling noise. The wind stirs the tops of the trees. The ground seems to leap towards me. I realize that the small dark spot that has been bobbing about beneath me is my shadow and I rush towards it. I remember to keep my legs together. The harness bites into the top of my thighs. I hold on tight to the Contax and slam down into the earth. I feel the thud inside my lungs. Ngh.

I lie face down for several seconds, checking myself for injuries, registering a remote ache in my ankle, a jarring pain in my knee. I must have fallen awkwardly, but nothing is broken.

The earth is hard despite the thaw. A few scraps of ice still lie in patches, exposing the colour of my fatigues. I get up, my legs wobbly, and roll up the chute like a skin sloughed off. Immediately I look for cover. To my left lies open country. The nearest building, with snipers inside, is five hundred yards ahead. A stand of birches is about half that distance to my right. I suck air into my lungs and run – a zigzagging path, my shovel waggling in my knapsack, the camera banging against my chest.

I choose the thickest trunk I can find, check the focus on my Contax, crouch down and listen. The sound of rifle fire, flattened by the landscape, ricochets off the trees, so that at first I'm looking in the wrong direction. Dozens of crows explode upwards. Rounds of shelling shake the earth beneath my feet.

The light is ghostly between dark branches as I frame the shot, the sky thick with transport planes and parachutes still gliding like giant spores to the ground. My fingers are freezing, but my legs and back are slick with sweat. I'm thirsty, my throat parched, and now I feel really desperate to pee – partly from the cold, but also a sense of fear. My knee still hurts. A taste of metal enters my mouth, making me swallow.

Dead cattle and horses lie frozen in odd postures across the fields. The stench touches my nostrils, adds to the feeling of nausea. The sun is unlocatable behind the clouds. I finish one film, seal it in a canister, clip another one in, wind it on, snap the back of the camera shut, and start clicking again.

3

The resistance is fierce but limited, confined to half a dozen farm buildings and an outhouse. The artillery does its job. The buildings burn. The first prisoners are smoked out, hands on heads, the barns mostly destroyed. The inner walls are exposed so that it's hard to believe there were people in there just a few minutes ago, and odd to see how small a space the rooms once occupied. The farmers are the last to flee – an old man with expressionless eyes, his headscarved wife rescuing what possessions she can, and their grandchildren, a boy and a girl, too paralysed with fear to cry.

By 11 a.m. I have several rolls of film, including shots of para-chutes slung over wires like stockings over a bedpost, medics tending to the wounded, and a transport plane bulking large and coming in low over the trees. I write *March 1945* on the canister. A good morning's work. Time for a cigarette and a hit of whisky from the flask.

And only now does it seem safe to pee. I dream of trees in leaf, fields ripe with wheat, an eight-page spread in *Life*, my pictures showing the world what happened here near Wesel. As the beatific vision continues, I imagine myself in the arms of a good woman, who strokes my hair and covers my face with lipsticked kisses, making everything all right.

The reverie doesn't last long. The tree I relieve myself against has only just started to darken when I see the sign: ACHTUNG! MINEN!

I spend the next four hours until the disposal team arrives standing motionless, smoking cigarettes, checking the focus on my cameras, doing my best to look unconcerned.

⌇

She almost ceases breathing, pulls her stomach muscles in, resists the impulse to fiddle with an earring. But she can't stop her mind racing or ignore the itch inside her, the little kick of ambition that drives her on.

Does she think she'll win? She can't think that far ahead. Does she deserve to? That's a different question.

She tries to slow down the pounding of her heart, works to control her breathing. Everything around her grows quiet. She hears the nominations read out by last year's winner, Jennifer Jones – her own, followed by Claudette Colbert, Bette Davis, Greer Garson, Barbara Stanwyck – each name announced with the same crisp excitement that holds out the promise of brilliant things. Like snow, she thinks.

There's a silence. An envelope is opened, its rustle amplified by the microphone that stands like a sunflower in the middle of the stage.

She holds her husband's hand to the left and feels the tightening grip of her producer, David Selznick, to the right. The room pitches. She finds it difficult in this instant to make connections between things.

When the four Scandinavian-sounding syllables of her name are announced, they seem remote, oddly foreign, unrecognizable. Applause fills the auditorium at Grauman's Chinese Theatre, quickening around her.

'That's you,' Selznick says. 'You've won. You've won!'

'Go get it,' Petter says.

Ingrid stands and the seat tips behind her. Everything is confusion: the sudden tumult of the music, the fan of lights, the fierce clapping and chasing spotlights.

She presses her neck forward, her senses alert, her eyes alive to the male attention that swims around her. It is harder than she imagines to walk in a straight line. Caught in a current of affection, she feels tugged along, her insides filling with warmth. The sensation enlarges. Her hands grow clammy and, as if she's had a glass of wine already, she feels the redness creep into her cheeks.

Photographers jostle and flashbulbs explode, capturing the evening in bright slices. Hatless, simply dressed, with a long beaded necklace that hangs down to her waist, in flat shoes and wearing minimal make-up, her effort at restrained elegance feels inadequate set next to the dinky hats and spotted veils of her fellow nominees. For a moment, she feels horribly exposed.

Unknown in Hollywood just six years ago and speaking with an accent that was mistaken for German as the war began, Ingrid still feels an outsider. But she got lucky with *Casablanca*, made her mark in *For Whom the Bell Tolls*, and here she is lauded for her performance in *Gaslight*, with *Saratoga Trunk* and *Spellbound* about to open in theatres across America, and shooting *The Bells of St Mary's* for a Christmas release.

Later she will regret that the evening went so quickly, that the moment like a dream was over so fast. Later she will feel cheated by the experience, and long to relive it. But in this instant, she almost runs onto the stage.

She remembers thinking it important to keep her head still. After that, everything is a blur. She remembers taking a breath to steady herself. If she remembers hovering over the microphone, it is only because of the lights splintering into a million filaments. If she recalls being conscious of the audience, their faces grey beyond the glare, it is only because of the collective hush.

'I'd like to thank the Academy for honouring me with this award.'

The microphone picks up a slight tremor in her voice, but the note is huskily feminine, not girlish, and noticeably lower than that of Jennifer Jones.

Her fingers play with the statuette, her palms mottled, her hands surprised by how heavy it is. She feels the tug of it like a gravitational force, clings to it, enjoying the sense of possession.

How she wishes her parents were alive to witness this. Or her Aunt Mutti. Someone. She thinks of Pia, her six-year-old, at home in bed, asleep. Will she understand what this means? Of course not. She's probably dreaming about riding her bike, the wobbly first attempts just yesterday, leaving her mother running to keep up, hands outstretched to prevent her falling. She feels a need to reach out and grasp her now.

As a young girl herself, Ingrid cultivated the shy habit of

glancing upwards through her long and perfectly spaced lashes and shooting a stare from under her fringe. It is the same look she offers now as the lights spear into her eyes.

Naturally she feels nervous, her heart racing, the words trying to line up and stand to attention inside her mouth. But she feels wonderful, too, and this slides into a sensation of calm that extends slowly to her legs, her head, the words that she says and that she hears herself utter as they are hurled by the sound system beyond her over many hundreds of raked seats.

Her face is lit, her eyes grow watery. She thinks she might cry, but she doesn't, not properly. This is what she's worked for, prepared for all her life, and she's not going to spoil it. The quivering that she experiences within her subsides.

'I'll do my best in the future to be worthy of it,' she says.

Applause, deep and appreciative this time, reverberates around the theatre in a series of overlapping waves as she moves with grace and without visible hurry from the stage, escorted by Jennifer Jones.

From the wings she watches Bing Crosby josh with Gary Cooper, the pair of them clowning together on stage, enjoying that male camaraderie and wisecracking energy she loves to be a part of on the set.

Afterwards, at the party hosted by David Selznick, when Ingrid returns to her husband's side, she notices how quiet and reserved he is. Perhaps he's having trouble absorbing the enormity of what has happened. He tries to look pleased but, she observes, something tugs at the corners of his mouth. It's obvious that he finds the adulation distasteful. He must resent the way everyone wants to talk to her, the fawning attention of the press, the way he is left alone at the table, working a toothpick at a stubborn bit of meat between his teeth.

She realizes he hasn't enjoyed a moment alone with her since she received the award. When eventually he manages to get near her, it is to urge her to leave early. He smiles stiffly and touches her hand just once as if in consolation for some great sorrow.

Later she won't remember agreeing or making excuses, but she does recall being driven home just minutes after midnight, Petter stone-faced and silent next to her, their legs not touching in the back of the car.

'Aren't you pleased?'

'It's nothing less than I expected.'

A sourness revolves in her stomach. 'You really thought I'd win?'

'They'd have me to contend with if you didn't.'

'You don't seem happy.'

She watches the tree-lined boulevards float by, with their manicured lawns and hacienda-style houses. North Fairfax Avenue dissolves into Sunset, which melts into West Sunset. She notices how the reflections swarm, shaky as a back projection pouring across the windows of the car.

'You understand what this means?'

The vibrations of the engine mingle with the smell of petrol to make her feel queasy. The fragrance Petter wears next to her becomes a part of that. 'What does it mean?'

He smiles, kisses her on the cheek. 'Nothing.'

The car pulls into Benedict Canyon. She realizes she's hungry. She's always hungry. It hits her now like a light switched on inside her head. They left before the dessert was served, before the dancing began. And though she knows she shouldn't, sitting here with the gold statuette in her fingers and her name on everyone's lips, with the city lit and flickering like a train outside, she feels more than a little flat.

2

I've learnt to sleep anywhere.

Tonight, though, it'll be a hotel room in Paris, with a bathtub, a bottle of Scotch and a buzzer for room service right by the bed.

In the streets on this May day, the sound of cheering mingles with the peal of church bells, the honk of klaxons and the smell of freedom released like a gas. Thousands of people wave home-made tricolours and brandish American flags with too many stripes or too few stars. The air-raid sirens sound a final all-clear.

Irwin directs two men with moving picture cameras from the Signal Corps. The cameras putter like small outboard motors and hum above the celebrating crowd. But the jeep jerks around so much and brakes so abruptly, it's a struggle to keep the lenses steady.

I sit braced in the corner as the jeep slews around, my Rollei-flex and Contax primed. In case one of the cameras jams, I alternate shots. And I'm snapping away like crazy.

All the young men want suddenly to shake our hands. Several have climbed trees and shinned up lampposts, clinging on with one arm and raising a free hand in salute. Women print our cheeks with kisses, fill our arms with flowers. Children are hoisted on their fathers' shoulders, lifted from the crowd to see. A nun wearing sunglasses waves her handkerchief. Two gen-darmes, caps tilted back, join in the revelry rather than attempting to keep the peace. Local mademoiselles, in floating skirts and light print dresses, belt out the Marseillaise.

The women look pretty, the way only French women can – that original girlishness, that poise and elegance, as if femininity were invented here, along with perfume, good cooking and saucy lingerie.

One girl, with sun-browned legs and hair piled up high above her forehead, rides a bicycle and tries to keep pace with the jeep. Her skirt, shaped like a lampshade, lifts as she pedals to reveal a rhythmical glimpse of voluptuous pink thigh. She knows this and smiles, holding her skirt with one hand to stop it billowing completely. She seems to enjoy the feeling of us looking and the sensation of wind on her skin.

I manage to get off several rolls of film, just taking what's there. People are crying, they're so happy. The whole population of Paris seems to press into the streets, spilling out so that they fill every space available, perching on ledges, massing on balconies, one boy poised atop a statue like a Cupid on a cake. A group of old men cluster round a board, reading of the German surrender, needing to witness it in print to be convinced that the war in Europe is finally over.

And it really is. I think about what that means for me. At last I'll be able to brush my teeth instead of using my finger. I'll be able to shave using a mirror rather than just by touch. It means I can pay some kid to polish my boots again. It means fresh bread and cheese instead of C-rations. Oranges, maybe. Soap and shampoo. A fresh change of underclothes. Whisky in a glass instead of a tooth mug. The freedom to come and go whenever I please and talk to whoever I want – and no one shooting at me when I raise my camera.

I don't go in for crazy angles or anything. Nothing fancy. I just concentrate on getting close enough to see the expression on people's faces, fix them in the viewfinder, then click. All it takes is a certain sensitivity to the moment and a steady pair of hands, a quick eye and a willingness to push yourself forward. With a camera you can't help but have a point of view.

Wine cellars bricked up during the war are re-opened. It's like opening the tombs of the pharaohs. The rich odour of casks and the stored perfumes of Burgundy leak from windows, inundate the streets, thread a delicate ribbon of scent down the avenues.

Everywhere, the brasseries and bistros overflow with grateful soldiers. The menus may be shorter and the prices higher, and some of the wine may be sour or corked, but after the first mouthful no one notices; each new glass tastes like a nectar specially brewed.

We drink to celebrate. We drink to forget. We drink because getting drunk helps to keep the nightmares at bay.

Irwin reminds me about the dance halls on the rue de Lappe, the casino at Enghien-les-Bains. If you have enough money, he says, there are girls who are also models around the Champs Elysées. If you're not so flush, there's always La Maison des Nations, with its Oriental room and prints of Mount Fuji and the girls unfailingly luscious and young. Or if you're down to your last sou, then there's still the Bastille. There amid the shadows and the sickly sweet scents, he says, you'll find women with kohl eyes and black chokers, and though they may be a little older, they'll still open their legs and give you a wild time.

It's a wonder the city doesn't crumble, he says, with all the fucking that's going on.

We end up in the Dôme around midnight. The tables are full. All the windows are open. A thick band of smoke moves levelly across the ceiling and wafts like the conversation into the air outside. The noise is tremendous. Men and women are pressed together so tight that you can almost smell the fermentation. The next thing I know, Irwin is disappearing off, one hand clutched by a long-lashed mademoiselle who stares up at him – adoringly or drunkenly, it's hard to say – the other raised to wave a helpless goodbye. The poor sap. He doesn't stand a chance.

At the same time, I become conscious of a shimmer of colour and scent off to my left. A woman's face flashes amid a group of friends, a face wide like a cat's. She keeps glancing in my direction, then pretending she hasn't. And when she tilts her eyes, the whole room seems to tip sideways. I make my way to where she stands, intent on restoring some kind of balance.

'American?' she says.

I shake my head. 'Hungarian. Budapest.'

She points at my uniform. 'You fight with Americans?'

I fish out my press pass, hand it to her.

She unfolds it, sees my passport-sized photograph with its official stamp, and reads. 'Capa?'

'You see that?' I say. 'Signed by Eisenhower himself.'

She nods slowly, impressed.

Amid the riot and clamour that surround us, she has the coolness of a flower shop. Her face is bright and open, her eyes meltwater-fresh. She twiddles her fingers, indicating that she wants a cigarette. She would have seen the GIs throwing packets of Camel from their jeeps. I pull a cigarette out of my pack and watch as she takes it with one hand, folding her other arm across her chest.

I pat my pockets for a matchbox.

She holds the cigarette cocked and ready. The blue flame illuminates her face. She pushes her hair back, tucks it behind her ear. Her eyes are green, her irises flecked with hazel. There's a blue tint on her eyelids, a dusting like pollen. The sweetness of her perfume cuts through the sourness of the bar.

'I like you,' she says.

'You don't know me.'

'We can work on that,' she says, this time in French.

With touching clumsiness, someone starts playing a violin, managing a few romantic spasms. If I close my eyes, I could be back in the Café Moderne in Budapest on a Saturday night.

She seems tense and expectant. I notice how she holds her cigarette some distance from her body as if she's ready to give it away. I notice, too, the pale band of skin on the third finger of her left hand where a ring has been removed. And there's something fragile about her that makes me want to protect her, to clear a space around her, and make sure that she's all right.

After a few shy words and a little kissing, and the kind of speed you associate with a dream, we're alone together in the warm shadows and silence of my hotel bedroom, the lights of cars re-tilting the angles of the walls.

She pulls the single pin in her bun. A plait unravels, slips down like a sigh. In lifting her dress, she gives off a sweet smell, an odour composed of shampoo, tobacco, lipstick, powder. She seems to pour herself upwards. Bits of her hair cling to the fabric as she tugs the slip over her head. And giddy as if we were breathing helium, we immerse ourselves, descend into each other. The night becomes all raw sensation, blind will, and I experience an incredible warmth across the whole of my body.

Afterwards, naked, lazy, sitting up in bed, we share a cigarette.

'I won't stay,' she says.

'You can if you like.'

I stroke her hair, which seems to spark in the darkness and change colour as my fingers move through it. I switch on the lamp. And it's only now that I see the thick pencil line she's drawn down the back of her legs to pretend she's wearing stockings.

'I'll be gone in the morning,' she says.

'I'll still be here in the afternoon.'

She smiles, looks around, takes in the room, its bare furnishings and mess of magazines and clothes. She sees the cameras on the floor in the bag next to my boots, but it's my helmet she seems most interested in. She's surprised by how heavy it is, and holds it with both hands for a moment as if measuring its weight. She tries it on. It's too big for her, and her hair squeezes out the sides in little blonde licks. She tilts it, regards herself in the mirror, watches it wobble on her head, and when one long strand snags in the straps as she removes it, I feel something take a deep scoop out of my chest.

⌣

Floor-to-ceiling white wardrobes contain rails of dresses, black at one end and white at the other, with all the other colours – navy,

13

camel, lemon, teal-green, magenta – pressed next to each other in between. Ingrid looks at them, hands on hips, and frowns. Evening dresses, cocktail dresses, ball gowns, a small mink coat. They hang like shadows of herself, clinging to an imagined silhouette. She runs her fingertips across them, enjoying the answer of the fabrics. A current shoots through her, a crackle of static, as she feels the textiles scrape against her nail.

Now that she's famous and acclaimed, she can't just pull something on; she has to think about everything she wears because she will be noticed, and the way she dresses will be commented upon in the magazines. This is a fact, a consequence of her success, and there's no point bitching about it.

She does her best to retain a private existence, to keep her feet firmly on the ground. She works hard, remains dedicated, professional. She's known for the commitment she shows to her roles, the conviction she gives to them. But it's as if, at times, the barrier between her public and personal life dissolves, the two blending imperceptibly together like adjacent paints. And she understands how easy it is to be seduced by stardom, to grow blind to its predations. She's seen it happen often enough. Her husband warns her daily of its dangers, reminds her she must stay on her guard.

One moment, she reflects, you're a young girl – virginal, uncertain – trying for bit parts in the theatre in Stockholm. The next you're a full-grown woman and a Hollywood actress accepting an Academy Award.

How does that happen?

She can scarcely believe it sometimes.

The strange thing is, this life enjoys its own kind of ordinariness after a time. The airplane travel, the swimming pools, the jewellery and expensive clothes all have their everyday texture just like everything else. And it's crazy, she considers, but for a time you can fool yourself that this is what you really want. Stuck in this sunlit bubble, sucked in by the luxury, it's easy to believe that you're just a beat from fulfilling your dreams.

Why does she want to be a movie star anyway?

Because being herself is never quite enough, she supposes. And she loves that strange, mesmerized state she enters when she's preparing for a role. The way she can hide away and transport herself to another time and place, immerse herself in a different life like a bath until it feels real. Then a point comes when she's taken over. An energy possesses her. She feels a heat behind her ears. It's as if she enters a secret existence, as if she's admitted into the mystery of another human being, and only she has the key. It's the kind of thrill you get when someone touches the back of your neck and you're not expecting it. It's incredibly intimate, and suddenly she's able to see everything at a slant, the way her character does. It's like living two lives at once, and she relishes that.

Her work gives her intense satisfaction; she loses any idea of time when she's on set; then when she's not working, she feels as if she's wasting her days not doing anything. The way she figures it, she owes a debt to the world and needs to add something, to create something worthwhile; she feels she must earn her place.

But that's not the end of it. There's something else, she knows. In her more vulnerable moments, she feels as though an impostor has taken over her body, colonized her somehow, as if a parasite is slowly eating away at her flesh. She feels this other woman's presence like a negative, a dark other, penetrating her skin and leaving its imprint. At times she feels it dissolving her insides like an acid, burning away what's left of herself, so that even after a standing ovation, she can still yield to an impulse to run to the bathroom and cry.

It has taken time, but she's reconciled herself slowly to the exposure. The photographs and films, she finds, grow to have a life of their own, a shadowy existence, remote from her. She manages it for the most part with the help of her husband, who is also her manager, and who works hard to puncture the Hollywood bubble, preventing success from going to her head.

Nevertheless, when she's invited along with Larry Adler and

Jack Benny to help entertain the troops following the end of the war, she grabs the chance to escape, to rediscover herself, to breathe the reinvigorated air of freedom on faraway shores.

She hasn't been to Europe since before Pia was born. It will be good for her and good for her career, enlarging her audience, Petter agrees. But when he comes in now and sees her contemplating the open wardrobes, sees the number of cases laid out on the bed and the number of dresses she's filling them with, he asks, 'How long is it you're going for?'

She needn't worry. He's only teasing. He gives her a kiss on the forehead, warm and tender, though with a vaguely patronizing note mixed in – not so she minds, though, because that's how he always is and she has grown used to it. She doesn't take offence; in fact she finds it endearing. She responds with genuine affection even if there's little heat in the embrace.

'Don't eat too much ice-cream,' he says.

'What will you do? Cut off my allowance?'

'Don't drink or smoke too much. It's bad for your complexion.'

'You could still come.'

'You know how busy the hospital is.'

'And check up on me night and day.'

'I'll leave that to Joe.'

Ingrid offers him a tolerant look. She knows he means well. He's a dear, really. What would she do without him? He organizes everything, attends to the arrangements, ensures every last detail is taken care of. She never has to worry and she loves him for that. She pouts, touches his nose with her finger and runs the same finger down the length of his tie.

Before leaving the room, Petter can't resist offering one last piece of advice. 'And remember, don't sign anything without me seeing it first.'

She goes on folding her clothes and nodding, saying, 'Yes, yes,' in a sing-song voice, though when it comes to closing the cases, she does so firmly and snaps the buckles tight.

★

A chain of hands ensures that her luggage arrives at the airport safe and on time.

She waits in the lounge with a hollow feeling in her stomach and remembers how she kissed Petter goodbye and hugged a tearful Pia tight. She has never been away from her daughter for this long before, nor has she ever been this far apart. She's discussed it with Pia, who is happy that her *mommy* – Ingrid still can't get used to the idea that her daughter has an American accent – is doing her bit for the war effort, doing her best to raise the morale of the troops. But it's one thing, she knows, to contemplate a parting in the abstract; it's another to sit in the airport and be confronted with separation as an actual fact. In this instant, Ingrid experiences a primitive need to be with Pia, an ache that for a few minutes approaches a consumptive hunger. She will miss her terribly. She pictures herself sitting next to her in bed on a Sunday morning, reading the newspaper, and remembers her smell, the exact aqua colour of her eyes, the golden freckle on her left iris. And she recalls how, in a desperately affectionate gesture, the girl had tried to copy her mother's wink. As Ingrid thinks of this, involuntarily she repeats the way Pia had wrinkled her nose, closing both eyes at the same time as though taking a photograph.

‿

In the morning, my head pounds, and I'm conscious of nothing but this fist knocking insistently at a door inside my skull.

Slowly, like something seeping towards me under the door, the realization comes: she's gone. No note, no address, nothing. Only a dent in the pillow and a crimp in the sheets, a faint flavour of perfume to remind me she existed and that she was here at all.

I smile to remember last night. It hardly seems real. Then a darker thought enters my head.

Everything I own in the world is in this room. I sit up quickly, check my wallet, run through all the leaves. To my relief, no money is missing. And my cameras? There's my bag on the floor under the bed next to my boots. In it there are forty-seven rolls of film still undeveloped, cartons of flashbulbs, a bundle of ID papers, the latest copies of *Life* and *Picture Post*. Packed in a separate compartment are silk stockings, French perfume, a silver hip-flask and a left-handed corkscrew. The cameras are still there. She's taken nothing as far as I can see. Not even my helmet. There it is still, with one long blonde strand of hair snagged in the strap. The details of my blood group lie snug in the lining with my two last letters: one to my mother – God bless her Jewish heart – and the other to a girl, only the name changes quite a lot.

Is it my fault if I defend myself badly against women?

I collapse back onto the bed. My head thumps from the effort. My mouth is parched, my tongue like sandpaper. I turn my face to the wall and try to sleep some more, but it's noisy up here on the top floor. The pigeons scrabble on the skylight, their tiny feet scratching the glass. Personnel carriers and trucks, each with a fat white star on the side, drone down the street, shaking the light fixtures, making the windows tremble in their frames. The sound of wooden-soled shoes echoes on the cobbles, clack clack clack, the Nazis having requisitioned all the leather during the war. A boy hawks newspapers enthusiastically in the square. It's all so noisy. The howitzers and bombardments I could sleep through, but not all this.

A telephone sits on the bedside table. A walnut dresser and cane chair are the only other furniture apart from the bed. I don't know what time it is or how long I've slept, though I suspect it's already mid-morning. I stare at the telephone, willing it to ring, and for someone to say something, to tell me what happens next. It lies there like a dark mouth, silent.

My toes protrude pinkly from beneath the white sheet. I wriggle them. Proof, at least, that I am alive.

I drag myself out of bed.

Half a dozen birds take flight as I open the shutters. Their wings make a *wap wap* sound like a flat tyre. I lean my head out the window and breathe, taking a slice of high cool air.

Sunstruck, the city stretches below: its pavements and roofs, its pigeons and brick chimney pots, its horse chestnuts and benches. Military jeeps and vehicles move like wind-up toys; bicycles glide as if on rails.

A few minutes later I'm standing, a white towel wrapped around my waist, shaving foam framing my face, a cigarette plugged in the side of my mouth, holding a razor while I turn on the tap.

The pipes chug and clank loudly. Rust-coloured water dribbles miserably into the sink. This can't be true. It's less the colour that bothers me, more the fact that it's cold.

I telephone through to reception.

'If you want hot water, Monsieur,' says the man, 'then you need to stay at the Ritz.'

'Tell the manager I'm very disappointed. I bet the Nazis had hot water when they were here.' I sigh, wipe a clot of foam from the mouth of the telephone and put down the receiver without quite slamming it.

It takes ages to fill the tub with lukewarm water, though at least it runs clear after the first few spurts of orange.

The level sways when I step in. The water is tepid at best. A rash of goosebumps extends along my arms and legs. I pinch my nose and slide back until my head is submerged and the water closes over me. I hold my breath for as long as I can. It's the best cure for a hangover I know – the best, that is, aside from an oxygen mask or a parachute jump at 6,000 feet. So I lie there, cold and motionless, my stomach hollow, my head still thick, the acid aftertaste of the wine mixing with the fact that I haven't eaten to produce a burning sensation in my gut.

I surface with a gasp. I hold my palms against my face and push back my hair. Through damp eyelashes, I can see that the water bends my limbs but straightens the hairs on my chest and shoulders. I'm so hairy. Everyone says so. If I were an animal, they'd hunt me for my fur.

My father was the same. Until he blew his brains out that is, having accrued the kind of gambling debts that can't be paid except with your life. I remember how the hair was plastered all over his body, his back like a mountain bear's. It was never enough to protect him. That Hungarian gloominess would descend without warning and cling to him like a mist. Poor papa. I like to think he'd be proud to see one of his sons now in Paris, with an American press pass, a room at the Lancaster and his pictures in the magazines.

I've always liked to read in the tub. Where else can you get peace and quiet? When I have a book and I'm on the move, I tend to pull the pages out as I read them so as to lighten the load. But I don't have anything with me, not even a Simenon. In the hotel room, someone has left a close-typed edition of *War and Peace* in English translation next to a French bible on the shelf.

I hold the pages with the ends of my fingers so as not to get them damp. The first ten pages start with a party. A society soirée. They end with the bare white shoulders and ample bosom of a woman called Hélène. She adjusts the diamond necklace at her exposed throat as she listens to a story. The heat of the blush that rises from her chest fails to infiltrate my body. The water grows cold, too cold to read much more.

Dressed and ready to face the world, I check myself in the mirror. I put on a smile, my best one. I tell myself I have the strength to continue, the stamina to go on. I take the stairs rather than the elevator. And when I step out the door of the hotel, I feel my heart lighten. My legs feel weightless. The sunlight hits me with the force of a blow.

⌐

On a two-day stopover in London before flying on to Paris, Ingrid consents to an interview with *The Times*.

She's already flown from Los Angeles to New York and taken the long ocean voyage from New York to Southampton.

Something of the endless expanses of air and ocean she's been exposed to, something of the vast distances and tilting horizon seem to have entered her, making her light-headed.

On the ship each morning she would stand at the stern, mesmerized by the long creamy wake unravelling like the train of a wedding dress. Always a strong swimmer, she recalled a time after her father died when her Aunt Mutti took her on a picnic to the lake, and she set out with a gentle breaststroke for an island a good half-mile away. She had never felt so lonely or at peace as at that moment on the verge of womanhood with her parents both dead, striking out for that far shore. Had she turned round, she might have seen the figure of her aunt reduced to a dot in the swarm of summer; she might even have heeded the calls for her return, the pleading with her not to do anything foolhardy or dangerous. But her aunt's voice quickly diminished to a murmur, a distant hum indistinguishable from the insects. Having reached the island safely, she then swam back before twilight, and was startled to find her aunt in an advanced state of panic, convinced her niece had drowned.

It was this same sensation of remoteness, light with inconsequence, that she experienced each morning at the stern of the boat; and she feels something of that dreaminess now, sitting in the lounge of the Savoy hotel, sipping tea with an over-dressed journalist as he licks the tip of his pencil and writes down everything she says.

She's used to doing interviews. She's endured hundreds of them. Those conducted in Hollywood are always carefully scripted, her responses dictated virtually word-for-word by the studio. Here, though, it's different. She feels an urge to speak her mind, as if it doesn't matter what she says, being so far away; she can be candid and careless, and her words will simply disappear like smoke into the air.

She says she loves food but doesn't use make-up. She says she doesn't mind whether she appears on the stage or in films, as long as she is working. She admits that she's shy, but declares that inside her there is a lion.

Asked why she chose to be an actress, she says she didn't choose acting, acting chose her, but without it now she would stop breathing.

Of future film projects, she says she has to trust the voice inside her that tells her what to do.

Does she believe in God?

She says that God hasn't exactly covered Himself in glory with the recent war.

The interviewer studies her before writing this down. Already she knows he won't include it.

Asked what she thinks of Humphrey Bogart, her co-star in *Casablanca*, she says that it is possible to kiss a man and not know him, and this is what it was like with Bogart because he kept himself to himself, but in the film he looked at her with such longing that it makes her blush whenever she watches it now, and her husband was worried something might be going on.

She doesn't say this last bit. But she thinks it, and the way the journalist shuffles uneasily in his chair makes it seem as if he has heard it, too.

She is quick to write him a note to thank him for his time, to compliment him on his professionalism, and to wish him well for the future.

The next day, her picture is featured prominently on the front page.

3

I sit with Irwin at one of the aluminium tables in an Art Deco café on the boulevard Saint-Germain: big smoky mirrors, burnished cutlery, glinting chandeliers.

The pâtisseries may be empty and the cakes just cardboard models; the menus may show less than half what was offered before the war and at more than twice the price, but the food still tastes wonderful. And that's not all that stays the same.

Despite the hardships, the women in Paris remain immaculately turned out. Every minute or so one of them rises from a table and heads towards the twisty stairs. At the bottom of the stairs, I know, is a lavatory with a dodgy lock. Inside, it's damp and fetid, with mosquitoes fizzing round the tiles. There's no toilet as such, just a single richly stained hole in the ground, with cleated blocks on either side where you plant your feet. And here's the thing – beneath all the elegance and chic, at the base of all these layers of refinement lies this dark stinking hole, and just like everyone else, these women have to squat above it, balance their heels, hitch up their skirts with one hand and somehow dab themselves with the other.

What's marvellous is the way they return afterwards – poised, graceful, even fragrant – to their tables. The waiters go on waiting, the coffee cups sit exquisitely in their saucers, the poodles sit panting in the taxi cabs outside, and not a word is said.

That's Paris for you. The tints and smells and textures change around me like a new season. Beyond the window, a blue sky presses everything together. The leaves of the sycamore trees, their dense greenness, seem especially lovely under the sun.

Irwin and I laugh about last night when two women came to

blows over him in a bar. A real fight, with hair-pulling and cat-like scratches.

A thickset and tough-looking Brooklyn Jew, with a barrel chest and tight curly hair, Irwin is a writer. He enjoyed some success with his stories and plays before the war, and now he says he's amassed enough material for a novel. He kids me that I might be in it, and that I'll recognize myself, either in the figure of the debonair photographer who knows his stingers from his whisky sours, or in the shape of the undersized Hungarian forever jumping onto a train with a bottle of champagne and someone else's wife.

I make to punch him and we spar for a moment, shadow-boxing, much to the disdain of the patrons, who look at us as though we are crazy.

One thing that has changed: the price of drinks across the city. Champagne and brandy cost $30 a bottle. It's difficult to get hold of whisky or gin, but the cognac is good value at ten cents a glass, and you can mix it with Coca-Cola to make it last.

The key thing is to remain on good terms with the bartender, and to call him by his first name. Alain stands behind the coffee machine that gleams like a locomotive boiler. The levers hiss as they release their steam. I ask him to add a shot of cognac to my coffee, to give it a kick.

'You want some?' I ask Irwin.

'A bit early for me.'

I realize something terrible. It hits me for the first time. 'You know what?' I tell Irwin. 'It just occurred to me. I'm out of work.'

'Peace doesn't make good copy. You know that.'

'Thirty-one and no prospects. What am I going to do?'

'You could move into portraits, weddings, set up a stall on the Pont Neuf.'

'Maybe I should get some business cards printed: *Robert Capa: War photographer – unemployed.*'

In the meantime I order another shot of cognac. In the same instant, a large-eyed man runs into the bar, starts talking in rapid

French to some friends in the corner, beneath a cartoon of Napoleon and Charles de Gaulle. A rumour like a gust of wind runs abruptly round the tables, lifting people to their feet. They seem excited, military and civilian alike, while the girls on the barstools start chattering like parrots. Everyone starts to leave without finishing their drinks.

'What's going on?' Irwin asks.

No one stops to answer. They're all in too much of a hurry. The café empties except for one elderly, red-nosed gentleman who sits, bored and stubbornly unimpressed, reading a newspaper. He sees us looking puzzled, speaks in French without taking his eyes off the paper. 'Some Hollywood stars are on their way to entertain the troops.' He turns a page. 'They're stopping over in Paris.'

'Who?' I'm thinking, Bob Hope, Jack Benny. Rita Hayworth, maybe?

He looks up at us for the first time, evidently sceptical, his cigarette smoked within millimetres of his fingers. 'You really care?'

Irwin and I exchange a look. Yes, we care.

He returns wearily to his copy of *L'Humanité*.

We finish our drinks, throw some money on the table, including enough for a tip, and leave.

I glance back at the old man who shakes his head as he turns a page, holding the paper upright for a second. Realizing that some wineglasses have been left on the tables, he leans over and pours the remains of one glass into the remains of another until his own glass is brimful. I wish I had my camera to capture the smile on his face. The old devil. Satisfied, he sits back, sips at his drink and returns to his newspaper, which he spreads across the table like a wealth of cloth.

Irwin and I head straight for the Ritz. I decide not to go back for my Contax. Too many photographers already swarm outside.

The lobby is hot and crowded, tense with expectation. But for an hour or so, nothing happens. Then, just when everyone is growing restless and frustrated, a black limousine enters the place Vendôme, with a low rumble on the cobblestones. There's a flurry of activity. Doors are opened. A woman steps out. Everyone presses to see.

Touched by sunlight, she pulls a hand through her hair, which glitters brilliantly, and then gives a little wave. Quickly she's surrounded by a crowd of fans and photographers, many of whom have been waiting for hours. All of them are calling out her name. She's handed a big bouquet of orchids and a spray of pink roses, both so large that she hands them to the man behind her – a tall, dark-suited, stern-looking fellow who shepherds the pressmen, directing the entourage towards the hotel.

There's such a crush as she enters the revolving doors, it seems there's a danger that she might get stuck. The glass panels reflect split-second glimpses of her face. Animated, smiling, and unflustered it seems by all the pushing, she is swept through the lobby where I stand with Irwin, each of us on tip-toe, straining to see.

She's beautiful – more beautiful even than she appears on the screen. She walks as if against a light wind, a slightly absent look on her face. And something in the tone of her body and the way she holds herself seems to give off a flare, a sense of exhilaration, a heightened air of expectancy. All through the lobby, amid the sheet lightning of cameras, an electricity is generated by her passing, by the sheer vividness of this woman. It's as if there's something charged about her, a crackle of energy, as if – were you to touch her – you'd probably get a shock.

I feel my vision tighten around her. My eyes take her in, her image stored. Long white gloves. Black polka-dot neckerchief. Ice-blue eyes. Her cheeks are high in colour as if fresh from a bath, her face luminous in the afterglow of flashbulbs.

A narrow skirt constricts her movements, so her steps are whisperingly quick. Her heels click on the floor. But there's nothing fussy, no visible hurry in her walk, just a rather restrained sense of grace that makes everything else around her look gaudy. Effortless, she seems to glide, and if her skirt did not constrain her motion, did not somehow manage to tug her back, the impression is she might just float away. Her existence is frictionless. The forces that work to pull the rest of us down, appear merely to buoy her up. The mirrors, light fixtures, carpets, serve only to support her progress. She negotiates her way unresisted through the throng.

I nudge Irwin.

'Oh, boy,' he says.

She has the kind of glamour that has little need to declare itself, yet is always on display. Blessed with beauty, she's unable to diminish its impact on those around her. It simply glows from her, blinding us, an inner incandescence spilled. She slips through an encircling group of pressmen who instinctively part to make way. It's as though magnets contend around her, at the same time pushing people away and pulling them towards her.

Familiar to those assembled as a giantess on screen and billboards, here she is among us now. It's as though we know her already. She has spoken to us, stared us in the face, her fears and desires exposed, her dreams and disappointments projected into our heads. And though remote and brilliant as the stars in the sky, nevertheless there seems something shy about the smile she bestows.

She sails towards the elevator, which a trembling bellboy holds open. Flashbulbs go on popping like champagne corks. Her face takes on a shine from the lights. Her dreamy progress continues into the lift. And then as the door sucks shut, she is gone.

I can still smell her perfume trailed like a ribbon behind her, haunting the foyer, still hear the tick of her heels. The murmur and buzz that follow her are sustained as a high hum. No longer solid, she hovers among us, a rumour in the stirred-up lobby, a ghost in a photograph.

We grab some lined paper and a pen from the desk, and busy ourselves scribbling at a table. We make several false starts and screw up many pieces of paper because we want to get it right.

The note needs to be witty and intriguing, bold and provocative; otherwise she won't bother to read it. The thing is to project an attitude of casualness, but for the message to be urgent underneath.

'Okay,' Irwin says. 'Read it one last time.'

I recite it in a whisper that only the two of us can hear.

SUBJECT: *Dinner.*
DATE: *6 June 1945.*
PLACE: *Paris, France.*
TO: *Miss Ingrid Bergman.*

1. *This is a joint effort. At your service, Robert Capa and Irwin Shaw.*
2. *We planned to send flowers with this note, inviting you to dinner. Consultation with our financiers, however, reveals it is possible to pay for either flowers or dinner but unfortunately not both. Dinner won by a close margin.*
3. *Our taste is for champagne but our budget is for beer. Our supply of charm is unlimited.*
4. *We do not perspire and we sleep standing up.*

   We will call you at 18:15.
   Signed: two veterans of love and war.

We give the bellboy a dollar to push the note under her door.

A little after 18.15, I slip a second dollar bill to the receptionist and phone through to her room.

To my amazement, she answers. My scalp freezes, my stomach does a flip. I can see my face in the mirror opposite. My eyes have a faraway look.

I'm surprised by her Swedish accent. It sounds much more pronounced on the telephone than it does in her films, where I guess she suppresses it. Her voice is huskier, too; husky and lovely like velvet brushed by the back of the hand.

Irwin is impatient. 'What did she say?'

'I think I've just glimpsed paradise.'

'You mean she said yes?'

'She's never heard of us,' I say, teasing him. 'But she's hungry.' My arms spread wide to enlarge my smile.

We whoop like cowboys in the movies after they've lassoed a steer. Across the lobby, behind his desk, the receptionist regards us over his pince-nez with a look of utter contempt.

The shops in the square are full of jewellery and perfume. The air is warm and light. The slam of a car door makes me flinch for an instant. A pigeon explodes upwards towards the roofs.

We race back to the Lancaster to wash and take a shave. I straighten my eyebrows, comb back my hair and put on a favourite white shirt and dark tie. Today is one of my handsome days, I decide. The soak in the tub, the shot of cognac in the coffee, the apparition in the Ritz. It's all coming together, mixing like the ingredients of a dream.

Irwin sits on the bed and finishes counting every last bit of money. He puts all the coins and notes together in his wallet.

'We have enough for one good evening,' he says. 'And that's it.'

'What do we call her? Ingrid?'

'Too familiar.'

'Miss Bergman?'

'Too formal.'

'Mademoiselle?'

'She's married, isn't she?'

'Is she?'

The restaurant is noisy, crowded. I check my watch. Irwin keeps looking towards the door. It's gone nine o'clock and still there's no sign of her. The maître d' approaches. Irwin makes a star of his hand and signals five more minutes. But it's clear we won't be allowed to hold the table for much longer.

'Do you think she's coming?' he asks.

Just at the moment we're about to give up, Ingrid arrives,

wearing a green silk dress, cherry-red lipstick and a red gardenia in her hair. A touch of the exotic.

It's hard to believe that she's here. Everyone looks astonished. Conversation ceases in the restaurant as Ingrid Bergman, the movie star, walks tall and straight towards our table. A circle of silence opens up around us, with people pointing and the waiters conferring in hushed tones.

We shake hands. Her touch is a little icy. Her palm is bigger than I'd anticipated, her fingers long, her grip surprisingly firm. Our problem with names is resolved as she introduces herself simply as 'Ingrid'. Ingrid it is, then. I like the taste of the word in my mouth.

She apologizes for being late.

'We're patient,' I say.

'Good,' she says. 'I won't hurry next time.' Her smile draws us in, shifting in tone between mischief and simple goodness.

We remember our courtesy and compete to stand behind her chair.

She sits down a little warily as if balancing something on her head.

'So, you liked our note?'

'It made me laugh,' she says. 'Though I'd always rather eat than stare at a vase.'

We both lean forwards.

She sits back.

'Are you hungry?'

'Starving,' she says, picking up a menu.

I stare at the menu but don't take much in. All of a sudden, I've lost my appetite.

'I hope you have enough money,' she says, without looking up. 'I'm used to having a good time.'

I offer her a cigarette. She refuses.

Irwin says, 'You must be fed up with men asking you out.'

'They rarely do.'

'I can't believe that.'

She sets down the menu. 'I think they're afraid of me.'

I expected a touch of hauteur, and maybe this is what she tries to convey, but instead what comes across is a playfulness, an irrepressible merriment expressed through a light in her eyes, a self-shining thing like phosphorus. I notice that she never stops smiling.

Within a few instants, the champagne arrives. Glasses are filled by the maître d', who is suddenly obliging and endlessly attentive. It's funny to see his attitude transformed from surliness to servility as he fawns around Ingrid, placing the napkin tactfully across her lap, straightening a spoon.

'I thought you said your budget was for beer,' she says.

'Have you tasted the beer?'

Her hands come together on the table. She touches her glass without lifting it. The imaginary object balanced on her head has yet to slip.

Around us, people continue to stare. They must be amused to see her coolness and our desperate attempts to impress.

'You look different from your photographs.'

'Is it the hair?'

'It's more that you're in colour.'

Ingrid wrinkles her brow – her way of signalling that we might be trying too hard.

The maître d' withdraws. Ingrid raises her glass. She understands the situation perfectly, of course. Her eyebrows arch. She smiles to herself. I guess she's relishing the attention as well as being entertained by the spectacle of two grown men making fools of themselves.

We chink glasses, drink. And as we drink, she begins to respond more encouragingly to our stories. I know that she'll laugh if they hit her at the right angle.

I tell her about the time I found myself in No Man's Land, with the Nazis shooting from one side because of my uniform, and the Americans shooting from the other because of my accent and German cameras.

'Lucky they were both bad shots,' she says. She removes the gardenia from the side of her head and places it on the table. It looks green in the dim lights, like something from the ocean floor. 'Where did you learn English?'

'I just learnt,' I tell her, 'by talking.' I resist an impulse to pick up the gardenia and play with it.

'How many languages do you speak?'

'Five.'

'What do you dream in?'

I make the sign for clicking a camera. 'Pictures.'

'Don't ask him what kind of pictures!' Irwin says.

'You know the stills they used of Spain in *For Whom the Bell Tolls*?'

'That was you?'

I wonder for a moment whether she still thinks in Swedish, and if she does, whether she thinks differently and whether or not I'd like what she's thinking.

This time, when I offer her a cigarette, she doesn't refuse.

Irwin says, 'It takes a lot of courage to come on tour and perform in front of a bunch of sex-starved GIs.'

'I dine with some of them afterwards.'

'You mean the generals?'

'The regular men.'

'Is that what you're doing now?' Irwin asks.

If Ingrid is in any way offended by this last remark, then she doesn't show it. I feel like kicking him under the table, but settle for a pointed stare.

'They show me photographs of their wives and sweethearts.'

'You do this often?'

'I call their families when I get home.'

'You do? Really?'

'Really.' She takes the gardenia from the table, places it back in her hair.

'If I give you my number, will you call me?' I say.

She laughs. Her head tilts. The object I imagine poised on top slips off at last.

We head to a nightclub in Montmartre. A small dance band plays 'I Can't Get Started'. Irwin takes Ingrid's arm for the first dance.

I watch the two of them flicker in and out of the shadows, shimmer and twist with feathery grace. As the music quickens, Irwin spins her out confidently across the floor. He holds her lightly around the waist like a fragile vase. They look good together, and she seems to be enjoying herself.

I cut in. Reluctant to yield, Irwin mutters something under his breath. He might even swear at me.

Ingrid's face shines in the light from the bar as we dance. In fact everything about her shines. She seems lit from within, and the glow spreads outwards to brighten the chairs and tables, adding a gleam to the orchestra and the couples dancing in the room.

She slips off her shoes, dangling them both over my shoulders so that the heels graze my back.

I tell her I might crush her feet.

'You don't mind that I'm taller?'

'Next you'll tell me that you make more money.'

'A smart woman would never say that.'

When she smiles, I notice, this crimp appears at each side of her mouth, tense little dents of muscle.

I point to the ring on her finger. 'You're married.'

She nods. 'To a dentist.'

I need to lean close so she can hear me above the music. 'It's true.'

'What is?'

'You have great teeth.'

Her mouth widens in an irresistible smile.

We dance some more, and I surprise myself by blurting that she's beautiful. I need to shout because of the dance band and the hum of conversation in the club. 'What's it like to be beautiful?'

'Stop.'

'To wake up every morning, look in the mirror and see how beautiful you are?'

33

'In Stockholm everyone looks like me.'

'I've been to Stockholm,' I tell her. 'No one looks like you.'

The air inside the club thickens. The band plays 'Sunny Side of the Street', followed by a few fast trumpety numbers. Finely tuned to the rhythm, Ingrid spins. The animal gladness of dancing makes her happy, her body twisting in response to the beat.

'You dance well.'

'My husband taught me.'

'I hate him already.'

She doesn't respond, just dances in a kind of tranced, absent way.

I look at her. And after all the horror and atrocity, all the cruelty and injustice of the war, it's astonishing to see the loveliness of this woman, to see the way she smiles, her lips glistening, her legs moving in time with the music. It feels good to laugh, not out of fear or self-defence but because something is just funny.

Having worked up a thirst, we join Irwin at the table for a drink.

He wastes no time in asking, 'Is Bergman your husband's name?'

She doesn't answer straightaway, but lets the ice at the bottom of her glass play across her lips. When she puts the drink down, the ice rattles like dice in a box. 'He's a Lindstrom.'

'You don't look like a Lindstrom.'

'I don't feel like one.' She looks sideways, glancing at the dark sea of couples swaying on the dance floor. She turns to me, shouts over the music. 'And what about Capa? Is that really Hungarian?'

'When you're deported under one name,' I tell her, 'you return under another.'

Ingrid laughs. And there is in her laugh something flirtatious, the way she tilts her head. 'Why Capa?'

'My girlfriend invented it.'

'Your girlfriend? Is she a dentist, too?'

I speak directly into her ear. She bends her head forwards to make it easier. My lips for a second touch her hair. 'No magazine would buy my pictures, so she hatched this plan and claimed they were taken by a glamorous American photographer called Robert Capa who was famous in the States. The editors bought them straight away.' My palms open as if to reveal a secret.

In straining to listen, her mouth stretches wide. 'And where is she tonight, this girlfriend?'

I hear her laugh. It doesn't fit in with what I'm about to say. I say it anyway.

'She was crushed by a tank near Madrid.'

Ingrid recoils as though she's just touched a hot pipe. 'I'm sorry.'

A waiter comes over, looks questioningly at me, then at the empty glasses on the table.

'Let me get another,' I say.

'No, I'll get this,' Ingrid says.

Determinedly she takes out her purse, insists on paying and will not be persuaded otherwise.

Before we know it, it's three in the morning. Irwin is slumped in his chair at the table. His eyes are hooded. He's completely soused.

Ingrid and I drain our glasses.

'Well? Are you surprised?' she says.

'At what?'

'Admit it. You were expecting a Swedish milkmaid.'

Maybe not a milkmaid, I think, but there's still something peachy-cheeked and eatable about her. 'You had a nice time?'

She doesn't answer, but instead looks over at Irwin and glances back at me to indicate we should do something.

With her help, I escort Irwin out of the nightclub. Together we bundle him into a taxi. I hand some money to the driver, give him the name of the hotel.

'I'll see you tomorrow,' I tell him, gently slapping his cheek in an attempt to rouse him.

He stirs, grabs me aggressively, even threateningly by the lapel.

'Be nice to her,' he whispers.

'What?'

There's a strained expression on his face and an odd emphasis in his voice.

'Just be nice to her, that's all.'

Ingrid hangs back and doesn't hear.

I close the door. The taxi drives off, with Irwin laid flat in the back, struggling to keep his eyes open.

'Is he going to be okay?' Ingrid asks.

'If he can survive the Nazis,' I tell her, 'he can handle a few bottles of Krug.'

The roads are empty but lit, the cobbles shiny as if immersed in water. A light breeze flickers across our faces.

Ingrid drags a strand of hair away from her mouth. 'It's such a beautiful night,' she says. 'Let's walk.'

'You're not tired?'

'I want to see the river.'

We descend the steep narrow streets that curve gently from Montmartre, continue down along the rue de Clichy, carry on past the Opéra, and head towards the Seine.

Hard to believe there were swastikas on the Champs Elysées not so long ago. The city is dusty but miraculously untouched either by artillery bombardment or street fighting. In fact you'd hardly know there'd been a war on or that Paris had been occupied by the Nazis except for a few bullet holes on the rue de Rivoli.

Though power cuts afflict the suburbs, the city centre remains mostly lit. The sky is suffused with a dull electric glow. The day's heat is released like a sigh into the darkness. Across the river, I can make out the blue silhouette of roofs. Above us, the moon floats sad-faced and tragic. Beneath one of the bridges, two barges are moored. A light is on in one of them.

Ingrid bends low to remove her shoes for a second time tonight. She holds them in her hand while inspecting the holes in the feet of her stockings.

I light a cigarette.

Without looking up, she says, 'I have to leave tomorrow.'

'An appointment with your dentist?'

She doesn't smile. 'I have a show. In Berlin.'

'That's too bad.'

I hold the moment of quiet that follows.

She stands straight again. 'Maybe we'll meet some other time.'

'I'd like that.'

An impulse to do something athletic enters my head. The fresh air, the energy of the alcohol and the exhilaration of the moment combine within me. I perform a handstand at the corner of the Pont Royal.

'What are you doing?' She looks around to see if anyone else notices. The streets are deserted. The moon's reflection crimps in the river. Something in the water gulps.

'Trying to show off.' I can hear the note of strain in my voice. I stagger a little, trying to hold my balance, a cigarette still clamped to the corner of my mouth. The ground is damp under my hands. Little bits of grit adhere to my fingers.

'Am I supposed to be impressed?'

'Yes.'

I can hold it no longer. My legs fall to the ground. I stand up, rub the dirt from my palms, look at her. She's tired now, I can tell. She wants no more fooling. Her eyes grow solemn.

A gentle wind frets the river. Reflections tremble in the water. Ingrid lifts the same slipping strand of hair from her eyes. The moment becomes serious. I feel myself brushed by her look.

'You're a crazy guy, you know, Capa.' Her head hangs at a contemplative angle, her hips tipped outwards, her torso leaning sympathetically the other way.

'You call a guy crazy for being in Paris with you? The crazy guys are the ones who are elsewhere.'

She takes the gardenia from her hair, and hands it to me. A gift.

As I hold it shyly, she kisses me, just once but properly on the cheek.

'Thank you,' she says.

'For what?'

I didn't even take her photograph.

The breeze continues off the river. The water stinks, but its wrinkles glimmer with starlight like bits of metal in the dark.

We walk on through the Tuileries back towards her hotel. When we arrive at the square, she stops.

'Good night,' she says.

'Good night,' I say, matching her formality.

Without looking back, she heads across the place Vendôme towards the revolving door of the Ritz hotel and the uniformed porters now standing inside.

I look down to see her feet, pale and slender on the cobbles, her toes making splinters of silver, her steps leaving not the remotest trace behind.

That I would eventually meet a woman like Ingrid, there has never been any doubt in my mind. I've always taken it as a given, like a card in the pack that must turn up. But where and how this would eventually happen has long remained a mystery, as remote as the notion of a long-lost twin. I always imagined that it would be announced somehow, foreshadowed by some sign, but in the blind way of things, it never occurred to me that she might arrive just like this, in a hotel lobby in the first weeks after the war.

What astonishes me most, though, given who she is, is the ordinariness of it. Still, it's as familiar as all miracles turn out to be.

Am I sure that I've met her now? As sure as I can be with the dark of the night and the quiet of the city around me. The conviction grows within me. She exists, as solid as any object, as fragile and alive as the heartbeat in my chest.

Something about her corresponds to a shape inside me, a shadow stored within. I pursue the intuition and recall how my chin touched her hair while dancing, remember the rosiness of her ears, the smell of her perfume rising to my nostrils. And already, bathed in moonlight, the moment lives in my memory, one note short of golden.

Already I'm conscious of a hum inside my head. The sensation makes me, as I return to my hotel room, for an instant a little dizzy.

⤳

She's exhausted, yet exhilarated. From the moment she stepped onto the metal staircase of the airplane and tasted the air wavy with the plane's vapour, saw the grass nubbly like an old jumper, she knew she felt at home. And then tonight she had a ball with the two pressmen, one of them charming, romantic, with eyes so dark she wanted to wash them. She was able to forget herself for the first time in ages, able to drink, to dance, to walk freely in the warm night air.

Her publicity manager, Joe Steele, is less than happy, though. He has waited up, worried something might have happened to her. No one knew where she was. The war might be over, he tells her in the lift up to her floor, but it's still dangerous on the streets, especially for a woman alone at night. What was she doing out until the early hours? She knew she had to get up early in the morning. If Petter or the studio were to find out, they'd be furious with her, with both of them. She's here to work. He doesn't want it to happen again. He hopes she understands.

Released from his onslaught by the opening doors, Ingrid waves away his concern, reassures him that she's a grown-up and can take care of herself, that he can trust her. And when she says it, she believes it, and has no reason to think otherwise. At the same time, something inside her feels gleefully disobedient. Who cares what this man thinks? She wants to enjoy herself, wants to experience everything this city has to offer, and she's not going to let Joe Steele prevent her from doing that. This time there is no script, no restriction, and there's a limit to the influence even the studio can exert from five and a half thousand miles away. The sudden sense of freedom she feels is dizzying, like a blast of pure oxygen.

Reaching her room, she unlocks her door and is quick to wish Joe good night.

She sleeps soundly for five hours before the wake-up call, and then she's amazed to find she doesn't have a hangover. She kept the window open so there was fresh air in her room all night and drank lots of water before going to bed. Was she really dancing in a club until the early hours with those two newspapermen? And who is this Capa?

She sets the bath taps running. Removing her nightdress, she becomes conscious suddenly of how she looks in her own skin, away from everything. She strikes several sideways and backwards poses in the mirror before the glass steams up. Then she twists her hair and pins it up briskly. Her skin goes pink with the heat as she immerses herself luxuriously in the tub. The room around her warms and reddens as she closes her eyes.

4

The *Life* offices are packed and smoky, with the usual crowd of newspapermen playing poker in the locker room.

Though he confesses that he can't remember how he got back to the hotel or how drunk he was in the taxi, Irwin still seems sore about what happened the other night. I join the table and he wastes no time in getting even. Usually extravagant, he establishes himself as a tight better and folds early, so that when he stays in and raises, the rest of us guess he must have a strong hand. It's as though the cards are transparent to him. We're completely suckered.

'You can't have all the luck,' Irwin says, his eyes avoiding mine.

Luck?

I remember my father one year at Passover chewing on a cheap cigar, pointing at the rabbit's foot dangling round my cousin's neck. 'It didn't do the rabbit much good,' he said.

Irwin collects his winnings, dragging a wrinkled heap of bills from the middle of the table.

My editor chooses this moment to retrieve a piece of paper from his pocket. 'By the way, Capa, the accounting department sent this back. It seems they won't allow you to put your gambling debts on expenses.' He holds it between finger and thumb as if finding it distasteful.

I take the piece of paper, leaving him still holding his thumb and finger like pincers in the air.

Isn't it great, I think, the way they keep the negatives and retain the copyright, the way they own everything you do, yet they won't even agree to cover a few lousy poker losses? 'It was worth a try, no?'

He looks at me with the same scrutiny he shows hunkered

over contact sheets with his magnifying glass and blue pencil. 'You may be the world's greatest war photographer, Capa, but you're a terrible poker player.'

I break into a smile, wonder what I've done to deserve this hostility all of a sudden.

'When is she back?' Irwin says, looking at me for the first time.

Sunday, it's hot. The church bells seem sluggish, the leaves sticky in the heat. Only the river churns coolly under the sun.

I carry an outsize bottle of Arpège, over half my height, through the doors of the Ritz hotel and into reception. It's heavy and square, the glass slippery in my fingers. I can just about manage to hold it sideways. The task is made more difficult by the cameras dangling round my neck. I drag it the last few yards screechingly across the floor.

The clerk at the desk winces, a look of horror overtaking his face. Hands on hips and clearly outraged, he regards me as if I'm mad. A gold tooth flashes inside his mouth.

I ask to see Ingrid. I know she's returning from Berlin.

'She's not here,' he says. And he can't tell me when she'll be back. He refuses to give me her room number. Nor will he disclose how long she's intending to stay. He says, 'It's the policy of the hotel never to give out such information.'

I explain that it's important.

'They all say that,' he says, peering over his pince-nez.

'No, really.'

I ask him to check if she's left a message.

He checks, tells me that she has left no message.

'Perhaps she didn't get my telegram.'

'That must be it,' sniffs the clerk.

At this moment, as if conjured by an act of will, Ingrid appears at the bottom of the stairs. She's wearing a long navy skirt and a matching turtleneck sweater. Her hair seems a little longer and curlier since we last met.

The clerk looks astonished to see her, though he tries to hide the fact. He slips into silence, busying himself and fussing with some papers on the desk. It is obvious that he has not passed on any message. Ingrid in turn looks surprised to see me, and startled to see the monstrous bottle of Arpège standing there, attracting the stares of the staff and other guests. She seems more embarrassed than amused, and not the least impressed.

I brush some dust off the shoulders of the bottle. 'It's for you,' I say. I spread my hands like a conjuror revealing the final trick of his show.

A giant clanking and hauling starts above us as I call the lift. A system of pulleys moves upwards as the counterweight falls.

'Where did you get it?'

'I liberated it.'

'You mean you took it?'

'You don't approve?'

'You have to take it back.'

'I thought you'd like it.'

'You thought wrong,' she says, with irritated quickness.

We exit the lift, the bottle squeezed between us, its contents sloshing audibly inside. With some effort, I drag the enormous bottle of perfume into her room.

She closes the door. 'How did you know I was back?'

'I'm a newspaperman, remember. I know everything.'

She remains standing, folds her arms. 'I'll remember that.'

I notice how big the room is, how light inside, with long windows overlooking the square. The bed, its white sheets and coverlet, dominate the right-hand side of the room.

She sees me looking.

I look away. 'Aren't you going to smell it, at least?'

With a huff and a reluctant tug, she unseals the bottle. As I tilt it, she sniffs, dabs a little scent on her fingers and then sniffs again, first curious and then sceptical. She shakes her head. 'That's not Arpège.'

'What do you mean?'

'I'm pretty sure it's just water.'

'You're kidding.'

She sniffs again. 'Coloured water.'

'What are you talking about?'

She inhales once more. 'It's a display model,' she says, with a hint of triumph. 'Can't you see? You think they make bottles of scent that big?'

'They might.'

I smell it myself just to make sure. I can't believe it. No distinctive scent or sweetness, no hint of a fragrance. Just the flat bland smell of water. I scratch my head.

Ingrid begins to laugh, relaxing. Her mood switches from mild anger to hilarity. Her smile widens to reveal a ring of white teeth.

I've never felt so dumb.

'Capa,' she says, adopting a schoolmistressy tone and shaking her head as though to scold me.

But I see with relief that she's still smiling. And her blue eyes fall on me, two small bright things in this big grey city. Searchlights in the dark.

The afternoon is blue, translucent. The shadows on the ground look sharp enough to cut. Ingrid wears dark glasses. We sit under the alcoves of the place des Vosges, drinking white wine and smoking American cigarettes.

'Did the tour go well?'

'Yes,' she says. 'Well, mostly.'

'Why, what happened?'

She hesitates. Her nose wrinkles. 'The soldiers started waving condoms above their heads.'

'What were you doing? Dancing?'

'Reading a poem.'

I laugh out loud.

She crosses her legs. 'What was I supposed to do? I can't tell jokes, I can't sing, I don't play an instrument.'

'I wouldn't worry. It's not as if they have much chance to use them.'

'I guess not,' she says, blushing.

'I use them all the time.'

She doesn't look at me.

I sit back, remove the cigarette from my mouth. 'They keep my cameras dry.'

Still she doesn't meet my eye, but slowly her solemn expression melts into a smile. She reaches for her drink. Sunlight hits the glass and the reflected brilliance wriggles on her cheek. 'How's Irwin?'

'Irwin's fine.'

'He got back all right the other night?'

'He was drunker than he should have been.'

'He wasn't mad?'

'No, why?'

'At leaving me alone with you?'

'You mean, was he jealous?'

'I don't know.'

'Should he be?'

A silence follows.

She puts out her cigarette. Her stockinged legs whisper as she re-crosses them. She glances at her watch. 'I have to go.'

'Already?'

She scribbles something on a piece of paper. 'Here. You'll be needing this.'

'What is it?'

It's her telephone number in Berlin, where her contract requires that she return for another week. I hold the piece of paper, look across at Ingrid, but she's already gathering her pocketbook and scarf. I fold the paper carefully and place it in my breast pocket, over my heart. And it occurs to me suddenly that, if all the cryptographers in the world were asked to decode the mystery of a woman, to unlock her secret and discover some invisible key, then maybe this is what they'd come up with: a telephone number freely bestowed.

Standing, ready to leave, Ingrid removes her dark glasses and adopts a purposeful tone. 'Come on, then. I thought you wanted a photograph.'

Afterwards I float down the streets feeling weightless. I'm running suddenly, full of energy. I run until my legs grow tired, until a stitch afflicts my side and my lungs begin to burn.

She likes me, I think. And I like her.

I feel suddenly invulnerable, handsome and alive. It's like one of those photographs of a war-torn city where, amid the ruins, one building stands upright, glittering in the sun. The one clean note: happiness.

Then back in my room, I think of all the terrible things that have happened in the last few years, the people who have gone, who are lost for ever, the lives destroyed, of Gerda crushed by a tank, and without warning I begin to cry.

The next day, Irwin sees me.

'What's going on between you two, anyway?'

'Nothing. I swear it.'

'Really?'

'We're just friends.'

Irwin shakes his head emphatically as though talking to a child. 'Men and women can't be friends.'

'You don't think?'

'Are you fucking her?'

I don't respond.

'Well, are you?'

'What do *you* think?' I say.

At the market near Les Halles, I buy half a dozen peaches, soak them in Courvoisier, pour champagne over them, and wait.

∽

Ingrid makes her way to the salon next to the swimming pool in the Ritz.

She feels the hairdresser kneading her temples, straightening her face, as if forcing her to look at herself in the mirror, as though compelling her to think about why she's here, what she's doing, making her examine the vast pattern of accidents that have led to her sitting in this particular place at this precise moment in time.

The stylist speaks good English and smiles a lot. She works without hurry, attends luxuriously to Ingrid's scalp.

Ingrid closes her eyes and relaxes, happy to place her head back in the rest and submit to the slow massaging of her temples. She relishes the two rich applications of shampoo, the needling rinse of warm water. It feels wonderful.

The hairdresser asks, 'You have children?'

'A girl. Seven years old.'

A thick white towel is lifted from her shoulders to rub the wet from her hair. 'The same as me.'

'Really?'

For a fleeting instant, Ingrid experiences one of those forks in her imagination. She entertains the mad idea that perhaps they could exchange places, swap lives for a time. The hairdresser might become a movie actress and she could become a hairdresser in Paris. They're about the same age, she guesses, with similar figures, and they're both tall. A parallel life. Think of it. It's not impossible, she considers. Just imagine. Like those stories of paupers and princes swapped at birth.

It's funny, she decides. Most women dream of being a movie star, while sitting here in the salon she fantasizes about being a normal citizen.

She suggests it to the hairdresser, who laughs, dismisses the thought instantly. 'You'd soon grow bored.'

Ingrid considers for a few seconds. 'So would you.'

After a silence, the hairdresser asks, 'Where is she now, your daughter?'

'She's at home.'

'Here in Paris?'

'In Los Angeles.'

A look of puzzlement, perhaps even a hint of disapproval, registers itself as a frown on her brow. 'You don't miss her?'

'Of course.' She puts her hands together and stares at them. 'Her father takes good care of her.'

'He must be wonderful.'

'I wouldn't leave her otherwise.' And it's true, she reflects. Pia is her father's darling; he dotes on her. She's always so gentle and compliant with Petter, whereas with her, things can be more of a battle, whether it's going to bed on time, getting up in the morning, or simply eating her food. Ingrid recognizes that she is more the disciplinarian, and she tells herself that this is because she cares; Petter spoils Pia, she thinks, though at least she's consoled that, while she's away, Pia will be happy. 'We also have the most fantastic lady who helps out.'

'Are you getting her a present?'

She meets the woman's eyes in the mirror. 'I don't know how I'm going to carry home all the toys.'

Ingrid thinks of Pia, the way they often sit together on the long beige sofa in Benedict Canyon. Sometimes they hold each other for so long of an evening that Pia falls asleep and has to be separated stickily, peeled from her mother's cheek, where a round red blotch remains. Ingrid especially loves, as she lifts Pia away from her face, that tickly, flickering sensation of her lashes brushing against her cheek. She can picture it now: Pia's delicate, freckled nose, her lips deliciously pink and wet. She remembers when she was first born. It was like falling in love all over again; she recalls feeling touched by her own tenderness, and knowing for the first time what her own mother must have experienced – that strange and unanticipated sensation of holding a part of your own self wrapped in your arms. The detail pierces her.

Before Ingrid leaves, the hairdresser asks for her autograph. Ingrid consents, graciously. How can she resist that smile? She borrows a pen from the counter and starts to trace the shape of her name. That first big lopsided letter. Those airy, rounded, confident strokes making little dents in the paper, the childlike loops of her signature. Herself.

Back in her hotel room afterwards, she is startled to find it transformed into a garden. A whole room full of flowers. Strange, showy blossoms, with a single white rose, and a short note.

She pushes her nose into some of the petals, savouring their heady scents. The mingled fragrance is overwhelming. Odours swarm as in a hothouse.

Sweet, she thinks, but she also feels a little uneasy.

Joe comes in. He looks round warily. 'I see you have an admirer.'

Ingrid reads the card and smiles.

'Anyone I should know about?'

'Just a photographer.'

'Oh, one of those,' he says.

'Yes, one of those.'

'I'll see they're taken out.'

Ingrid watches him move towards the door. 'Joe?'

'Yes?'

She picks up the white rose, hesitates, puts it back with the other flowers. 'Nothing,' she says.

5

She's due back today. Two weeks of waiting. Two weeks of going to the racetrack and countless hands of Red Dog with Irwin.

I can't sleep. I wake with the birds at five o'clock. My throat is dry from too much wine and too many cigarettes. The cups, the stuff on the floor and the chairs seem startled into an absolute stillness. Objects lack a dimension at this hour. I pull back the curtains and unhook the shutters. The sky is pink and milky. Pigeons scrabble, their claws loud on the skylight. Lines of washing, strung from windows, stretch across the street.

The sun bubbles behind the rooftops. As the shadows harden, slowly the objects in the room begin to tremble. They come alive and are themselves again. Beyond the window, things begin to glint.

A half-pleasant chemical whiff, a hint of toxicity, hits me when I open the bathroom door. Bottles of developer and fixer surround the sink. Long thin strips of film like flypaper are hung up to dry. And amid these there she is, her image haunting several of the negatives, transparent, vivid in her lipstick, sticky.

We take an evening stroll through the shaded arcades of the rue de Rivoli, and across the Pont Neuf towards the iron fences of the Luxembourg.

There's a small bistro around the corner from the gardens. It's warm enough, we decide, to eat outside. We order steaks and drink spumante, and watch the waitress disappear through a beaded curtain into the kitchen.

At dusk, bulbs hung from the trees illuminate the courtyard. They tremble gently in the breeze and mix with the scent of lilac and the faint strains of a guitar inside.

'Capa,' she says, looking at me.

'What?'

'I'm just getting used to your name.'

'Did you read them any more poems?'

She blushes. 'I stuck to the funny stuff this time.'

A dent appears in one corner of her mouth. As she lifts the drink to her lips, I notice her wedding ring click against the side of her glass. I see her glance at it, possessing it for an instant, giving it weight.

I fumble for a match.

Something in the action prompts her to reach for her pocketbook. 'I got you a present.'

'You did?'

Ingrid pulls out a purse, a tortoiseshell comb and a couple of photographs; then, following a moment of deliberate suspense, she produces a silver-plated harmonica. 'There,' she says.

'You got that for me?'

It's a lovely thing, with a metallic gleam like vodka, and a sliding button at the side to sharpen the notes or make them flat. The name of the make, Hohner, is italicized across the front.

I hold it up admiringly. It's cool to the touch and heavier than I expected, about the weight of a small pistol. For a second I balance it on my palm, registering its density. I blow into it, whizzing my lips across the holes. It makes a surprisingly loud noise. Guests at a table close to us turn around disapprovingly. One of the waitresses looks over. She's holding several plates on her arm.

'Shh! Not here,' Ingrid says.

I run my mouth over it the other way, going down the scale this time. I do it so fast that my lips begin to burn.

'You have to practise.'

'I promise.' I look again at the craftsmanship. The holes along the side in the dark resemble a strip of celluloid.

Ingrid adopts a mock-stern voice, wags her finger. 'And don't you dare pawn it!'

I open my palms in protest.

Her look of scepticism softens into amused tolerance. She begins repacking her pocketbook, including her comb and purse, but I stop her before she returns the photographs. There's one of a girl with honey-blonde hair and a cloche hat.

'Is that your daughter?' I lean over to get a closer look. 'She looks sweet.'

'She's spoilt,' she says, though immediately a look of pride fills her eyes. 'But she's adorable, too.'

I spy another photograph. A man, this time. 'Your husband?'

'Father,' she corrects me. She puts it away. 'You remind me of him.'

'I do?'

'He owned a photography shop in Stockholm. He was always pointing a camera at me.'

'Is that how you learnt to act?'

She laughs.

I notice the girlish way she draws in her cheeks, then looks up over her glass as she drinks. Her eyes seem mobile, liquid. I point at her glass, now empty. 'Another?'

'I'll start saying things I shouldn't.'

I call up another round of drinks.

Ingrid plays at being cross.

'Your father didn't mind all the boyfriends knocking at your door?'

'There were no boys. I was far too shy and awkward for that.'

'You were a daddy's girl?'

'I was still an infant when my mother died.'

'I'm sorry.'

'And *your* father?' she asks quickly, not permitting an instant of self-pity. 'Was he a photographer?'

'He was a gambler and a drunk.'

'Does that worry you?'

'Not if I don't think about it.'

'How do you avoid thinking about it?'

'By drinking,' I say. 'And gambling.'

I whizz my lips across the mouth of the harmonica, making a low sound.

Ingrid says nothing for several seconds, just squeezes her eyes in a way that makes her nose wrinkle. 'I worry about you sometimes, Capa.'

'Don't.'

'You know something?'

'What?'

'I'm never sure when you're joking.'

'Is that bad?'

'I don't know. I haven't decided yet.'

Our eyes lock. It is she who looks away first.

I lift my wrists as the waitress takes my plate away. We watch her retreat into the kitchen. The beads click and close behind her, sway like a grass skirt.

Walking back to the hotel, I take Ingrid's arm. A little tipsy, she doesn't resist. With the fresh air, I'm conscious of the alcohol, its warmth, and the shine of it inside me.

In this crazy time just after the war, an odd democracy seems to be emerging. For the first time, it seems possible to meet and speak to anyone, no matter who you are or where you're from. The war has mixed things up, made them topsy-turvy so that anything seems possible. And here we are, the two of us, walking arm-in-arm. It's summer and we're in Paris, with the trees in leaf and dense with blossom.

There's a moment, I know, when you can kiss a woman. A trusting, vulnerable look enters her eyes. You hear yourself utter nonsensical things, and you feel this pull suddenly, an otherness. Shadows place themselves sympathetically. A face is lifted into brilliance. A vibration starts inside your chest.

I recognize the sensation. It overtakes me for an instant. I imagine I see it in Ingrid's eyes; that tender, defenceless look, and I feel a mad impulse just to reach out and touch her face, feel the need to pull her towards me and press her lips to mine. Every

53

fibre of my being, every instinct wills it, but something stops me, draws me back.

What am I thinking? I must be nuts. I tell myself not to be ridiculous. She's married, with a family, for God's sake. I remember who I am, who she is, and I wonder if she's thinking the same.

Just before we reach her hotel, without warning it begins to rain. A heavy summer downpour, sudden and glorious, the raindrops fat and splashy, drenching us both.

We run the last hundred yards or so, our feet sloshing in puddles.

She's laughing.

I try to hold my jacket over her. As we near the revolving door of the hotel, she disengages her arm, pushes the damp hair back from her brow.

She stands there wet-faced and expectant. 'Don't fall in love with me, Capa.'

The tone is light and allows us both to enjoy the moment.

'You mean, I have a choice?'

An instant before she enters the hotel, I see her turn. For a split-second, she stops and smiles. I move off, glad of that last look, oblivious to the rain that falls warm and aimless, soaking me through.

When I get back to my own hotel, it is late. The air is hot and sticky.

The elevator arrives. Stepping in, I pull the slats back until they are fastened. The brass diamonds of the gates repeat themselves around me. A hollow forms in my stomach as the lift clanks upwards towards the top floor.

⌇

She sets off early in the afternoon wearing her dark glasses. She has no map and no particular plan in mind except to strike out beyond the confines of the place Vendôme, with its shop windows full of perfume and shoes.

54

Heading south, she decides not to take the Métro – heeding Joe's advice, for once – but to stay above ground so she can see everything and breathe it in. She enjoys the anonymity of the city, the feeling that no one knows her here and that she can toddle along as if invisible, with little fear of being recognized or pursued. She likes the world as seen through dark glasses. The green of the trees seems more vivid, the clouds above her more sharply defined, and she likes the feeling of being hidden, the power it confers.

She walks down rue Castiglione towards the Tuileries, registers the geometrical line of the trees. Paris is such a planned city, she considers, everything designed in squares and circles, laid out in careful symmetries. It makes her realize how planned her own life is, how organized, and how much she longs to do something spontaneous, to break free. She hasn't thought about it much but, approaching her thirtieth birthday, she knows this is an obvious time to take stock. Seeing so many young men on the streets using crutches, with just stumps left where there should be limbs, and noticing the number of young women dressed all in black, makes her realize how lucky she is and reminds her of her duty to live the best life she can.

She heads on towards the river and walks along the embankment. Bits of orange peel and blue cigarette packets whirl in tight circles, tugged by the current. A film of oil glimmers in the sunlight with the iridescence of fish scales. The reflection of the water runs across her shadow as if the blood in her veins were suddenly exposed.

She walks until her feet grow tired, sauntering along the quai Voltaire, then down rue Bonaparte and rue Jacob, and across place Saint-Sulpice with its fountains scattering droplets in thin clouds of spray. She stops at a fruit stall where she buys two dusty, succulent peaches, the juice spilling on the ground around her and making her fingers sticky.

Refreshed, she sets off again, strolling through the Jardin du Luxembourg and then back along the boulevard Saint-Germain, where the traffic is busy and where political posters and slogans fill the walls. Everywhere she goes, she's conscious of men's eyes upon her, their lingering and languid glances, conscious of the way she swims across the net of their attention on this sultry afternoon. At least she knows that, if they look at her, it is not because they realize who she is, but because she's fresh-faced, tall and pretty, and this is Paris in the summer, the radios bleating love songs and sap rising in the trees.

As she walks, she turns her wrist silkily this way and that as if trailing her hand from a boat in low water. Without her realizing, the feminine lilt of the motion operates like a siren song. She's approached by at least three men who try to talk to her, and she smiles but waves them away. Another proves undiscourageable and only leaves when she threatens to call the police. Still, continuing up to the Ile de la Cité, she becomes aware of a strange sensation – a feeling that she could pick up any man and take him back to the cool of her hotel room, where they could undress and make love. The thrill she feels is partly that she knows she can do whatever she wants and there is no one there to stop her. Instantly she feels guilty, and a little ashamed. It's not so much the thought she finds shocking, more her willingness to entertain it. In the same instant it surprises her to realize that she has thought little of Petter or Pia all day. Nor has she responded to Hitchcock about her character in the RKO feature due to shoot in the fall. It strikes her that, beyond the confines of the hotel and away from the oppressive attentions of Joe, she experiences none of the dependency she feels in America; she's able to move at will in the streets, democratically to visit whatever shops, galleries, bars she wants, and enjoy the promise of a full-pulsed life. This seems genuinely amazing, and retains the weight of a revelation. It surprises her also quite how liberating it feels, and somehow this results in a lackadaisical impulse to swing her arms freely as she walks on. Attached to the action is a series of thoughts, including the knowledge that if Pia were here with Petter, she would make her mommy and daddy hold hands, and she becomes conscious, too, as never before, of the earth revolving constantly and the clock subtracting precious seconds from her life.

Her feet are really killing her now, and she slows down as she re-crosses the river and turns into the rue de Rivoli. The air thins, grows cooler, and the ache in her feet mixes with a hunger she feels in her stomach so that on an impulse she sits outside at a restaurant close to the Palais Royal, where she orders a lamb cutlet, a potato salad and a glass of lemony wine.

She'd intended to go back to the Ritz before dinner. Joe, she knows, will be furious with her for having been gone so long. But she's happy sitting here, watching the world go by, the leaves of an elm tree spreading over her as if delivering a blessing.

The streetlights come on. A radio plays inside. But even though she eats until she's full and her feet in time recover, the ache within her remains. She feels it like a gap inside her, and it lingers there as she returns with an obscure longing to the hotel in the near-dark on this hot night in July.

∾

Wednesday night. Fouquet's. After the first bottle, we both feel a little heady. After the second, she can't remember my name. Following a third, Ingrid almost falls from her chair.

The room gains space, takes on an elastic sense of depth, while the things in it, the tables and glasses, the waiters and guests, begin to wobble.

In trying to stand up, she jars her arm against the chair. Her glass falls from her hand. We both expect it to break, and I listen for the high-pitched splinter and crunch. Instead, the glass just bounces and remains undamaged. Bits of ice skid off across the floor, sparkle on the carpet.

Baffled, she looks at the empty glass for a moment and blinks slowly. Her eyes have that drowsy, faraway look, and she's leaning tipsily against my shoulder. She says she's very tired now and wants to go to bed. She sways and presses against me, her hands coming together for a few seconds around my neck before we break apart.

When we get back to the hotel, she's still struggling to hold a straight line. There's a man waiting in the lobby, seemingly asleep in a chair.

'Shit,' Ingrid says.

This is my first real glimpse of Joe Steele. He's been dispatched as a chaperone by International Pictures. It is his job, apparently, to see that Miss Bergman wants for nothing, that she remains safe, that nobody bothers her. He fields her incoming calls, orders her food, books her in wherever she wants to go. There is nothing Joe will not do to keep the bubble secure around her, nothing he will not do to ensure that her reputation for sanctity remains intact.

'Let me go in first,' she says, ducking out of sight of Joe. She tells me to wait a few minutes, tip-toe past her sleeping guardian, then go on up to her room.

I do as she says, and five minutes later I knock softly on her door. It seems an age before she answers. She leaves me to close the door behind her and totters back inside.

'Open the window,' she says, with a quickly raised and quickly falling gesture of her arm.

Cool air enters the room, stirring the blue curtains. The sound of a passing car reaches up, diminishes to a hiss.

Beyond her bedroom door, there's a loud clank and an ascending hum. Down the corridor, the lift doors open. Footsteps tick along the hall. A man's footsteps. The sound grows louder. The light under the door darkens. Ingrid puts a finger to her lips. She's obviously worried that Joe is on the prowl. I feel anxious for her suddenly, sense her girlish fear. Then she stretches her mouth wide as if relishing her own mischief, and gives me a conspiratorial grin.

The sound of footsteps fades away. Whoever it is continues on. We both giggle with relief.

Exhausted, Ingrid sits on the edge of the bed, her face in shadow, her head slumped to one side. Her body sways a fraction before she catches herself. She makes a conscious effort to sit up straight. After a moment, she starts to rise and tells me to help take off her dress. She raises her arm in a failed effort to manipulate the zip. 'You see?' Her fingers make a doomed attempt to stretch the extra inch.

The silk of her dress feels cool beneath my fingers, like a trickle of liquid hardening. It parts in two halves from the back, revealing a V of white skin. A blinding flash like the bare shoulders of Tolstoy's women. The whiteness of wood once you peel the bark. The white flesh of a pear.

With an effort, she straightens, relieving each arm of its sleeve. There's an automatic quality to her motions, a learnt routine. The dress tumbles forward onto her lap. The two black arcs of her brassière become dark staring eyes.

Clumsily she stands, sloughing off her dress with an instinctive shimmy and a final kick of her legs. It falls in a wrinkly heap at her feet. She motions groggily for me to pick it up. Her eyes are hooded with tiredness. 'Thanks,' she says, as an afterthought.

Shoulders hunched, she sits again on the edge of the bed. Her stockings glisten like nets catching the light. The skin of her arms and shoulders glows. The black of her underwear seems a kind of armour.

My mouth grows dry. The back of my throat feels scratchy. A tingling sensation enters my limbs.

With difficulty, she stands and walks towards the bathroom.

She is gone a long time.

I wait for a while, then knock.

No answer.

All I can hear is the thin continuous drizzle of water in the basin. I knock again, ask if everything is all right.

The water ceases running.

After a moment's delay, she says, 'Everything's fine.'

There follows the soft tumult of the toilet flushing and a click as she opens the door. She has changed into a nightdress, a rich creamy gold. She falls backwards onto the bed, where she lies in a languorous zigzag.

I hear her say she likes me. I hear her say I have nice brown eyes.

She rubs her legs together, lifts both arms above her head as though about to dive into a pool. The lamplight creates a circle round her shoulders. Obscured by her hair, her face remains in shadow. I can see that her eyes are open now. She props herself on one elbow. Her hair tumbles to one side.

She stares questioningly at me.

'What?' I say.

A look of drunken puzzlement overtakes her face. 'I don't fascinate you?'

My heart turns over. A door slams far away. I'm conscious of her body's warmth, her perfume, the rustle of the bedclothes.

'You've drunk too much,' I tell her.

'Come here,' she says, patting the space beside her. 'I want you next to me.'

The bed feels soft and shifts with the addition of my weight.

She turns on her back, yawning like a big cat, and I see the pink wet insides of her mouth. Her legs slither amid the sheets. Her arms extend until they meet the headboard. She seems to enjoy the resistance this gives her. Her fingers push for an instant against the wood. By way of an answer, I reach for it, too, and feel a sweet straining sensation in my arms.

Her face glimmers with the cream she has put on. Lying there side by side, our shadows mingle on the white sheets of the bed. Light from the lamp prints a gold bar on her shoulders.

In bringing her knees up, feet together, the nightdress climbs a little over her legs. She makes no attempt to adjust or tug it down.

She closes her eyes and tells me to close my eyes, too.

The silence deepens, with only the sound of our breathing to underline how quiet everything is. And at first I think I'm imagining it, but then I feel it, infinitely soft, effortlessly gentle – the touch of a single fingertip against one eyelid, then the other. The pressure is so delicate, my skin scarcely registers it.

I bend towards her the way you bend towards any source of light. My hands are trembling, my heart pounding. Here she is right next to me, open, gorgeous, feminine, and I feel achy and half strangled inside.

'I'm tired, now,' she says. Limply her hand falls onto the cover.

It is enough. I never thought it would be, but it is enough for the moment just to be here, enjoying a few minutes of intimacy, experiencing the warmth of her breathing as she begins to sleep. And though I'd do anything in the world to stay here beside her, I know that, sober, she'd probably want me to go.

Moving from the gloom of her apartment to the brightly lit cage of the lift, I have the ghostlike sensation of moving into another world. The lift descends through the darkness of the early hours, gliding downwards noiselessly like a diving bell through the floors.

Back in my own room half an hour later, I lie awake, my eyes open, staring at the ceiling. The bed is cool and empty. The bleaching sweep of car headlights generates sly angles across the walls. I find myself wanting to lean against something, to find the resistance of her skin. Her touch stays with me where her fingers lingered. The hum of the lift continues on inside my head.

I feel myself fall into a long nothingness. A steep sorrow. Sleep.

〜

She wakes and feels wretched, groans, holds her head in her hands. She experiences an instant of vertigo, fights it. Slowly she gets up. The room begins to spin. She closes her eyes. Seconds later, she attempts to re-open them, slowly focusing.

Where is Capa?

She remembers him being here, but can't recall him leaving. Well, he's not here now, so he must have left at some point. He must have pulled the covers over her, which was sweet of him.

Did anything happen?

She doesn't think so, though she can't rule it out. And she finds

61

herself wondering how she'd feel if she discovered something had gone on between them. Is this the kind of adventure she had in mind? Is this the unscripted excitement she was after? She's not so sure. Rather than liberated, she feels guilty and conjures an image of Petter and Pia sitting patiently at home in their vaulted living room back in Los Angeles, Petter reading in his easy chair, Pia frowning over a drawing, crayon in hand. The image enjoys a remembered glow, remote but wholesome, inside her head. It is, though, overtaken in her imagination by another scene: cameras flashing and journalists pushing as, pale-faced and drawn, she fights a way through a jeering crowd, denounced as an adulterer and taunted like a witch. Shame and humiliation are heaped upon her. Scandalous banner headlines burst, the thick type falling like rain over her head. Her heart freezes for an instant just contemplating the disgrace. The shadow of her downfall seems to darken the world around her. Nevertheless, when she spools back in her mind from this darkness to what she can remember of last night, and sees the sun against the curtains, hears the sound of French voices in the square outside, her anxieties seem distant and unreal.

She had a nice time again with Capa, she considers. She feels happy, relaxed, at ease in his company. She tries to recapture the sound of his voice, his way of walking, his sad smile, the way his cigarette waggles up and down in his mouth when he talks. It is only later, when she sees her underwear crumpled on the bathroom floor and recollects the way she stretched out next to him on the bed that abruptly she feels her face grow hot.

As the morning goes on, she's surprised to find she can't concentrate; surprised to find herself staring out of the hotel window at nothing; startled to find herself contemplating images of herself with Capa. The rightness of the images jars with the wrongness of the feeling and the clash serves to paralyse her for a few seconds.

Slowly she grows aware that, within the cool, composed centre of her being, a faint splinter has appeared, a spidery crack, from which, as if from a long-dormant crater, something molten and irresistibly liquid threatens to spring. She feels again a premonitory heat suffuse her cheeks.

When it comes to lunch, she doesn't feel hungry. Instead she's conscious of an ache inside and out. She takes another bath. Afterwards she experiences a sudden need for chocolate. She eats five large squares one after the other, and immediately feels queasy.

Then when she sees Capa in the afternoon, any feelings of tenderness contend with an obscure sense of unease, which her nerves twist into a knot.

At the corner of rue Mouffetard, he asks for another picture. She sees his camera swing towards her, his eyes squinting as he focuses.

'Absolutely not,' she says. She raises a hand to cover her face.

'Why?' he says. 'Afraid I'll steal your soul?'

'You believe in souls?'

'I've seen a lot of dead bodies,' he says, 'but no evidence of souls.'

She tucks a piece of hair behind one ear. 'You don't think I have a soul?'

'I'm willing to be convinced,' he says.

She watches his arms drop to his sides. She notices how the camera hangs like a religious icon against his chest. He lights a cigarette.

She tries in her mind to connect how things were when she arrived in Paris – the sensation of complete liberty and ease – with the gnawing feeling she experiences now. She can't, and within her forms an unstable mixture of tenderness and a feeling close to grief. The discomfort, though it lasts no more than a minute, seems to writhe like a living thing inside her.

He says, 'Shall I see you tonight?'

Immediately she knows that she wants to say yes. 'This is becoming addictive.'

'I like being with you.'

'Addictive isn't good, is it?'

'It means I don't want to stop.'

'Nothing addictive is good.'

They both stand motionless in silence for a few seconds. Smoke rises like the evidence of a spiritual essence from his mouth.

It is now that she realizes something new: that she likes the person she is when she's with Capa; she likes the person he allows her to be. She senses the difference inside her, the fact that something has changed. She finds it hard to identify or locate the sensation, but then she remembers; it revives the adolescent excitement and awkward need she experienced as a girl, putting on lipstick and practising kissing. She would practise against her arm, against the mirror, pressing her lips so hard that her teeth would click against the glass.

Her brain catches up. Something squeezes inside her chest. 'I'd better go,' she says.

Then she sees him smile. It happens like this. He turns to go and she notices how he looks across at her one last time, and smiles. He may not believe in souls, she considers, but he is still capable of acts of grace. A woman could go through a lifetime, she thinks, and never be blessed with such a look.

She feels the muscles around her mouth rise into an uncontrollable smile of her own. The expression still hovers and must linger on her lips when she enters the hotel, prompting Joe to ask as soon as he sees her, 'What's the matter with you?'

6

After hearing the news of the second atom bomb, we commandeer a car and drive out of the city to the Bois de Boulogne. I remember the wine. I remember the bread and cheese, and the glasses, but I forget the corkscrew. Shit.

Irwin says, 'You don't even have a knife with you?'

A small laugh. 'Do you?'

'When was the last time you organized a picnic, Capa?' he says, closing and folding his newspaper. 'You're hopeless.'

Ingrid says, 'Maybe I should have brought Joe after all.'

The bottle of wine was expensive. Château Margaux. I'm determined not to waste it. 'Watch this,' I say.

When I tap the neck of the bottle with one hand smartly against a stone, nothing happens. I try again a little harder, without success. The blow – a high tinkle – echoes under the trees. I smile nervously, look up, conscious of the others looking on, watching the experiment unfold. I shift my feet, concentrate. When I strike it more fiercely at an angle, this time with both hands and a little lower down, not only does the neck break, but the whole bottle smashes, spilling gouts of red wine across the bare grass, leaving the jagged remnants of glass in my right hand and a long thin cut across my palm. I don't believe it, the whole thing drained away. And only yesterday I was giving blood in the Pitié-Salpêtrière hospital, the tube springing in an instant with blood from the tender, swabbed place on my arm. It surprises me there's enough left to spill.

Irwin groans as the wine leaks away. Ingrid laughs, and at first the blood that wells from the cut mixes indistinguishably with the red stain of the wine. Once she sees me examining the gash, though, and realizes what has happened, she leaps up from the ground. Spurred into efficiency, she takes hold of my hand. She's quick to dab the wound clean and to make her handkerchief into a small poultice. She attends to the wound with exceptional tenderness. I watch her eyes dart in and out of shadow, notice how her eyebrows are darker than her hair; her mouth pinches at one corner as she concentrates. Lovely. The white handkerchief absorbs the worst of the cut. Soon the bleeding stops. My fingers tingle, retain the warm touch of her hands.

'Hey, nurse, what about me?' Irwin says.

'What's wrong with you?'

'Something much worse than that,' he says. 'And something only you can heal.'

Ingrid plays along, shoots a knowing glance at me. 'Oh?'

Irwin withholds it for a moment, desolately clutches his chest. 'I've got a broken heart.'

I laugh. Ingrid smiles, acknowledging the flattery involved in the joke. 'I'm afraid my expertise only extends to cuts and grazes,' she says.

Though we mourn the loss of the wine, at least we get to eat the bread and the cheese. Irwin and I sit still in the sun, our backs to the bole of a cedar tree. Neither of us can take our eyes off Ingrid as she lies on her front in the thin grass. We watch as she moves her legs airily in a kind of semaphore, first making a U shape, then crossing them into an X, the ankles touching lazily, then widening to make an inverted V. Her skirt has fallen above her knees to reveal the muscles in her calves and thighs, which look as though they've been moulded from a sculpture. There's silence for a time while we watch, giddy with cigarettes, and absorb the peace and calm, trying to work out the message conveyed by her legs.

Irwin says how strange it seems that people can just walk around as though nothing has happened, as though everything is normal. He sniffs the air, searches around with his eyes as if looking for a hole covered-up or detecting, instead of the green leafiness, a whiff of devilry, something elemental going on.

Ingrid nods but says nothing. I look around at the blameless landscape, and see no evidence of anything nasty waiting to claim us. Not yet, anyway. Everything is still and quiet, the only movement a tiny breeze in the tops of the trees and Ingrid's fingers as she picks a bit of grass from her hair, plays with it. She continues to exercise, though now it is just her feet striking odd angles. A group of GIs walks past. They boast noisily, saying it loud enough so we can hear, how in Berlin they sold $4 Mickey Mouse watches to Red Army soldiers for $500 apiece.

Irwin tries again. 'You don't think that's odd?'

'I never did like Physics,' Ingrid says, without looking up. She twiddles the blade of grass in her fingers.

'But if it puts an end to the war?' Irwin says. 'To all war. . .?'

'Isn't that what they said about dynamite?' I say.

Irwin won't give in. 'Maybe it's a way of saving the rest of the world.'

'Of controlling it, you mean.'

Hostile, cocky, he says, 'It makes perfect sense.'

Ingrid sits up, leans forward as if pushed. 'But it feels all wrong,' she says. She pulls her skirt down over her knees, roughly brushes some bits of dead grass from her lap. And she asks us to imagine what would have happened and how we'd feel if the bomb were dropped here. 'Would you like that?' she says. 'Think of the woods obliterated, all the trees, gone. Think of Paris smashed like a matchstick city, and everyone in it – including you, me, all of us – everything, turned to dust.' Her voice drops. 'Where's the sense in that?'

Irwin seems stunned by the intensity of her attack. He loudly exhales, stabs out his cigarette against the bark of the tree.

Ingrid gives her skirt one last quick sweep, brushing away nothing.

I want abruptly to feel the touch of her hand in mine again. I peel off the handkerchief, which comes away stickily from my palm. I offer it up to her like a flag bloodied in a heroic struggle. 'I'm sorry for ruining it,' I say.

Had I been told some weeks earlier that I'd meet a woman who would not only make me feel unutterably happy, but also make me willing to leave the bars of the city to sit here in the woods, I would have scoffed at the idea, dismissed it as so much fantasy and nonsense. But here I am now, and here she is, and after recent events, I'm not sure anything would surprise me.

'Let me look at that again,' Ingrid says, rising from the grass, and needing something to do. She inspects my palm like a gypsy seeing in my future something wonderful but troubling. 'You should wash it when we get back. You don't want it to get infected.'

Recovering himself, Irwin says, 'I can understand it might feel wrong, but why don't you think it makes sense?'

Ingrid traces the line of the cut on my hand with her fingers and kisses it better. She looks up, blinking into the sunlight. 'I'm thirsty,' she says.

The newspapers are full of the Japanese surrender. V-J Day. People swarm in the streets with renewed fervour, waving flags and handkerchiefs, many clustered around boards where the front pages of the newspapers are displayed.

Ingrid is with me on the back of a jeep as I take photographs. We're driven slowly as part of an improvised victory parade through the wildly celebrating crowds.

Even though I'm snapping away like crazy, I can't help but feel at an angle to all the rejoicing. No matter how close I get or how partisan I am, things seen through the viewfinder seem to happen at one remove.

Ingrid has no such problem. She involves herself fully, sings heartily and brandishes a large flag borrowed from an obliging GI. It's as if something is released within her, as if she feels newly at ease. The festive energy seems to infect her, making her heady and self-forgetful.

She has to shout so I can hear. 'It's just like the newsreels.'

It's probably the first time she's come across history as other than a series of props, with generals wearing medals and talking tough on screen. But here she is involved in the moment, actively engaged as a witness and participant, and not just re-enacting it afterwards.

I re-load the camera.

She continues to wave and blow kisses to the crowd. She can hardly contain her sense of fun. It spills from her irresistibly, all her usual poise and diffidence pouring into unrestrained joy.

As if impelled to do something reckless, she turns to me suddenly. 'Watch this.'

'What?'

'I'm going to kiss one of the soldiers.'

'What about your husband?'

'Shouldn't I put my country first?'

'It's not your country.'

'Do you have to get so technical?'

'You have anyone in mind?'

She points at a GI in the crowd – tall, blond, Viking-jawed – and slips me a mischievous grin.

'Isn't he a bit young?'

She shouts for the driver to stop. He slows down enough for her to clamber off. She threads her way to the soldier with an unswervable sense of purpose.

She looks back at me to make sure that I'm watching, perhaps because she's acting and requires an audience to see her latest role, but the spontaneity of the act argues against that. She takes the GI by both shoulders and pushes her face up towards his as if emerging through water to meet her own reflection. I see it all through the lens of the Leica. She kisses him, tilting her head, giving herself without hesitation.

I stop taking photographs for a moment and just watch through the viewfinder. The sound of the cheering seems to diminish to a dull background echo, a remote seething noise like insects, and it's as if I'm listening with several walls in between.

Ingrid kisses him on the mouth for several seconds. The soldier looks stunned. He probably can't believe his luck. He returns her kiss and their lips seem welded together like bits of metal after a fire.

It is Ingrid who pulls away first.

The startled look on the soldier's face is worth a picture. Is it who he thinks it is? Surely not. But for once I don't take a photograph.

It's only when she scrambles back onto the jeep that I feel my face unfreeze. The walls muffling the sound dissolve, the noise of the celebrations returns to my ears and I remember what I'm supposed to be doing. The world quickens into colour again, and I do my best to catch up.

What is she trying to prove? Is she trying to provoke me? Is she telling me she wants to be free? She's obviously very pleased with herself and clearly moved by the occasion.

Ingrid waves back at her blond GI who is calling, beckoning her to come back for more. Around him, his friends whoop wildly and whistle, their fingers in their mouths. Ingrid wags her finger as if to say, 'Enough'. But she's smiling widely, and her eyes have a startled look as if she's just been plugged into an electric socket.

Now it's my turn, I decide.

'Here, hold these,' I say, unfastening my cameras and handing them to her.

She seems a little bemused, wondering what to do with them, and it takes her a second to untangle the straps. She places them awkwardly around her neck. 'What are you doing?'

'Don't drop them,' I tell her.

I leave her struggling with the cameras, and jump off the jeep while it's still moving, jog forwards towards the crowd and make a beeline for a pretty brunette with large dark eyes in the second row.

She stands out, not because she's tall, but because she has a perfect face, with everything symmetrical, and this perkiness bursting from her chest as she waves. She's wearing a simple print dress, her hair curled, with a vivid strip of lipstick like a danger sign across her mouth.

I press through the crowd to get to her. I look her full in the face, give her a winning smile, take her waist in my arms and kiss her. She resists at first, leaning back, but then slowly closes her eyes. Her mouth opens and the sensation is glorious, floral. Though I don't count the seconds, I'm conscious of kissing her for longer than Ingrid kissed her GI.

I clamber back onto the jeep. I can still taste the salt of her kisses on my mouth. I reach for the cameras, take them from Ingrid, knowing full well that she's been watching me with the same appalled attention that I reserved for her. The straps tangle again as she tries to unburden herself too quickly.

'Did you enjoy that?'

'Did *you*?' I say.

'You made your point.'

'What are you talking about?'

'I didn't realize it was a competition.'

I fasten the cameras back around my neck. 'I thought we were just having a bit of fun.'

She doesn't look at me.

'You're not angry, are you?'

'You want me to be?'

She still can't bring herself to look me in the eye. She stands straighter, readjusting her collar, subdued for a moment, but she soon recovers her toughness, lifting her chin. She recommences singing, accepts another extravagant bunch of flowers. The actress in her emerges in a determined smile.

I check the focus and start taking photographs again.

For the next few minutes we are careful to ignore one another.

I try to concentrate on getting some pictures. But the jeep jolts a lot as it battles through the crowds and I struggle to keep my balance. One dizzying lurch coincides with a moment when a big white cloud hurries over a tall building. And it seems for one terrifying instant, the way I see it through the lens, as if the building might fall on top of us.

*

71

We get back to the Ritz in the late afternoon. The bar is crowded, teeming with people, with no place left to sit down.

There's a kind of defiance, a mania even, in Ingrid's wish to celebrate. A desperate edge laces her suggestion that we work our way through the cocktail list.

The glasses grow sticky in my fingers, the taste of the liquor over-sweet.

Ingrid is combative, fuelled by the drink. 'How do you think the French feel,' she says, 'when the GIs whistle and offer stockings to every pretty girl they see?'

'Can you blame them?'

'When people are starving, and Allied officers dine free?'

'You eat pretty well.'

'I pay my way.'

'You can afford it.'

'When there's no fuel, yet military jeeps are everywhere.'

'Is that why you leapt on your GI earlier?'

She turns on me, a fury fed from within. 'You think I don't see through you? Your pathetic attempt to get even, your childish effort to prove yourself?'

I hold a silence.

She almost spits at me. 'It's about time you grew up.'

'That's good coming from you.'

'Oh?'

'Someone who spends her days making *The Bells of St Mary's* while the rest of us fight a war.'

'You think it's more grown-up for a man to click a camera?'

'While you behave like a schoolgirl on a dare?'

This stings her, I can tell. She gathers herself, leans forward. 'I know your game, Capa. You do your best to appear light-hearted but you don't fool me.'

I finish my drink. A last ice cube slips into my mouth. I crunch it noisily between my teeth.

Her lips tighten as if crushing a bubble between them. She rolls the glass between her hands. 'You act like life's a joke. You shrug things off and move on, to the next girl, the next war, the next poker game or whatever it is you do to pass the time.'

I can see from her braced look that she fears I'll mock her. And she's right, this is my instinct. I ask her if she knows what it's like to be arrested, if she knows what it's like to be beaten, what it's like to be shot at for no reason – or worse, because you're a Jew. Instantly I regret it.

Her eyes are shiny as she drains her glass. She says no, she doesn't know what that's like, but she knows what it's like to lose a mother at three, her father a few years later, and she knows what it's like for men to treat her as though they own her, and she knows what it's like to feel adored by people all over the world and still feel empty inside.

I sit there blinking while the tirade breaks like the ocean over my head.

'Can't you be serious for a moment?'

I match her defiance. 'What do you want to be serious about?'

She slams her glass down on the table. 'Anything,' she says.

'Are you trying to frighten me?'

'I thought you were fearless.'

'I'm scared of *you*.'

'You see?' She slaps the table.

'What?'

'There you go again.'

'I try to make you laugh, that's all.'

'Well, maybe you try too hard.' She looks around as if conscious for the first time in a while of other people, and the fact that they might be listening. She begins chewing her lip with worry.

'Ingrid, can I ask you a question?' I say. 'Why are you here?'

She regards me dumbly.

I speak as softly as I can. 'Why aren't you home with your family?'

The hardness in her eyes melts into what seems a vengeful pleasure. 'Tell me, Capa,' she says. 'Where's home for you?'

*

With the firecrackers going off outside, we go on in silence to her room. She doesn't invite me up, I just follow. And when she sees me coming, she does nothing to stop me, just tells me to grab a bottle of Evian from the bar.

From the window of her bedroom, we look out. People are on their balconies, watching a small fireworks display flash like summer lightning in the dark. For a few minutes, we listen to the high crack and watch the scattered stars and rain of gold-dust falling everywhere.

Back inside, we leave the shutters open. Ingrid asks me to draw the curtains. She switches on the bedside lamp.

The room is hot and seems glazed after the cocktails. I pour two glasses of water. The carpet takes on a stretchy quality, a special vividness of its own.

She's going to ask me to leave now, I'm convinced, and I try to think of something to say, some way of rescuing the situation, some way of restoring good faith. But then she does something I don't expect.

I watch as she removes her tortoiseshell grip and shakes her hair beautifully loose. It spills like a liquid onto her shoulders. Then, as though performing the simplest operation, she begins undoing the buttons of her blouse.

The glass of water is still in my hand. I feel its cold weight in my fingers. Without warning she moves towards me, extending her arms, laying them flat across my shoulders.

Trembling, shy, she looks at me.

Accidentally the glass touches her belly. She flinches a little. Involuntarily she shivers, half-closing her eyes. Her lips pull apart with a moist tug of flesh. 'It's cold,' she says, with the beginning of a giggle.

I put the glass down.

Her perfume wafts at me, wild and magical.

I lift her hair and press my lips to the shadowed side of her neck. A rose colour deepens across her throat. Her whole skin changes tone. My hands reach inside her blouse, my arms encircle her waist.

She puts her head on my shoulder and hugs me. She says that I'm her gypsy newspaperman, that she's glad she met me, and glad to have shared this day with me in Paris. She'll never forget it, she says.

'You're far too lovely for me,' I tell her.

'Don't say that.'

'It's true,' I say.

'You're the brave one. I just pretend for the cameras.'

'Are you pretending now?'

She looks at me and confesses, 'I've tried pretending. It didn't work.'

Cast down, her lashes are so long, I notice, they almost touch her cheeks. When she looks up, her face lifts out of shadow. Her eyes are slices of paradise.

Shifting her weight onto one leg, she reduces her height by several inches, lending her an air of submission. The dabs of red on her lips and cheeks seem a leaking through of something brilliant from beneath.

As she tilts her head upwards, a sweet scent is released, a mixture of lipstick, perfume and another nameless odour – a distillation probably of her skin. I sense the swell of her breasts, feel the inward female flare of her hips. At the base of her neck, I notice, are these tiny blonde hairs, a down so delicate and golden that I want to cry out.

My hands rise inside her blouse, steady as though holding a drink, brimful. My lips are within an inch of hers. I feel the warmth of her breathing. Her eyes close slowly. Her mouth opens and we kiss.

My fingers enjoy a sudden mad freedom. There are straps to negotiate, stocking tops to unroll, webs of elastic and silk to unravel. With a snap, the long light weight of her is exposed. And there she is, bright as a light-bulb, with that electric texture to her skin, a fine-grained pallor that seems almost unearthly.

'This isn't supposed to happen,' she says.

Shame becomes a vapour in the heat. I sense something widen inside her, a warm space open, soft and shapeless.

Through the curtains the lights of fireworks splinter, drizzling in a fan of vivid sparks. The room shivers with each new explosion, the window shakes in its frame, and there's a kind of animal snarl on her lips as she whispers to me to make love to her, please – except the way she says it is not so ladylike.

Her body stretches to a thinness, golden. Blindly her eyes slide upwards. The room tips in the direction of her neck.

I sense her fall through space with a luxurious shudder until the waves in her subside, and the different colours of the fireworks mix with the festive energy inside us as the two of us become one, all the colours turning suddenly to white inside my head.

For the rest of the night, with my eyes shut tight in silence, I feel the tiny pressure of her breath, delicate, trembly, like a bird's feather on my neck. And from somewhere deep inside me, her smell – locked up and stored as though for a long time – is released like a perfume, and I just sink, the way water does sometimes without warning over a ledge, into the deepest, sweetest sleep.

Like snow that falls in secret during the night, then presents itself vividly in the morning, it's wonderful to wake up and discover Ingrid next to me, sleeping. She lies with her arms spread above her head, braced as if for a fall, her hair mussed and fanned across the pillow.

In the dim light of the early morning, she seems the only thing that is real. And waking next to her, my heart feels crowded. I'm afraid of nothing. I can feel myself breathe.

'What are you thinking?'

'I'm not,' I say. 'I'm feeling.'

We look at each other lying together, arms touching, in the long mirror. My head feels different, as though a space has been cleared, and I don't care what anyone says or thinks because I'm happy. I feel like I want to run and fly.

In the bathroom, I look at myself in the mirror and wonder how I came to be here with her in this place now. If I'd been told this was a possibility even a week ago, I wouldn't have believed it.

The pipes sing with the luxury of hot water. The taps sparkle. Steam issues like a blessing from the long white mouth of the tub.

'If I'd known, I would have brought a book,' I say, when she enters the bathroom minutes later.

'What book?'

'*War and Peace*.'

She tuts. '*Anna Karenina* is much better.'

I watch as she twists her hair into a bun and pins it. She takes a small bottle from her toilet bag, drops its contents like a magic potion into the bath. A sweet smell lifts to fill the air. She swirls the water until it froths. Then she steps right in, one foot testing the water, the other following. She slides in opposite, her legs astride mine, her arms stretched along the sides of the tub.

The water swings for an instant, rises. She sinks down, lifting the bubbles to her nose. Suds slop over her breasts. And when she sits up again, skin glistening, the water spills from her body like torn silk.

I think of Tolstoy's women as the glossy tops of Ingrid's shoulders shine above the water. Her knees form small islands. Her throat grows rosy from the heat.

She slips one foot onto my thigh. I run my finger along the scribble of a blue vein on her ankle, then feel the toughness of her heel, the tautness of her calf, the hollow at the flat back of her knee. The muscles twitch in her long clean limbs. Her eyes close slowly.

Come to think of it, I wouldn't have done much reading after all.

Irwin can't believe it.

'The answer to your question,' I tell him, 'is yes.'

'You're not serious.'

'It's true. I swear it.'

'You're bullshitting me.'

'It's your fault.'

'Mine?'

'You told me to be nice to her.'

'So?'

'So I was. *Very* nice.'

'All right, then,' he says. 'What does she have for breakfast?'

'Guys like you,' I say.

I glance up to see if there's any detectable change, any afterglow or far-flung radiance staining the sky above us. There's nothing. Just the usual sunshine, the birds in the trees, pretty women in floaty dresses, and the tinkle of cups and saucers in the café.

Maybe I'm mistaken.

Did I imagine it? It does seem incredible.

Maybe nothing happened after all.

∾

Ingrid has felt this mixture of fear and wonder before.

There was that exercise in the Stockholm Theatre where she was told to close her eyes and fall backwards, trusting her partner to catch her before she hit the floor. She recalls the instant of fear before the sensation of sinking blindly but faithfully through space. And she remembers a school visit to the caves at Lummelunda: the guide leading them down into the echoey cavern, the walls slick with moisture, the shape of the rocks menacing but beautiful in the electric lights. The guide asked if anyone had experienced darkness before – *real* darkness. She wondered what he meant by that. A starless night in the country? The dark of her bedroom once the curtains were closed? 'When I say *real* darkness,' he said, 'I mean *absolute* darkness, the total absence of light.' The guide then counted down dramatically: 5 – 4 – 3 – 2 – 1 – and switched off the lights. Ingrid wasn't sure for a moment whether in her fear she'd closed her eyes or not. She tried opening and shutting her eyelids but the effect was the same. She could see nothing. Dense and impenetrable, this was a different order of darkness to anything she'd experienced before. And the silence, too, was unnerving; it was as if no one breathed. She wanted to reach out and touch someone, to make sure that the others had not deserted her, leaving her in the cavern alone. It was then that a bizarre thing happened. First of all, the silence was broken by a dripping sound, which sounded loud and close even though she knew it was probably far away. And then more fantastically, her eyes staring wide, she began to see something. Within the darkness, slowly there began to appear little blue glints, pale glimmers of blue light. Was this a flaw in her eye, an optical illusion, a visual trick? No, she was convinced it was something outside her, a mineral brilliance, a glitter coming from inside the rock, and the bits of blue began to burn like tiny stars in the dark until, without warning, the lights were switched back on and voices filled the space of the cave again – nervous, excited, relieved – as at the end of a great play.

The memories revolve obscurely in her head, mixing in a mysterious way with the dark of the hotel room as she feels Capa reach across to touch her hand. The touch, though not unexpected, electrifies her. The air turns thin. Her heart bumps, and she laughs, which is all she can think to do.

Her arms and legs turn watery. The vibration widens to afflict her fingers and stomach. The sensation crowds her chest and stretches her from within.

It surprises her at first to be on his left side. With Petter, she habitually takes up a position on his right. And it seems to her for a minute as if she's in some odd, reversed world that mirrors her own, where everything is slightly tweaked.

His face passes inside the focus of her eyes, filling the inches between them. They kiss, and it's as if an icicle enters her head. It feels like his mouth is inside her. The sensation spreads to between her legs, where she feels splayed and achy.

She understands that he has opened her up, this man, this Capa, that he has dismantled her.

A blind sense of will attaches itself to her actions. She's startled by the violent need she feels. A balance swings within her. She feels for a second her flesh melting, her inner space rising to the surface.

Afterwards they remain almost motionless for several minutes, rocking in a kind of seesaw, an impression of fullness ebbing, and though a gentle dip and swaying motion continues on inside her body, she feels drowsy and becalmed.

She knows that it has happened, that there is no going back. She feels the shift inside her, subtle but transfiguring; she understands that a line has been crossed.

7

Picture this.

Ingrid sits cross-legged on her bed, reading a script the studio has sent her. She's underlining things with a pencil, scribbling notes in the margin, the tip of her tongue touching her upper lip in concentration.

She gets up, looks at herself in the mirror, feels in a flat mood, glances out the window distractedly.

There's a knock on the door.

She moves to open it. And there stands one of the hotel waiters with a trolley on which lies a bottle of Krug in a bucket of ice, and two sparkling glasses.

'Your champagne, Madame.'

'I didn't order this.'

'No?' The waiter stands there, uncertain what to do. He begins to retreat.

'No, wait,' she says. 'Bring it inside.'

She sneaks a look down the hotel corridor as the jiggling trolley is manoeuvred into the room. There's no one.

At least that's how I imagine it. Perfect.

But what I don't reckon on is the fact that an increasingly suspicious Joe, hearing Ingrid's voice down the corridor, will emerge from his room to see what's going on. And of course, he sees the trolley with the champagne and two incriminating glasses being wheeled into her room.

He surmises correctly that someone – probably me – must be about to make his way up, and in that instant resolves to intercept me. After a quick check of the stairs, he makes his way to the elevator.

So there I am downstairs, oblivious to this, waiting until the desk is busy and heading beyond reception to call the lift.

The light pings on, showing the top floor. It seems to take an age to descend. The waiting grows steep inside me. I watch the fan of numbers above the door. The light snags on 4, then 3, and 2. And by the time it finally reaches the ground floor and the doors slide open, there is Joe towering above me, standing ready, keeper of the castle, protector of the Queen's bedroom. He recognizes me straightaway. His eyebrows form one unbroken line of dark hair. The line rises as he speaks. 'Excuse me, sir, are you a guest here?' He knows full well that I'm not.

'I'm meeting someone,' I say.

'Are you registered?'

'It's all arranged.'

The doors slide shut.

I push the button. The bellboy opens the doors again, throwing a rectangle of light on both of us.

Joe looms over me, blocking the way. 'I'm afraid it's against hotel rules to allow visitors up to the rooms.'

'I see.'

'Yes.'

'I didn't realize that.'

'I'm sorry, sir.' He's enjoying this pantomime.

I notice a small gap between his two front teeth, which accounts for his slight lisp.

'My friend will be disappointed,' I say.

He smiles, relishing the power he holds over me. 'I'm sure your friend will understand.'

It's clear he's not going to budge. I slope back through reception. But when he isn't looking, I dart across the lobby.

At that exact moment, some instinct makes him turn and he catches sight of me as I head up the stairs.

I see him rush towards the elevator, but it's too late. The doors have already closed. The lift has gone up again, so he'll have to press the button and wait. I have a few seconds on him. I run up the stairs as fast as I can, taking them two at a time.

It is enough. Just.

I race down the corridor, its subdued lights and rich carpet, the oil paintings and smell of cleanliness.

By the time Joe exits the lift, Ingrid is already answering the knock on her door.

She sees first me, then Joe, and is quick to see what's going on. 'Is there a problem, Joe?'

'No, ma'am.'

'Have you met Mr Capa?'

His strength drains visibly, his shoulders falling. 'He's not on the list.'

'He's a friend.'

Joe says nothing. His eyes avoid mine.

'You'll be seeing quite a lot of him, probably.'

'Does Mr Selznick know about this?' He says the name with an odd emphasis. It's clear he's trying to intimidate her.

She stares at him.

He doesn't back down, returns her gaze.

'Mr Selznick and I understand each other.'

'It's my job to protect you, ma'am.'

'You needn't worry, Joe. Mr Capa was in the war. He can handle things.'

A look of subdued fury puts a kink in his brow. His fists clench and unclench, and his instinct is probably to slug me, but he knows he can't, and that must make him mad.

Ingrid plants a kiss on his cheek as though removing a thorn from his paw. But if she's hoping to placate him, she's mistaken.

He walks away stiffly, humiliated.

Inside, I see Ingrid has already poured the champagne.

She's late. I've been waiting at a restaurant on avenue George V for over half an hour. She isn't coming, I think. She's thought

83

better of it. I take a sip of wine, then another, and resist the urge to check my watch again. Instead I consult the menu for the tenth time.

Maybe she misheard me, thought I meant somewhere else.

I try to remember details of the conversation. I'm convinced it was here. The arrangement was clear. I tell myself to stop looking at the entrance, to stop watching everyone who comes in the door. I decide to give her five more minutes.

Five minutes pass.

Does she have to spell it out?

She's not coming. She's changed her mind, had second thoughts. Isn't it obvious that she regrets what has happened? Isn't it clear she considers it all a dreadful mistake?

What begins as a tiny seed of doubt swells to a terrible certainty. She realizes how much she loves her husband, her daughter, her home. She realizes how much she values her career. She wants to erase everything that has happened, pretend that nothing took place. She has no wish to hurt me, but at the same time she needs the message to be clear and unambiguous. It's over, and she wants me to leave her alone. Either that, I think, or maybe Joe has got to her, issued her with some threat.

Then, just as I'm about to give up and leave, I hear a few light footsteps, the rustle of stockinged legs, the long swish of a skirt.

I stand up. 'I didn't think you were coming.'

She sits down. She doesn't smile, doesn't remove her jacket.

I signal to the waiter.

'Why didn't you call me?' she says.

'I wasn't sure you wanted me to.'

'You're right. I'm not sure I did.'

'Meaning?'

'Maybe you'd better not call again.' A silence follows. She plucks a petal from a vase on the table, begins rolling it into a thin tube.

'You're joking,' I say.

'Of course,' she says. 'And you?'

*

84

The next day, I figure she'll be late again.

I'm wrong.

With a cigarette in my left hand and concealing a bunch of flowers in my right, I arrive mid-morning at the table where Ingrid is waiting.

'Where were you?'

'In the tub.'

'All this time?' A glass rests in her hand like a translucent piece of fruit.

'I was reading.'

'*War and Peace*?'

I smile.

She chews her lips for several seconds before making her announcement. 'I've extended my stay for another few weeks.'

I nod, take this in. 'What about your dentist friend?'

'My husband?'

'He won't be upset?'

'I don't suppose so.'

'You're sure?'

She re-crosses her legs. 'Maybe it's me that won't,' she says. 'Anyway, it must be a relief not having to look after me.'

'And your daughter?'

Her mouth seems suddenly a hole through which everything drains. She puts down her glass. After a silence, she says, 'Apparently she's been trying on my clothes.' She half-laughs, but the thought clearly pains her in its sweetness. She pushes her drink away, looks at me unflinchingly. 'You know what scares me most in all this?' Solemn, she doesn't give me a chance to answer. 'I'm getting to like you far too much.'

Not knowing what else to do, I hand her the flowers. 'Happy birthday,' I say.

Though still touched with sadness and not as happy as I'd hoped, she seems genuinely surprised. Slowly her face brightens. 'How did you know?'

Her head tilts to one side like a bird's. Her face widens into a smile before squeezing inwards in an attempt to contain it, like water brimming to the lip of a glass.

'What do you want to do?'

'Honestly, I haven't given it much thought.'

'Anything special?'

'Why don't you surprise me?'

'You'll be disappointed.'

She pouts, a little wearily. 'I'm used to being spoiled.'

'I can tell.'

She shifts her hips, makes a face. 'So what *do* you give the woman who has everything?'

I consider for a second. 'Penicillin?'

I buy her a scarf, organize more flowers – white roses – and present her with a photograph I took of her at the Étoile.

For lunch, I take her to a Hungarian restaurant in Montparnasse and order pepper-and-egg casserole. It's the dish that most reminds me of home.

When I ask her what she wants to do for the rest of the day, she says she just wants to eat and drink and make love, and then eat and drink and make love some more.

I'll do my best, I tell her, to fit in with her schedule.

We have late afternoon drinks at the Crillon, then dinner at Chez Anna. Tipped off, the waiter makes a little ceremony of presenting a cake.

'Happy birthday,' I whisper.

It takes two attempts to blow out the candles. With her eyes squeezed tight shut, she makes a wish.

I cut through the fine-spun icing sugar into the fruit cake below. We wash it down with a glass of Marsala.

I ask her if she feels any different.

She lifts her napkin with both hands to her lips. 'I feel happy,' she says.

Without moving her head but tilting her eyes, she indicates a middle-aged couple seated at the table next to us. They are silent, chewing their food. Since we've been here, they've barely exchanged a word. Ingrid leans forward, tactfully angling her fork. 'Can you ever imagine us sitting together like that?'

'Maybe they're content.'

'They're not speaking.' She pops a forkful of cake into her mouth, looks at me for a response.

I move closer. For once, it is me who wants to be serious. 'What is it you want in life?'

'Oh, the same as any woman.'

'And what's that?'

She considers for an instant. 'The perfect pair of red shoes.'

I smile, lean back.

Her eyebrows rise as something occurs to her. 'I forgot to tell you. A man asked me to marry him yesterday.'

'He did? Who?'

'I've never seen him before. He just came up to me in a café. He said he'd been observing me.'

'A journalist?'

'He said that from the moment he saw me, he knew I was the one, that I wasn't to worry, that I could take as long as I liked to decide, that I'd realize in the end it was inevitable and that we were meant to be together.'

'What did you say?'

She smiles, adds sugar to her coffee. 'The wedding is next Thursday.'

'Am I invited?'

She laughs. 'You're the photographer, silly.'

'Is that how you think of me?'

She stops eating for a moment. 'Who says I think of you?'

I look at her, her chin resting in one hand, and laugh. She's funnier than any woman I know. We hold each other's gaze for several seconds. The moment grows serious and we both recognize it. Having acknowledged this fact in silence to ourselves, I feel the need to make her smile again. 'I should tell you,' I say, 'when I was born, they thought I was special.'

'Why?'

'I had an extra finger on one hand.'

She glances at my hand. 'What happened?'

'They cut it off.'

'Ouch.'

'At the same time as my foreskin.'

She winces.

'More cake?' Smiling, I hold the knife up, glinting, ready to cut another slice.

At Ingrid's favourite nightclub, Chez Carrière on the Champs Elysées, we dance very close. The stately wail of the saxophones makes us cling closer. Neither of us wants to let go.

At five in the morning, we walk home in the city's smoky light. The air is cool after the shock of rain. The streets are damp and lit. It's funny: when you're out so early in the morning, you can't understand why more people aren't up enjoying the start of the day. It seems criminal to miss the first light, the birdsong, the delicious chill in the air. You feel privileged because you're in it from the beginning, getting an edge on everyone.

The metal shutters of the shops are still closed, the leaves glisten, and a film of mist hovers over the river. The only sound is that of our feet on the cobbles.

We stroll up the avenues, walking in the cool darkness as the dawn comes, sending away taxi cabs as they slow down next to us.

We watch as the light rises, giving the world shadows. The grey shapes of the trees on the boulevards hold their breath for the heat of the day. And behind the buildings the sun comes up with its liquid edges. The sky folds itself into layers of red and pink and blue.

'Sleep well?' I ask.

'Really well,' Ingrid says, stretching.

'What did you dream about?'

'Lots of things.'

'You're blushing.'
'I'm starting to remember.'
'Did I feature in any?'
'We both did.'
'What did I do?'
'What didn't you?'

⌒

It's only now that she discovers desire. Not the duty enjoined by the conjugal act, but the profound abandonment, the soft wet melting sensation of sexual love, with its heat and freedom, its wild crackling charge and head-clearing energy, the feeling that her body is being pulled inside out.

She is overpowered by longing. Capa has stirred the sensual depths in her so that she feels almost deranged. At times, she's aware of the intensity of him looking, becomes conscious of the intimacy involved, and blushes. It's as though, she considers, she's been undone suddenly, as if she no longer belongs to herself. She finds the sensation unsettling and electrifying at the same time.

If only it were just that and not this other thing, she thinks. She feels inundated by an imprecise feeling that gathers shadows to itself, and to which she hesitates to attach the word love. The feeling grows scarily dense inside her. She reflects how he appeared out of nowhere, this man, this Capa. There he was, on her first night in Paris and then again when she came back from Berlin. And on the day of the Japanese surrender he lay down next to her and, as she turned her face towards his, he moved through her defences like a stone through a net and kissed her hard on the mouth – just like that.

And because he entered her life so unexpectedly, she was unable to prepare herself or erect her defences. Her guard was down, leaving her exposed.

Had she been aware of him from a distance, she might have

been ready to parry his attacks, to fend him off. But there he was, suddenly. And now before she can gather her thoughts or get things in perspective, she finds herself smitten.

She never thought that this would happen. It never occurred to her that there'd be someone else. But here she is, seized by the need to love this man who is here, as real as the walls of her hotel room, the table in front of her, as actual as the air that surrounds her, and which she breathes.

She thinks of this as he lies asleep beside her, watching car headlights re-draw the angles of the room. At the same time, she feels a pull, as though a hook has lodged itself within her guts. And it's not until his fingers twitch with the slightest pressure against her skin that she realizes they are still holding hands.

Following a warm dreamless sleep, she wakes, stretches her hands above her head, a ray of sparks under her arms, a single white sheet clinging silkily to her skin. She's conscious of the sunlight and the sound of water running as the streets are cleaned outside.

'I should go,' Capa says.

She nods, her eyes liquid with sleepiness, her cheek creased from the pillow.

He dresses, pulling on his clothes, it seems to her, with the practised quickness of a soldier used to leaving a hotspot in a hurry. She reaches for her dressing gown.

'What's going to happen?' she asks.

Impudently he tugs the belt that cinches her robe. 'Come here.'

He embraces her for what seems like a long time. The scent of sleep is still on each of them.

She smoothes a crease in his shirt, straightens his collar, brushes some fluff from the shoulder of his jacket. But the thought claws at her and she looks up at him, large-eyed. 'Don't hurt me. I couldn't stand it,' she says.

There is, she realizes, a kind of concession involved in this, a sense of dependency established. But then, she reflects, he's not the one who's married, who has a child, and a career that hangs upon how the public judges her. The stakes are far less high for him. Everything that seemed so open and free and spontaneous before now seems reined-in and difficult. She feels sick in her stomach, and very much afraid.

He smiles, strokes her hair.

'I mean it,' she says. Contained in her voice is an element of warning.

He nods, opens the door.

She feels the draught against her ankles.

After he's gone, she retreats inside, returns to bed. In pulling the covers up over her, she pulls herself tight shut like a purse.

For a long time, she lies unsleeping. She grows aware of a shadow that takes up no space yet has a weight that drags alongside her.

She has felt like this before.

As a girl she used to imagine her mother coming up behind her at night, putting her arms around her and whispering into her ear, and when she turned round to look, there was her mother just as she appeared in photographs. She'd be squeezed tight, kissed and feel reassured, only a few seconds later for her to wake up, sobbing, clutching the pillow, the bedroom empty, her mother gone.

She thinks of Pia. No matter what else happens, she considers, no matter what shame, suffering or humiliation she endures, she knows one thing: she cannot give up her daughter; she cannot give up Pia. She can't do that, and she won't do that. But she can't think that far ahead.

⌒

Some cards arrive late for Ingrid's birthday, including one from her husband and another, home-made, from her daughter. They each say they miss her, that they love her very much. They both ask her to come home soon. Petter finishes with a single kiss. Pia includes a row of wobbly Xs in crayon after her name.

She also receives an envelope full of clippings from the studio – reviews of *Spellbound* and *The Bells of St Mary's*. The flattering passages are helpfully underlined in blue pencil.

It's odd to think of Ingrid leading this other life with a husband in Hollywood. For a moment I think of it as a secret existence, some kind of shadow life or mirror world, unreal in a way. Then I remember that the secret life is the one she shares with me.

She emerges from the bathroom in a white bathrobe, her head at an angle, rubbing her hair with a towel. She catches me glancing at her cards, which sit on top of a pile of letters, franked with US stamps.

'Is he a jealous man?'

The delay in her response contains a hint of disapproval that I might have been looking at her mail. 'Yes, very,' she says. Her voice seems deeper after the shower. Her gown is tied with a large floppy knot.

'How can he stand you being away?'

'He can't.'

'Then why does he allow it?'

Gathering her hair in a thick twist, she wrings a bit of wet from the back. 'I get paid a lot of money.'

'He's not stupid.'

'You don't think?' She begins hunting for underclothes in a bottom drawer. She doesn't bend at the knees, just stretches effortlessly, retrieves what she wants. 'He doesn't like my leading men.'

'That I can understand.'

'He accuses me of having affairs.'

'And do you?'

She closes the drawer firmly and stands up straight as if to defend her honour. 'That would be unprofessional.'

'Poor guy.'

'He nags me. He doesn't like me eating.'

'He wants you to starve?'

With an efficient snap, she pulls on her underwear beneath her dressing gown. She continues in a sing-song voice, 'He doesn't like me slouching and tells me to stand up straight. He complains about the way I project my voice. He doesn't like it when I laugh – he says it isn't ladylike.' She loosens the belt of her robe, which falls to the floor, releasing her breasts like fruit, sumptuous, glossy. Her normal voice resumes. 'And the annoying thing is, he's almost certainly right, so I don't stop him. He's a good teacher. It's what I need. It's good for me, probably.'

She adjusts her bra, rolls her stockings over her legs. Tan-coloured, they swarm with dabs of shadow. Beneath the clinging skin of material I glimpse a bit of cracked red nail varnish on one of her small toes. It strikes me as exquisite. 'If it were me,' I say, 'I'd also want you all to myself.'

She wriggles into her dress, presents the back for me to zip. 'He never wanted me to be a star. Thought it would turn my head.'

'I thought you said he liked the money.'

'He does, but he hates the films.'

'He doesn't like you in them?'

'*Not bad*, is about the best I ever get. There's always some niggly little criticism. He tells me not to be complacent, but it can be hard sometimes.' She sits down and applies her lipstick in the mirror, her lips stretched wide as in a grimace. 'He thinks they're out to exploit me.'

'What if it's true?'

'Do I seem like a pushover to you?' She dabs her lips with a handkerchief, leaving the crinkly imprint of a kiss on the linen. 'I use them as much as they use me.' She smacks her lips, glances at me in the mirror. 'More, maybe.'

She lifts the hair at the nape of her neck, and with a deft expert gesture fastens a thin gold necklace at the back. Finally she touches some perfume under her ears.

'What does he want, then?'

'For me to sit there looking pretty.'

'It's something you do very well.'

She flashes me a sardonic look.

I'm conscious of her profile reflected in the glass. It adds to the impression of a second, shadow life.

'You know, he didn't even want photographers at our wedding.' She has trouble meeting my eyes.

'Are you afraid of him?'

She stands up, smoothes her dress, gives an instinctive flick to her hair on either side. I watch as she shifts her weight from one leg to the other and tilts her head heartbreakingly the other way.

~

Benedict Canyon
Los Angeles

Dear Ingrid

I trust this letter finds you well. It must be amazing to be in Paris at this time. I wish I could be there with you, seeing it all happen and witnessing it first-hand.

Pia, of course, misses you terribly. She can't understand how you can be so far away and gone for so long, although I keep trying to explain it.

She's very funny. She's discovered this terrific need to finish things and hates being interrupted. There's no stopping her if she's in the middle of doing a puzzle or trying to complete a drawing. I think she's going to be stubborn and determined, just like her mother.

I enclose a recent photograph of her.

Don't worry, it wasn't me who did that to her teeth. She's lost two on either side and the fairy has been busy putting nickels under her pillow.

Work at the hospital is hectic, with ships and planes coming back from Japan, and the men with injuries you wouldn't believe and that I hope you never have to see. Not just mangled limbs either, but more invisible damage – cases of severe psychological trauma, so that many of the boys have trembling fits, drink heavily, and have trouble sustaining any relationships. This is not so easy to heal.

What you're doing is excellent, I know, supporting the troops; we're both very proud of you, and it's good for your career, but the tour must be over by now and we'd love you to come home and help us get back into a routine. The house is quiet and empty without you and we look forward to you restoring order to our lives.

We're keeping the cuttings. Did the script arrive?

Selznick is going crazy and Hitchcock keeps asking after you, as do the people at RKO. I think Hitch is scared you won't come back. But I told him that you'd never let him down.

Anyway, take care my love and we'll see you very soon.

Pia sends many kisses.

Yours, ever
Petter
x

8

This warm September evening, a power cut darkens the capital. A fat tomato-red sunset fills the sky. Dusk falls and, when the electricity comes back on, the streetlights lift the city into brilliance. Traffic streams down the avenues. Music springs from the cafés. And just now I feel a surge within myself, an inflationary sensation. My life seems abruptly full.

In this mood, I want to say yes to everything. I open doors for people, perform a thousand small courtesies, greet everyone with a smile. The generosity of spirit extends to everything around me, so that I surrender my place in a queue for cigarettes, drop coins into a begging bowl. The feeling of largesse fills me like a gas – part of a larger gratitude that widens to include the scent of coffee, the leaves on the trees, the sun in the sky.

Amid the several million or so souls that inhabit this city, what a happy accident it is, I consider, what an obliterating coincidence that we have found each other. What have I done to deserve this, to be so singled-out?

I imagine I see her everywhere: obliquely in shop windows, coming up the stairs of the Métro, through the windshields of passing cars. It's as if I'm surrounded by these versions of her. Traces of her seem to exist all over the city, fragments jumping out at me as if from a splintered mirror.

If asked why I love her, until recently I would have been struck dumb. She's stubbornly herself, utterly mysterious, impervious to words. What could I say? I love the way she writes me notes with a single question, the way she holds her coffee up with both hands, the way she has of pushing the hair from her eyes with her fingers. The mere fact of her being alive is enough to make me happy.

I've seen her almost every day for almost a month now. Every minute, every hour away from her seems wasted. That poise, her voice – that accent, its foreignness. I'm completely under her spell.

It's wonderful to drink too much wine, to smoke too many cigarettes and to wake up with her in the mornings, to feel the weight of her next to me.

It's hard not to feel that, somehow, this is all too good to be true.

I take photos of her everywhere. I'm not used to having anything so luminous in the viewfinder. The light floods in through the lens, and I have to be careful not to over-expose the shots.

Why does the camera love her so much? Something magical and mysterious must happen in that moment when her image hits light-sensitive paper.

In the darkroom of the *Life* offices, I watch a series of prints emerge from their tray of chemicals. I see her redefined, traces of her developing so that here she is, posed like a tourist on the steps of the Sacré Coeur, arms raised at the Trocadéro, laughing dramatically outside Notre Dame.

Her image appears each time from the blankness, precisely outlined. In the red light, I hold the photographs with a pair of tongs, rinsing them in trays of developer and fixer before hanging them up to dry. Sometimes I need to rub the surface of the print with my fingertips or blow on it to develop the tone. The fumes can be overwhelming. My fingernails are brown as though I've smoked a million cigarettes.

The shots of Ingrid differ from my usual pictures, which are quick and improvised. Instead these are lovingly composed, soaked with light.

We sit in a café on the boulevard Saint-Michel, watching the day transform into a late summer's afternoon – trees in leaf, colours brimming, the windows taking sun. The radio plays 'Exactly Like You', and for a few seconds its rhythm seems to match the rhythm of the city outside. I don't know whether it's the music or Ingrid sitting there, her spoon poised over her ice-cream, but everything merges at this moment – the leaves, the sunlight, the scent of vanilla, the street with its sliced shadows – and if I had to define happiness, its one clean note, well, this is the closest I've come to it. I want to hold onto the feeling, to keep a part of it.

And it's funny, but whenever I talked to the GIs and they understood there was a chance they might die the next day, each of them became anxious to tell you about his girl. When things grew tense, many of them would start speaking about this marvellous young woman waiting back home, and you just knew in your heart they couldn't all be telling the truth. You knew there was no way that the poor girls sitting in their cosy parlours back in Gary, Wichita, Poughkeepsie or wherever, could possibly measure up to the image of them desperately projected inside these men's heads. But there they were, imagining their sweethearts as starlets and – this is the amazing thing – really believing it. They had to, I suppose. Because the alternative – the idea that there was nothing wonderful to return to, nothing worth staying alive or fighting for – was too damn hard to face. And in time, from their wallets, each would pull out a crumpled snapshot of a girl, as ordinary and pretty and snaggle-toothed no doubt as any other young woman in her home town, and no different from the fat-ankled girls in Budapest.

These were men, remember, for whom cynicism had become second nature, whose daily existence was atrocity and horror; men who'd seen that viciousness has no limits. Yet these soldiers, so routinely tough and worldly-wise, would sit on their bedrolls and fish letters from their breast pockets, showing them off with all their misspellings and large childish handwriting, with all the cracked and lovelorn phrases that could have come from any dime novel.

I never said anything, of course. In fact the hardest thing has always been just to stand aside and record what's going on, and not to interfere. I've been called callous and morbid, and a lot worse because of it.

The simple fact is, you have to concentrate. Your job is to hold the shutter open when everyone else is busy closing their eyes. You can't allow yourself to flinch, not even for an instant.

And if you want to take a good photograph, if you really want to capture what's going on, then there's no alternative: you need to get close. Fear might squeeze your stomach, terror press at your head, and you might recall every warm and comfortable bed you've ever slept in, but you can't allow those things to get in the way. There's no time. Reason kicks in afterwards. It's only later you have the leisure to consider that you might have been brave or reckless. It's only later you understand what an idiot you've been, only later you realize how lucky you are to have come through in one piece. And in war, when you get close, you learn one thing: there's nothing one man won't do to another in order to survive.

One of the editors knocks, sticks his hand round the door. 'Everything okay, Capa?'

'Why do you ask?'

'You've been in there a long time.'

'I'm working.'

'On what?'

I don't like being interrupted. 'When do I get paid?' I know he doesn't like talking about money. 'Can you give me an advance?'

'Are you kidding?'

'I just need a couple of hundred.'

'I'm sorry, Capa. You know I can't do that.'

'Have I ever let you down?'

'We're full with stuff from Japan. I'm surprised you're not there.'

'You can't get close to an atom bomb.'

'You'd find a way.'

I recall one story that came over the wires. Apparently the light from the explosion was so intense, it developed previously undeveloped film through the walls of a laboratory. I slide a thumb across my eyebrow. 'I don't deserve a rest?'

'Since when have you ever wanted a rest?' He looks round and sees some pictures of Ingrid hung up, twisting slowly in the red light. His lips lift into the tension of a smile. 'You thinking of retiring, Capa?'

'Me?'

'I didn't think you were the type to follow a woman.'

'I didn't follow.'

He tilts his head as if guessing at something. 'No?'

'I was pulled.'

'You still got the stomach for it?' There's a hint of mockery in his voice.

I say, 'It's my liver I'm worried about.'

I'm broke. Nothing new about that, I suppose. I'm always broke, with no regular source of income, other than a small retainer from *Picture Post* and *Life*. And the magazines have their own staff photographers who are desperate for work. They won't keep me on for ever.

Methodically I go through all my clothes, checking each of the pockets of my jackets and trousers. I find notes and dollar bills in the unlikeliest places, including five tucked inside an old sock.

I make a small pile of notes on the bed. Enough for a game, at least.

And this time I get lucky. The cards go my way. I don't count or memorize them – I don't have the patience. I follow no strategy or plan. The trick is always to remain optimistic and only to fold when loss seems unavoidable. It's important to think and play as if you know you're going to win.

Baffled, Irwin scratches his head. 'What's your system, Capa? Have you been taking lessons?'

'No system. I just go on my nerve.'

'I seem to be losing quite a lot at the moment.'

'Hey,' I say, knowing exactly what he means. 'I thought you were married.'

He looks straight at me. 'So is she.'

'You disapprove?'

Irwin reveals that he's going to leave soon. He's had enough of Paris. He plans to head back home to the States. He's moving with his family to a beach house in Malibu, where he intends to write his novel.

'Isn't that close to Hollywood?' I say.

'It's close to the ocean.'

'Do you know anyone there?'

'Are you trying to be funny?'

I smile.

He stabs out his cigarette.

I pat him on the back. 'Think about it,' I tell him. 'We're all winning.'

'How do you figure that?'

'We're alive, aren't we?'

She brings a small overnight bag with her, which seems astonishingly to hold the entire contents of her bathroom cabinet as well as a change of clothes.

Mid-morning when I wake up, I hear a shushing noise, then a series of low scrapes. I wonder at first if it's a mouse scurrying about the room. We're only two doors from a bakery, after all. But the scuffling is thicker, more regular and pronounced. I open my eyes, sit up, and there is Ingrid, up and fully dressed already, with a pan and brush in her hand. Her head is bent towards the floor.

I watch for a few seconds. 'What are you doing?'

She rises, smiles. Her voice like sunlight floods the room. 'Good morning.'

I can't believe this. She's cleaning up after me, tidying my things, folding my clothes, putting my shoes together under the bed.

'There's a maid who does all that.'

Ingrid rolls her sleeves up. 'She should be fired.'

I've never lived in a place so neat. 'I won't be able to find anything now.'

'I couldn't stand it. It was such a mess.' She pronounces this last word with particular distaste. 'How can you live in such squalor?'

I sit up and fold my hands behind my head. 'It's the way I am.'

'Well, it's not the way I am. I have a clean Scandinavian soul.'

'You do?'

'And you'll have to get used to it.'

I light a cigarette, shake out the match, drop it, tinkling, into an ashtray. 'No wonder the Nazis loved you.'

She straightens, stung by this. 'You can be a real bastard sometimes.'

'Weren't you one of their pin-ups? Blonde hair, blue eyes . . .'

'I don't have blonde hair.'

'It looks that way in the movies.'

'Pictures can be deceptive. You should know that.'

'Hey!'

'What?'

'Come here.' I motion her over to the bed.

Arms akimbo. 'Why?'

'Because. . .' I raise my arms, signalling an embrace. 'I want you to.'

'Why are you so cruel?'

'I didn't mean to be.'

'No?'

'I was only teasing.'

'My mother was German. Did you know that?'

'So was my girlfriend.'

'Did she have blonde hair and blue eyes?'

'She was Jewish.'

'And I'm a shiksa. Is that it?'

'Come on. I'm sorry.'

She allows me to kiss her on the cheek, but no more. 'You haven't washed yet. You don't smell too good,' she says.

The zipper on her bag makes a high tearing sound. She puts on her dark glasses, straightens her jacket, places her hat at a fetching angle. And within seconds I'm listening to the regular beat of her heels as they tick-tock down the hall.

⌒

She's checking her face in the bathroom mirror. Expecting to see something changed, expecting not to recognize herself, she's surprised to see her features unaltered, except for a hint of pinkness in her cheeks and something rubbed about her mouth where she's been kissed. Yet inside she feels completely different, utterly transformed.

It's like that sensation you get in a lift, she thinks, when you're not sure whether you're going up or down, and all you're left with is a queasy feeling and a faint impression that your insides are failing to keep pace with the rest of your body.

A trace of herself, it occurs to her, is left behind each time a movie is completed, each time a photograph is snapped, an impression taken and sustained beyond her physical body. Something of her essential self, it seems, is arrested and kept.

She thinks of the photographs Capa has taken of her in the last few weeks. It wouldn't be hard, she knows, for anyone to guess her relationship with the man behind the lens. She touches her fingers to her throat, lifts the hair from her neck and lets it fall.

There's a knock at the door. The spell is broken.

Joe steps in. 'I checked your room. You didn't come back last night.'

'I'm a grown-up, Joe. What do you want me to say?'

'You said you were staying in.'

'I changed my mind. Is that allowed?'

'I need to know you're safe.' After a silence, he goes on. 'You know what this holiday romance could do to you?'

Ingrid stiffens. 'You think that's what this is?'

'Isn't it?'

She feels her insides slip. Has she deceived herself? Are her feelings really that shallow? No, she decides. It's not possible to be so deluded. She knows in her heart it is much more than that. Why else does she experience such torment? Why else would she delay seeing Pia? She longs to see Capa, when she thinks of him now, and wants to feel his arms around her, holding her. It comes to her as a revelation. The idea makes her want to smile. It's only now that she absorbs the fact.

'You needn't worry,' she says. 'If there are consequences, you won't be to blame.'

'You're sure about that?'

A small silence follows. 'Joe, I'm going to need your help.'

'Don't ask me to be a part of this.'

'I'm asking you to trust me.'

'You want to buy my silence?'

'Don't insult me.' She seems thrown out of gear.

'You know the score. You're valuable property. They've invested a lot in your reputation.'

'All I ask is that you let me live for a few weeks.'

'You've had a few weeks.'

A smile rouses creases in her cheeks. 'I'm not exactly Mata Hari.'

'You're not Snow White either.'

'This is very difficult for me, Joe.'

He nods, turns to leave, but his essential chivalry wins through. 'All right. But I'm not taking sides.'

She feels a surge of gratitude. 'Thank you, Joe.'

The door closes quietly.

She goes over to the bed and lies down, exhausted. She crosses her arms over her eyes, considers.

She wants to live life intensely the way she has the last few weeks, to enjoy the kind of love Petter would probably think improper. It's as if she's been granted a kind of permission, the liberty to do things, and she wants to seize this freedom, even though she finds it frightening. After all, there's nothing and no one to hold her back; no one, that is, except herself. She feels invulnerable and wants the feeling to last for ever. At the same time, she knows the whole thing is impossible and struggles to see how it might be sustained.

Her mind follows an invisible bias to a place she visited on holiday as a child at the northernmost tip of Denmark. There, she remembers, two seas – each moving in opposite directions – meet and clash spectacularly. The wind tears at you, swallowing all sounds. Gulls flap like bits of paper. You become conscious of an edge where the horizon ends. You can go no further. This is the limit, the final boundary, and you go right to the point where the land comes to a stop and, trembling like the heather, put one foot in each of the two seas. The water is freezing, but you can still feel the pull of the current in different directions on your legs.

Even now, thinking about it, she feels something open and close, open and close inside her like a jellyfish.

9

There's a full-page advertisement in *Life* for *The Bells of St Mary's*, in which Ingrid plays a nun.

'That's funny,' I say. 'I never imagined you in a habit.'

I pass the magazine across the table. And there she is, a picture of sweet innocence in her dark wimple and robe. Her eyes stare upwards devoutly, shining. Bing Crosby stands in the background looking droll.

'I always wanted to play a saint.'

I give her a sceptical look. 'Really?'

'Joan of Arc is my favourite character.'

'Wasn't she a witch?'

She looks at the magazine, shakes her head, smiles. 'If only people knew the truth.'

'What if they did?'

'It's quite simple. I'd never work in Hollywood again.'

I laugh. She doesn't smile. 'Look,' I say. Below the photograph is an article about her. It begins worshipfully: *She doesn't drink, doesn't smoke, doesn't stay out late at night . . .*

Ingrid raises her wineglass in one hand, her cigarette in the other, and nods.

'Who writes this stuff?'

'The studio has a whole team of people working on things like that.'

'Can you be a saint and eat ice-cream at the same time?'

'It's no joke. You don't realize. The press would destroy me.'

'It wouldn't make you more interesting?'

'People would feel betrayed.'

'Which people?'

She regards me as though I'm stupid. 'The public, of course.'

'You really care what they think?'

'I want them to love me.'

'You're sicker than I thought.'

Again she doesn't laugh. 'It's all right for you. You're not the one who's married.'

'Who said I wasn't?'

Ingrid looks up at me, incredulous. The waiter comes over and pours two more glasses of wine. During the silence Ingrid snaps the pages of the magazine.

The waiter retires.

'Your girlfriend? The one crushed by a tank?'

'No.'

'Who, then?'

'I needed residency.'

'Capa, that's terrible. I don't approve.'

'I threw in a year's dancing lessons.'

'I can't believe you did that.'

'She liked to dance.'

'You know what I mean.'

'I was about to be deported back to the Nazis. What would you have done?' I look at her and she shakes her head. She doesn't believe me. 'I'm serious.'

'You're never serious.'

'I am about this.'

'Did you love her?'

'I hardly knew her.'

'Did you sleep with her?'

'I tried it on in the car afterwards. She slapped my face and ran off. We didn't even say goodbye.'

Ingrid tuts. 'Have you seen her since?'

'No, never.'

'And the dance lessons?'

'I'm still saving up.'

She begins fiddling with a spoon, tapping it against the side of her glass. It makes a series of high clinks. A woman at a nearby table looks over, irritated by the sound.

'It's typical of you. Frivolous.'

'It saved my life.'

'If you want to save your life, don't be a war photographer.'

'It's my job.'

'It's your job to get yourself killed?'

'I'm short enough to avoid the shells.'

'All for what? For just a few pictures?'

'Hey, I risk nothing for less than a four-page spread.'

She blinks for longer than is necessary. Her back remains very straight. Her eyes grow solemn. 'Don't you ever get scared?'

'Let me tell you, it's not easy changing your pants under fire.'

At first she looks challenging, then frustrated. She shakes her head, begins pulling on her gloves. 'You're insane,' she says.

I don't say anything, just watch her face tighten, the hair on her scalp slide back.

'You ought to be careful, Capa,' she says. 'One of these days, your luck will run out.'

It happens like this.

My legs ache from all the walking, and my face aches from the rain that soaks me through and drips miserably from the tip of my helmet onto my nose. It's been raining for days. Everywhere is mud. The smell of shit rises like steam from the fields.

The rain quickens, heavier this time, relentless and drenching. The wind narrows between the farmhouses. You can see the shape of it in the trees, swaying as if in layers of water. A ripple of wind must enter an opening in my sleeve because I feel a chill run up my arm and spread across my back.

A split-second later, there's a flash. The explosion deafens everyone, a concussive shock, sending clumps of soil and grass a hundred feet into the air. There's no suspense or hovering, no moment at which you're conscious of a shell screaming its way towards you. The sound comes after it hits.

Things in this instant fly off at all angles.

My ears ring. My heart slams inside my chest. My skin stings as if flayed.

There are screams of pain, terrible cries of anguish.

I run to get close, to get closer, through the smoke and the noise and the confusion, to where the shells landed, so I can see first-hand what's happening. I hold the camera in front of me like a torch.

There's a rhythm to the shelling, a heavy *pom pom pom*, with the space of a few seconds between each new launch of ordnance. Gaps are smashed into the farmhouses and hedges. The holes smoke as though the explosions come from underground.

One guy is hurt. He pitches sideways and staggers as if tipsy. He's coming towards me, stupefied.

I get off several shots, framing him in the viewfinder. I watch him, paralysed for a moment, not so much with fear but with fascination, because he's looking straight at me.

His eyes are staring, intense, and it's as if he's asking me a question and waiting for a response, or as though he's accusing me of something. With an odd, otherworldly roll, his eyes turn inwards. For the first time he must glimpse with appalling clarity what is happening, recognize the vast space opening up beneath his feet. His head lolls at a dreadful angle. His eyes, still open, are fixed into the distance. He stands for a moment in a strange motionless pose before falling to the ground.

'No,' is all he says.

At this moment something inside him seems to collapse. Frightened, he starts to pant, inhaling desperately in shallow gasps.

It's not long before his whole body is convulsing. He cries, not quite soundlessly. One of his arms makes a violent movement, and abruptly the convulsions stop.

The blood turns his uniform crimson, mixing with the grass and the mud as it spills on the ground around him.

'It's all right,' says one of the men tending to him. 'It's going to be all right.'

But I know just from looking at him, with his face already grey like water half-frozen, that it is not going to be all right. He is not going to be okay. He stares ahead dumbly as if at some dark secret place, a hidden inner landscape, cold as the space between the stars.

And the only way I know of answering that look of his is to show it, to expose it, somehow to communicate the stink and the hell and the waste of it, so that in the end there exists no gap between the camera and the action – so that, even though you can't smell the sweat and stench of decay or feel the rain on your face, nevertheless when you look at the photograph you'll feel as if you're there, while those who *are* there won't even notice because I'm so much a part of what's going on, and when they see the images later they'll be moved to say, 'That's how it was.'

It's only when something tragic happens that the fact hits home and the men remember why I'm here. And they recognize that I'm here because I want to be and not because anyone compels me. I'm here because I've chosen this job. It's my decision to risk my life. The more conscious they become of this, the more they consider me plain crazy, even dangerous. They can't understand why any sane person would do such a thing, and you can sense them getting edgy as if I might bring them bad luck. Because it's clear they'd do anything to get the hell out of here, seize any chance to take the boat home. I know what they're thinking. What son-of-a-bitch wants to take those pictures anyway? Doesn't that make me some kind of vulture? Or a voyeur, at least? Doesn't that make me one of the damned? And the more you see, the less you feel. So they loathe me at these moments for having the freedom of choice they never had, and for choosing wrong.

Ingrid tells me to get on the bed and to stand on one leg. I ask her why, and she says to just do it. So I stand on one leg on the bed, wobble a bit but hold it steady. The mattress is hard and springy beneath my feet.

'That's good.'

Once she sees I'm not going to fall over, she tells me to close my eyes.

'Still on one leg?'

'Trust me.'

'All right.'

'Try to keep your balance.'

I close my eyes.

At school in the gym, I remember, there was a yellow line that stretched the whole way down the hall. The teacher told us to walk along it, to imagine it as a tightrope strung high above the ground, understanding that one wrong step would cause us to fall off. It seemed easy, a simple matter of putting one foot in front of the other. In fact it proved surprisingly difficult. Very few of us succeeded in maintaining our balance the whole way. The teacher stood with his arms folded, laughing out loud as first one and then another tipped sideways, stumbling. I was one of the few who managed it.

Blind this time, I hold my balance for a few seconds but soon there comes a tumbling sensation. It starts inside my ears and extends to my legs. I become disorientated, feel myself plunging headlong, and the next thing I know I'm toppling like a log onto the bed.

Ingrid laughs.

I pull her down next to me so that she shrieks. Our heads are very close.

'Just one thing.' She props herself up on one elbow, keeps the hair out of her eyes with her hand.

'What?'

She looks at me intently.

'What is it?'

'I don't want to get pregnant.'

'Haven't I been careful?'

'When are you ever careful?'

'When it matters.'

'And it matters now?'

'Absolutely.'

She looks sceptical. 'What makes me so different?'

'Everything.'

'I don't want to get pregnant.'

'Trust me,' I say.

⮑

Tonight in Paris, the sky is purple, thin like the skin of an onion, layer upon layer making it opaque. The trees around the street-lamps seem apparitions. The air is stirred-up, the moon risen, obscurely tugging at something.

Ingrid is tired, her nerves stretched tight. Her head is buzzing from too much wine, too much coffee, too many things on her mind.

She stands for a few moments in the middle of her hotel room, as if trying to make connections between all the parts of her life. She finds herself laughing at some small funny thing that is private between her and Capa, and knowing it is small and exists just between them makes it all the funnier. At the same time she's shocked to find herself entertaining the idea of a little world which only the two of them inhabit – a world that her husband, Petter, has been banished from, in which he's invisible, in which he doesn't exist. For the first time, she feels life is possible, even preferable, without him.

She grows conscious of the night outside, its late fragrant flowers and simmering insects, the seethe of people, the city's lazy nocturnal warmth, and the lamps that hang like fruit. And with it comes a heedless sense, a refusal to feel afraid or regret anything, only a determination to keep the excitement going, and never to look back.

Ingrid stands by the long window in her room, when Joe enters clutching yet another telegram.

'They're getting impatient,' he says. Silence spreads like a carpet between them. 'What shall I tell them?'

She laughs, looks out of the window onto the square. 'Can I ask you a question, Joe?'

'Sure.'

'Do you think it's right to stay married to a man when you no longer love him?'

Joe looks on gravely, stares at the floor. His hand holding the telegram falls to his side. 'You realize what you're saying?'

'You think I'm crazy?'

'I think you're lucky to have a husband who loves you, a healthy daughter, a beautiful home. Most women would kill for what you have.'

The thought chases through her brain. 'Well, what if I want more?' She says this not from any sense of triumph, but out of despair.

His look is full of pity. 'If you're not careful, you might end up with a lot less.' He stands motionless for a moment. He makes a scroll of the telegram and slaps it several times against his thigh before turning and leaving the room.

Ingrid stands by the window, touches it with her finger. The glass feels cold. She presses the finger repeatedly to her hot cheek, then presses her cheek against the window. She has the sensation of life existing mistily on the other side. Her thoughts swerve towards Capa, and it's as if a rib of hers cries out. Flickeringly his image returns to her, spun on a dodgy inward projector, mingling with the lights of the city outside. She unsticks her face from the window, leaving a shapeless patch of redness where her skin has pressed, still warm.

~

When we come out of Maxim's, it's raining and we take a cab. The streets of the city appear inky, rinsed. Between the blur of the wipers, the streetlamps seem swollen then fractured for a moment. The shadows of the trees look dark and ragged. Headlights splinter to form Xs like kisses. And as if by magic, droplets of rain tremble upwards on the windshield, forced backwards by the wind and speed of the car.

We're pressed next to each other in the back of the car. She crosses her legs towards me, nuzzles her head into my neck and smiles. I enjoy the feeling of warmth, the sense that our bodies fit together, the knit of our limbs.

Still, when the cab stops outside her hotel and she motions almost routinely for me to follow her up, it comes as a surprise when I hear myself say no. I tell her that I'm tired, and that anyway I promised to meet Irwin.

'So you're not tired.'

'I said I'd see him.'

'You know what time it is?' Instinctively she looks at her watch.

'He stays up late.'

'As long as we're clear, then. You prefer to be with him than with me?'

'He's leaving soon.'

'So am I.'

There's a silence in which a host of different odours lifts upwards, composed of her raincoat, the tang of wet hair and the cool sweetness of her perfume. Cars move up and down the square.

She says, 'Come back with me.'

'Now?'

She pushes her hair behind her ears.

'You can get too much of a good thing,' I tell her.

We both know this isn't true.

She looks at me, startled for a second, and it feels all wrong, but something stubborn inside me, some pig-headed impulse, some crazy wayward instinct won't let me apologize or take it back, and I allow Ingrid to get out of the cab alone.

I feel the rush of cold air as she holds open the door. 'I'll call you,' I say. The door thuds shut, making me blink. A bus swishes past massively.

The seat is still warm next to me. I pick off one of her long hairs from my jacket. The traffic lights change, streaking the windshield with colour. Half of me wants to undo the moment, to stop the cab and run out and hold her and never let her go, but I don't, because whatever it is that is bloody-minded and obstinate in me takes over, and with a show of nonchalance that shocks even myself, I do not once look back.

We don't see each other the next day. The day after that, I take Ingrid to the races at Longchamp.

We buy programmes and one of the racing papers so we can study the form. From the infield we watch the grooms lead their horses round the ring. The heads of the horses nod rhythmically. You can spot the nervous ones, the jockeys patting them, talking to them constantly, and it's obvious which mounts carry themselves well. We're so close, we can see the muscles rippling tensely, the veins in their legs like little ropes, their big muddy eyes. The smell of liniment from the jockeys mixes with the animals, their pungency, to create a sharp stink under the late summer sun.

We make our way to the grandstand. Below the stands, in shadow, the betting booths are the same chestnut colour as the horses. The rails are white against the grass. The odds are posted high on boards.

Poised in the saddle, silks glistening, the jockeys canter their horses to the start.

It's Ingrid's first time at a meeting. She's bought a pair of binoculars for the occasion. She holds them with both hands, training them on the course. Magnified like this, she says, the horses seem to float over the ground.

We sit next to the long window in the bar overlooking the final straight. The sun runs a long fat rainbow across the glass.

She starts talking about her husband, how he's pestering her to go back home, sending letters and telegrams urging her to return.

I don't say anything.

'He's so mean,' she says. 'For years he's had me on an allowance. I have to ask permission even to buy a pair of shoes.'

'Why did you marry him?'

'I was twenty-one. He was handsome, strong . . .'

'Wealthy?'

She laughs. 'He had his own car.'

'And now?'

Through the big plate-glass window, we see the horses trot diagonally towards the stalls before the main race of the day, a seven-furlong steeplechase. I borrow the binoculars. The long oval of the course seems oddly foreshortened.

'I never thought I'd be unfaithful,' she says.

The last horse is blinkered and shunted in, the gates closed. The remote crack of the starter's pistol reaches us an instant after the blue puff of smoke. Wrens fly up from under the roof.

Ingrid studies her hands for a moment, twists her ring. 'It's not easy for me, you know. I was brought up to be very moral.'

The horses complete one circuit of the track. Having bunched at first, they begin to string out. There's a leading group of three.

She takes back the binoculars, lifts them to her face, hiding behind them. 'I know what you're thinking,' she says. Her tone grows needling, accusatory. 'You're thinking we shouldn't do anything hasty. We've only known each other a couple of months.'

I laugh, delay reassuring her. 'Would that be wrong?'

'I could have any man I choose.'

'So why choose me?'

'I'm used to getting what I want.'

'You deserve better,' I say.

Ingrid lowers the binoculars and turns abruptly, her eyes burning. 'Why are you like this?'

At first it's funny, then it's not. 'Like what?'

'If I were to give you my unswerving devotion, would you promise to love me always in return?'

'Of course not.'

The leading group of three becomes two as they sweep around in front of us again.

'Do you want children?'

'Me?' I laugh.

'Is that so absurd?'

'You've only just finished telling me you don't want to get pregnant.'

I weigh the silence that follows.

Her whole face has changed, her eyes look tragically unhappy. 'Marry me, Capa.'

My blood jumps. I expected something – perhaps a sharp remark or teasing riposte, something ironical maybe, but not this. It's not a question, it's a directive. It takes every ounce of my energy not to leap out of my seat. 'Are you serious?'

An announcement on the tannoy is so loud and crackly, it's inaudible.

My stomach falls. I'm not up to the moment. I find it impossible to be solemn. 'Can I have a few years to think about it?'

She shakes her head, regards the mangled end of a cigarette in the ashtray. 'I knew you'd laugh it off.'

I don't tell her how much I long to say yes. I don't tell her that I can think of nothing better. I don't tell her how every bone in my body aches, every sinew strains to respond positively, nor do I tell her how I need every bit of willpower, every ounce of self-restraint to stop me launching myself into her arms.

She looks at me, so lovely and naïve, as if I have answers to everything.

'I've told you already,' I say. 'I can't allow myself to get attached. If they say China tomorrow and we're married and have a child, I won't be able to go, and that's impossible.'

One of the horses begins to pull away.

'In my mind, you marry the man you love and that's the end of it.'

Needing to do something, I reach across for my drink.

'I believe in marriage,' she says, flatly.

The strain of stretching enters my voice without me wanting it to. 'As a fairy tale or an institution?'

'Both.'

'Suppose I'm not the marrying kind?'

The race moves into its final circuit. There's mounting excitement in the bar. Patrons wave their papers and shout encouragement. The lead horse, it seems, is slowing. The grey in second place is catching up.

'You're impossible,' she says.

'You made a mistake with your dentist. How do you know you're not doing the same with me?'

'You think this is a mistake?'

The window is blind with sun.

'What about your daughter?'

'You're happy that I'll leave and we'll never see each other again?' Her eyes are clouded with tears.

The race approaches its climax, the two front horses involved in a very close finish.

'Come to Hollywood, at least,' she says. 'The studios are always looking for photographers.'

'You want me to take publicity shots?'

'You should consider it.'

The feeling of resistance continues within me. I know what I should say, what I want to say. I hate myself for not saying it, realize how stupid it must seem, but I'm determined perversely not to appear impressed. My mouth opens like a bubble between my lips. 'I will,' I say. 'Consider it.'

'I could keep you.'

'I don't want to be kept.'

'You want to spend the rest of your life in crummy hotels?'

'I'm just not sure I'm ready.'

'If you wait until you're ready, you'll be waiting all your life.'

My leg jiggles. I hear the nail of her index finger tick against her glass.

The race ends. It's neck and neck at the finish. The horses are moving easy now.

The sound of a few cheers mixes with a more general groan of disappointment. People crowd around the bar. There's a renewed flood of sunshine through the glass. The angle of the light now blinds me, so that I have to avert my eyes.

The ticking of her fingernail stops. We keep our separate silences, become strangers for a few seconds. I'm not used to thinking beyond tomorrow, so it's bewildering to consider how the rest of my life might unfold.

She says, 'We don't have long.'

My mouth opens but I can't think what to say.

'You've got something against Hollywood?' she asks. 'Or is it just me?'

'That's where Irwin is headed.'

'I know. He told me.'

Another silence.

'You think they'd take me?'

She manages a smile. 'They let anyone in these days. That's why it's such a great country.'

'I'm not making any promises.'

'You can't die, Capa.' A new decisiveness enters her voice. 'I won't let you.'

A plane flies low over the race-track. Its wings sparkle for an instant. The noise drowns out the sound of an announcement. Numbers are slotted onto the board. The winning number looks familiar. I rummage in my pocket, check my yellow betting slip. 'Hey, look.'

'What?'

'We won!'

I plug my cigarette into the side of my mouth, double-check the slip. It's true.

Without smiling, Ingrid turns to the window and its view of a still brilliant sky.

★

Along with Irwin, I dodge a row of cars on the place de Clichy. The policeman's whistle is just audible above the traffic.

We go to Scheherazade, a favourite haunt of Irwin's, not far from Montmartre. The waiters are Russian. They wear tight red tunics with gold braid on the shoulders and wheel drinks and hors d'oeuvres along on small trolleys. Lit from beneath, the tables have transparent glass tops. The club is full of smoke and loud with gypsy music.

I tell him what happened yesterday with Ingrid.

'Are you nuts?'

'Probably.'

'Let me get this straight. The world's most beautiful woman asked you to marry her and then asked you to follow her to Hollywood – and you said no?'

'Guilty on both counts.'

'You could do a lot worse, you know.'

'I have,' I say. 'Several times already.'

'I can give you the name of a good doctor.' His tone of mockery shades into disapproval.

'I'm sure she only asked because she knew I'd say no.'

It's true, I'm certain. And what she said was not premeditated. I'm convinced of that. It was a rash offer, made on impulse, a sudden whim. She took me for a gambler and called me, but it was obvious that she hadn't thought it through. For all her pantomime of disappointment, a large part of her must have been relieved when I said no. I'm sure it would have scared the hell out of her if I'd said yes. Maybe I should have, just to see how she'd respond. Anyway, the whole thing has left me feeling utterly confused.

I tell Irwin, 'I've never been able to read a woman's mind.'

'If you don't know her mind, how can you love her?'

'For the mystery.'

'And when the mystery is gone?'

'Oops.'

He laughs. 'There's a larger mystery still.' He lights a cigarette, shakes out the match.

'What's that?'

'Why do men run away from women who want them?'

'It's not that men run away,' I tell him. 'The women just stand still.'

A column of blue smoke rises from his mouth. 'Maybe they stand still for a reason,' he says.

Ingrid finishes reading a letter from her husband and sits motionless, contemplative for several seconds.

Petter complains of her folly and self-indulgence in not coming back straightaway as planned. He tells her again how she risks compromising her career and breaching the terms of her contract; how, while she lingers in Paris, there are hundreds of pretty and talented young women knocking daily on Selznick's door, begging for a part. She can't take it for granted, he says, that the studio will have her back, and she has to be careful now that she's turned thirty. Few female stars survive long after that. And he tells her how much Pia misses her, crying often, feeling abandoned by her mother. She's grown afraid of the dark, he says, and needs her bedside lamp switched on all night so she won't be scared.

He's exaggerating, she's certain. It's not as if she doesn't see Pia. And she has not done what many of her fellow stars do, which is to ship any children straight off to boarding school. She sees Pia most days when she's not working, and pretty much every weekend, then for weeks at a time at Christmas and Easter, and for much of the summer holidays. They go cycling and swimming together. They go shopping in the stores, and for walks in the hills. Pia is no different from many other young boys and girls in Hollywood – pretty, spoilt, precocious, a little bit lonely maybe without a brother or sister to play with – but with every benefit of American plenty spent on her education and leisure. The loneliness she won't apologize for. Wasn't she lonely as a kid, being an only child? After all, her own mother was dead before she had a chance to know her, and she survived all right, didn't she, learning to be self-reliant? And wasn't it out of loneliness that her imagination flourished? And from that grew her love of dressing up, her love of dreaming and reading, her longing to act. And while she wouldn't wish the grief of orphanhood on her daughter for the world, it was out of this she knows that her inner life quickened, her sense of independence and self-possession thrived. This is a low trick of Petter's, she considers, to use their daughter's affections as a bargaining chip to get her back. It's wrong and simple-minded to think that a child can't survive without the constant attention of her mother. The important thing for Pia is to know that her mother loves her, and Ingrid loves her without reservation. She is confident that Pia recognizes this as a fundamental fact of her life.

Seeing children in the sandpit in the Champs de Mars this morning, though, playing with their mothers, made her want suddenly to hold her daughter's hand, to reassure her, to catch up on what she's been doing and to meet her friends. She thinks of the girl she saw who reminded her of Pia, skipping between two long ropes twirled in opposite directions, and experiences a pang.

As for her career, well, there may be lots of beautiful girls in Los Angeles, but few of them can act and fewer still are willing to put in the necessary hours of hard work. How many of them have slaved to learn the techniques? How many of them are determined to be professional like her? And while Selznick might be happy for aspiring starlets to bedamsel his couch, he will tolerate their simpering only for so long. In the end, he of all people knows that it's the box-office that counts, and he's smart enough not to discard his prize asset. Still, she knows there are limits and she needs to be careful not to overstep the mark.

It occurs to her again that she's been living her life, but not living in it, and only now does she feel she's beginning to pursue an existence that allows her to be true to who she really is. She loves working; it fulfils a profound emotional need within her, and she's desperate to be successful, but not at any cost. Her time with Capa has awakened a deeper ambition. Yes, she's happy that her movies make money, but she wants something more.

With Capa – and Joe, who sat behind rather than between them at the cinema as he had threatened – she went to see *Open City*. The film is terrific in depicting the work of the Resistance in Rome before the end of the war. The cast play themselves; none of them is a professional actor, and the vanishingly small budget makes her own films seem over-produced, glossy and contrived. Seeing the film moved her deeply; she appreciated its authenticity. She'd rather be remembered for a picture such as this, she thinks, which is fresh and unsentimental, than for all the money-making hits in Hollywood.

She takes her husband's letter and slips it back into its envelope, adding it to a growing pile of mail. Then she flops back onto the bed, face down, turns to stare at the ceiling, and lies there without moving for what seems like a very long time.

10

Traceries of light make nets on the low bridges. There's a wind off the river, a coolness. The water ripples, phosphorescent, nicked with white, its skin lifting and sinking as if something big stirs within. The moon revolves coldly. Clouds spin as in a bowl.

Inside, I lie on the bed, trying to read. The light above me buzzes, mingles with a more fundamental hum inside my mind. The print on the page swarms. The letters blur as if rained-on.

Like a bit of glass or shrapnel that takes years to work its way to the surface of the skin, the taste of bad dreams enters my mouth. I hear shouting on the street outside. A car back-fires loudly. I feel myself fall into the gaps between the words on the page, and without warning I'm crouched ankle-deep in bilge water and vomit at the bottom of a barge, my Contax taut in an oilskin round my neck.

The ramp is down and we're pouring out thickly like molasses from a jar. Immediately bullets spit and hiss at us, ripping holes in the water where we wade waist-deep.

The sea is grey and freezing. A chill, silvery sensation spreads upwards to cover my legs and my stomach. Planes hum over-head and boats throb in the water until the deep vibration mixes with the fear I feel and I stand open-mouthed, terrified. Shells explode in the water with a thunk, throwing up huge walls of spray. Bursts of gunfire flirt around me. My whole body shakes. Everywhere there's choking smoke and flak. My ears are full of confusion.

The next moment is lost to me. Gunfire rains down from hid-den pillboxes and machine-gun nests in the cliffs. They have a clear view of us. Lines of barbed wire make it easy for the machine-gunners. We're totally exposed.

The waterline is already stained red. Corpses roll like logs on the waves around me. And everywhere men are crying, blubbering like infants, their faces twisted with fear. My mind darts ahead but can't conceive of what to do. The only way to survive, I decide, is to keep moving. I ditch my overcoat, discard my shovel and bedroll in an effort to lighten the load. By some miracle, I make it to the beach.

I can't feel my legs under me. I've never been so scared. Mortars and rockets set fire to the sky. Smoke billows from burnt-out tanks and holed barges.

My stomach feels empty, my knees non-existent. I reach for my hip-flask and take a good slug. I lie flat and still for several seconds, slip the Contax from its sheath and get off a few shots.

I dodge from one anti-tank trap to another, get through several rolls of film, shooting blindly, head down, my hands in front of my face to click. But I'm shaking so much that, even before I can load a new film, the wet on my fingers ruins it.

The tide is coming in, pushing me on towards the barbed wire. A bible washes up in the scum. The shells land nearer. The noise is tremendous, deafening. Going to war is a wager, I know. So far I've been lucky, stayed ahead of the percentages, but it's only a matter of time before a bit of shrapnel or a bullet catches me.

I figure it's time to beat it. I turn and run, back to the water.

The nearest boat is fifty yards away. The riptide hits me, slaps me in the face. The water reaches right up to my chest. I hold the cameras high to keep them dry. Bullets ping close to me.

I'm just a few feet from the boat when it takes a direct hit and explodes. There's blood and debris everywhere. The stuffing from the kapok jackets drifts down in a blizzard of white feathers.

I'm shivering with cold. My head thuds with the endless shelling. I think of my mother, my brother, of Gerda, and in a series of lightning-fast thoughts I have the absurd luxury to wonder whether in her last moments she thought of me.

As if in answer, another boat appears ghostlike amid the smoke. I manage to scramble aboard.

I can still taste the vomit in my mouth, which mixes with the smell of oil and the scent of salt water to make me nauseous, so that even now as I try to collect myself, I feel the gorge rise in my throat.

And I endure all this only for some idiot in a darkroom back in London in a stupid hurry to overheat the negatives, let the emulsion run and melt almost all of the pictures.

Only a few shots survive. They blame my trembling fingers for the fact they're out of focus.

That was 6 June 1944. Exactly one year to the day later, I met Ingrid. The worst and best days of my life.

That must mean something, I think.

In an adjoining room, someone flushes the toilet. The water drains noisily, recalling that moment in a train when you press the pedal and see beneath your feet the blurred hurtle of the tracks, hear that sudden vortical roar.

Irwin is hunkered over his typewriter when I walk in. There are several screwed-up pages and abandoned drafts surrounding him on the desk. He's working to a deadline.

He doesn't stop typing, nor does he look at me, but he speaks with a cigarette still in his mouth. 'You know something?'

I sense from his tone that it's not going to be a compliment. 'What?'

'After a few days back in the States, she'll have forgotten you ever existed.' He pulls the carriage back hard, continues clacking away.

'Things are different now.'

'Don't delude yourself, Capa. These may be strange times, and it seems like anything can happen.'

'It has.'

'But when the dust settles, you'll see things haven't changed that much. The rich will retreat back into their palaces, leaving guys like you and me to press our noses against the glass.'

I look at him. 'I didn't realize you were so bitter.'

'Skip it.' He stops typing, rests his cigarette in the ashtray, stares at the page in front of him.

Silence.

He rips a piece of paper out of the machine, screws it up and throws it at the waste bin next to me, misses.

I don't pick it up.

He takes a clean piece of paper, places it on the roll together with a carbon, and starts typing again. 'Have you told her about Gerda?'

'Yes.'

'How much?'

'You think I tell her everything?'

He plants the cigarette back in his mouth. 'Don't you think you should?' He looks at me and carries on typing. His fingers clatter on the keys. The sound is like a machine-gun going off inside my head.

In the red light of the darkroom, I show Ingrid files of photographs and contact sheets. She inspects the images hung up to dry, watches as I rinse one print in liquid and lift it, still dripping, with a pair of tongs.

'You're an artist,' she says.

'There's nothing artistic about war. I just get close enough and click.'

'But you're creative, aren't you? That doesn't change. Why don't you photograph other things?'

When I ask her what she means by 'other things', she struggles to come up with stuff other than flowers and landscapes and faces. I need something more, I tell her. I'm tempted to say that I need to feel history going on around me, even if I'm only able to touch it in small ways. But that's not exactly true. The feeling is more immediate than that. What I need, I suppose, is the idea of the world moving ahead in a direction connected with me, and the direction is always dictated by war. So there's really no alternative. That's the way it is, and that's not something that changes either.

'Is it worth it?' she says.

'Someone has to show it.'

'Does it have to be you?'

'I remember in Spain, this one guy stood up. I had him in my viewfinder. And the instant I clicked the shutter, he was hit. Absolutely at the same moment I took the photograph.'

She eyes me sceptically. 'So you want them to be shocking, but you also want people to say, hey, great photograph?'

'It's a way of taking a stand.'

'I can think of safer ways.'

'That pay better?'

After a silence, she says, 'You really think you can change things?'

'You think I should stop trying?'

'You obviously enjoy it.' Now she's getting cross. When I don't answer, she goes on, 'My husband has spent the last three years treating soldiers, then having to send them back.'

I say, 'Maybe he shouldn't treat them so well.' I notice she doesn't laugh. 'Anyway, I thought you said he was a dentist.'

'He is. I mean he was,' she corrects herself. 'At least that's how I think of him. He re-trained as a brain surgeon.'

'That's even worse. A brain surgeon, and he still can't see his wife is unhappy?'

This touches off something in her. 'At least he's smart enough not to get himself killed.'

My mouth feels furry. There's dust everywhere – on the dresser, on the table, the long thin bed with its iron headboard like a grille.

I'm trying to read. But as the light beyond the window ebbs, a strange thing happens. Perhaps I nod off for a moment. Either that or I must have chosen to lie on an especially soft part of the bed because, beneath my weight, the mattress seems to give and I feel myself falling. It's a tiny instant, a split-second of terror like those moments when you tumble in a dream. My whole body seems to jump. I sit bolt upright, breathless. The blood thuds in my ears.

I notice a dent in the lampshade, the bubbles in a pane of glass, the pitted surface of bricks beyond the window. The world is full of holes and cracks, and people seem simply to disappear into them. I think about how mysterious this is. Nothing seems smooth or beautiful just now.

The city outside becomes a gap of darkness like a river seen at night. Slowly, as in a double exposure, a more intense darkness seems superimposed over the room. I'm conscious of a sweet smell, a perfume. And abruptly I feel something touch me, graze my arm.

The cold touch of fingers, is it? A hand against my skin?

I freeze, paralysed by dread, experience a hot panic. A sweat breaks out across my back. Ghosts swarm, flicker palely.

I hear a voice, a woman whispering. The suspicion hardens into a certainty. Blind, I can't see her but I know she's there. I can feel it behind my eyes. The idea seizes me, won't let go. Her presence hovers as in a fogged mirror.

The thought launches a terror within me. The grille behind me is cold as a stone. It's so black outside now, I cannot manage a shadow. The darkness presses, pinning me down.

∽

Ingrid listens to him tell her how her skin glows, how her eyes look dreamy, especially after wine. He says this as he puts his arm around her.

She has sensed in recent days and weeks a new self starting to appear, as if a fledgling identity were beginning to emerge. She has grown into the space left blank in her marriage. It's as if finally she's surfacing, having been submerged against her will.

It occurs to her that this might register in the way she looks, and wonders if a photograph would pick it up. It's at this moment that she notices something odd. Capa doesn't seem to have his cameras with him. She knew there was something different, something missing. There's an absence at the centre of his chest. Then she discovers that he's pawned them. When she asks him why, he says, 'To be with you.' He needs the money, he says.

She's appalled. How could he do that? That's just nonsense, she tells him. How could he believe that? It would be the equivalent of her giving up acting, of rejecting the best part of herself. Unthinkable.

She looks across at him, his hair with a glisten of brilliantine, a smile stretching the corners of his mouth. How can he live in such a disposable way, with no thought for personal possessions, no sense of tomorrow? She admires the sensibility, finds his heedlessness appealing, but there's something about it that also unnerves her, makes her feel uneasy, even scares her. An inner discipline asserts itself. 'You shouldn't compromise your work for me,' she says.

He touches the place on his chest where the Leica would hang. 'You wouldn't, I suppose.'

'No, you're right. I wouldn't,' she says. 'I practise something every day. Even now I'm doing my stomach exercises.'

'Why?'

'Why? So you don't notice the fat.' She rolls up her blouse to expose the convexities of her belly, pushes an accusing finger into her midriff. 'Petter wouldn't allow that.'

'What else wouldn't he let you do?'

'You leave him alone. He loves me. He's a good manager.'

'But a bad husband?'

She swats away a fly. 'I'm a bad wife.'

Ingrid feels angry with Capa. She also feels troubled by his question and by her over-solemn response to it. Behind it, the latest letter from Petter rankles. She feels the pressure of his words exerted from thousands of miles away, that implacable sense of will disguised as moral principle.

There's another thing that bothers her and now batters like an insect inside her head. It represents a hole in their conversation, a gap in their talk, and she can't ignore it or let it go. 'Tell me about your girlfriend.'

'*You're* my girlfriend.'

She rubs her hands together. 'The one who died.'

'Gerda?'

'Were you with her . . . ?'

His eyes flinch minutely. 'If I'd stayed, she'd still be alive.'

'You must have loved her.'

He shifts his weight uncomfortably.

She feels the trace of this other woman upon her like a stain. 'Am I very different?'

He kisses her on the forehead, puts one hand on her leg, a gesture of tenderness, and as if in a trance tells her how they met in Berlin, how Gerda taught him to dress with style, stopped him drinking and gambling to excess. In return, he gave her a Leica and showed her how to take photographs. Both Jewish, and each fired by a hatred of fascism, they joined the Republican side in the Spanish Civil War. The one time he came back to Paris, she stayed on near Madrid.

He read about her death in the newspaper, he says, of all things while sitting in the barber's chair, waiting to have his hair cut. Afterwards he saw the crushed buckle of her belt and learnt that as she lay dying, delirious with morphine, all she asked about was the camera and whether or not it had survived intact.

He doesn't need to explain any more. And though she's moved almost to tears by his story, she feels excluded, and that feeling merges with a deeper sense of him not caring enough about her, and in an unreasoning human way this upsets her. She's conscious of the unfairness of her thoughts, but can't help feeling the pain of her unhappy marriage, the pressure on her to return, and the urge within her, increasingly desperate, to do something before it's too late.

'What was she like?' she says. 'You're comparing me, aren't you?'

He says nothing, removes his arm from around her shoulders, maintains a baffled silence.

'I need to know.'

Things tumble inside her, become mixed up as in a dream. She knows she's being irrational, but the feeling gathers and quickens inside her, and there's nothing she can do to stop it. In the silence that follows she takes a deep breath to steady herself. 'Between the two of us, who would you choose?'

'What are you saying?'

Her blood bumps. 'If she were to walk in through that door right now, which one of us would you walk out with?'

'Ingrid, she's dead.'

There's a momentum that won't be stayed. She hurls the words at him: 'And you can't stand the fact, can you?'

He prevents her with his hand from leaving.

She feels the contending pressure of something rising up and pushing down simultaneously, the pull of love, the tug of the studio, the fear of jealousy, the flood of Petter's letters, the yearning to assert her identity, so that her heart feels squeezed and her lungs are filled with something dense like water.

She pushes him off.

'You should get your cameras back,' she says.

⤸

The darkness thickens. It's dead quiet. Once more the nightmares come. Unseen presences swarm. It's hard to describe the sensation. It's like being in a plane as it sinks through a gap in the atmosphere and you suddenly plunge a thousand feet. My chest and back are slick with sweat. My head is throbbing, swollen like a drowned man's. A rawness claws the back of my throat.

Renewed feelings of panic make me turn and look at Ingrid. Fear of not loving contends with a fear of not being loved. She's still there next to me, motionless, breathing. Her face is in shadow, but there's an oily shine where her eyes must be, a glisten.

For a moment I think that maybe she's awake.

Is she looking at me? Can she see me?

I pass my hand in front of her face. She doesn't stir. It's hot in the room, and she sleeps naked. As if a lamp is switched on within her, her skin gleams creamily in the dark. There's a warm smell, the mysterious sweet-sour scent of a woman asleep.

Gingerly, so as not to wake her, I put my bare feet on the floor and pad across the room.

'Capa?' The roughness of her voice suggests it's only now that she's awake.

I stop, but do not turn around.

'What are you doing?' She props herself on one elbow, scratches her head drowsily, squints in disbelief at the clock. She holds the sheets chastely above her breasts. 'What's the matter?'

'Just getting a drink. I didn't mean to wake you.'

There's a rustle as she puts a pyjama top on, the pattern like the back of a playing card. She switches on a lamp. A small brown spot on the lampshade becomes a full-blown stain projected on the wall. The glass in my hand glints suddenly.

I hear Ingrid walk towards me, feel her fingers cool on my back, sense her register the film of sweat.

'You don't have to drink,' she says.

'I don't have to stop myself either.'

With a few simple twists, I open a bottle of Scotch. The sound in the half-dark is an upwards slide, high and tight like a dress slipping off. I pour a large one, stir it with my finger.

'Are you all right?'

I realize with a shock that my hands are trembling. 'Sure.' I take a first sip of the whisky, taste its fire, cling to it as I would any source of heat.

She pulls her hand away from my back. I feel the chill her fingers leave against my skin.

She scans the after-image of terror in my eyes. For a moment she says nothing, just stands there, studying me. It's very quiet. Little tendrils of rain touch the window.

'Do you ever pray?' she says.

'Only when the water is up to my neck.'

'Is that often?'

I shrug. 'Often enough.'

She shifts her weight from one leg to another. 'You know, Capa, I like the fact that you're brave. It's admirable.' She strokes my hair, my cheek, fixes my gaze. 'But don't you see there's a difference between being brave, which is fine, and being reckless, which is crazy?' She puts her hands either side of my face and won't let me look elsewhere. 'I love the fact that you're fearless,' she says, 'but it also frightens me.'

Reaching over, she tries to remove the glass from my hand. I resist at first, but she won't give in. Her middle finger and thumb hold it in a kind of pincer. She gives me her stern, schoolmistressy look and tugs again. This time I let go.

For a few seconds my hand holds the ghost of a glass. I hear her set it down on the dresser. Then she walks over and embraces me.

Slow to respond, my arms hang for a moment before coming to rest on her back. I feel the strength of her body pressing hard, pinning me. It's an attempt, I realize, to drain the menaces from my skin, to absorb them into herself, an effort to inject me with her goodness.

'Why?' she says. 'Why do you do it?'

'Drink?'

'Go off to war.'

'I just go where the excitement is.'

'Am I really so boring?'

I search for an honest answer, find nothing adequate. 'It's in me. I feel it.'

She's trying her best, I know, to rid me of these demons, performing a kind of exorcism, and I love her for it. I feel grateful. She's willing to take them on, wrestle them for my sake, sacrifice herself perhaps.

For a moment we just stand there in silence, with only the door and the carpet, and a band of light between.

I ask, 'Have you ever saved anyone's life?'

She shakes her head. Her eyebrows flatten, become part of a frown.

'Save mine,' I say.

She looks at me for an instant to check that I'm not kidding. Her face shines benignly. She takes the bottle of whisky, removes the top. She stands over the basin and tilts the bottle until what's left of the whisky is poured away in long gulps. It takes several seconds to drain and leaves a sour stink in the room.

'Love me,' she says.

For the moment I feel consoled, but the devils, I know, don't go away. They merely retreat into a formless dread, vanish for a time inside me, scared away by the kind light of her face.

⤙

Capa is pouring champagne into a pyramid of glasses, each layer spilling like a fountain into the next. He's surrounded by admirers, who cheer him on, enjoying the virtuosity of the act. Even Joe looks on, smiling, won over by the vivacity and charm of the man.

Capa laughs, obviously loving this, a cigarette clamped to the side of his mouth.

Ingrid is astonished to see the transformation, from the chrysalis of fragility in the early hours of the morning to this evening's butterfly of social exuberance. She stands at a distance from him, chatting to Irwin, who has grown morose after several Scotches. His eyes, she notices, are dark and shining.

She asks, 'What are you writing?'

'Trying to write,' he corrects her. 'A novel.'

'You must let me read it some time.'

'By the time I finish it, you'll be long gone.'

Ingrid chooses not to answer. Instead she watches Capa finish his trick with the fountain of glasses.

'Irrepressible, isn't he?' Irwin says.

'You think it's an act?'

'You'd know about all that.'

'I'm just asking what you think.'

Irwin blinks slowly. 'You give a damn what I think?'

'You're his friend. I want to like you.'

'Is that hard?'

She smiles serenely. 'You could make it a bit easier.'

'Some people embellish their lives,' he says. 'Capa's invented a whole personality.'

'If you don't like him, why are you here?'

'He's the best friend I've got.'

'So what's the problem?'

'The problem is, he's everybody's best friend.'

'Don't tell me you're jealous?'

He shrugs, the glass at an angle in his hand. 'Who do you think redeemed his cameras?'

'Did he thank you?'

'What do you think?'

She looks away.

He jabs a finger as if ready to interrogate her. 'Have you ever caught him in the morning before he puts his smile on?'

She doesn't answer.

'It's in his blood. Can't you see?'

'See what?'

'The only time he feels alive is when he's photographing corpses.'

'That's a horrible thing to say.'

'He's a great war photographer.'

'He's a great photographer,' she corrects him. She recovers enough to declare with confidence, 'He'll come to America.'

'You think?'

'I know.'

Irwin laughs out loud. 'As your poodle? Following you around? He'll love that.'

'Like I said, I'm trying hard to like you.'

'The one time he became attached to a woman, he lost her.'

The stem of her glass feels suddenly fragile in her hand.

'She followed him. It killed her. And ever since, he's felt responsible.' He flicks a bit of ash from his lapel.

Ingrid looks straight ahead, impassive.

Irwin shrugs drunkenly. 'He can't help himself.'

'Then other people have to.'

'You won't be the first.'

'Maybe I'm more persistent.'

'But no less married.'

Her eyes harden, her face grows tense.

Irwin knows he has over-reached. His eyes are filled with self-loathing. He turns to look at her, his whole face narrowed to a hopeless appeal. 'You're very beautiful,' he says. He tries hard not to slur his words, not to spoil the moment, but the complex effort demanded of his mouth makes it seem all the more awkward.

Ingrid holds his gaze for a few seconds.

What started as a drunken compliment, she realizes, has developed into a clumsy attempt at a pass.

She smiles, but her eyes reveal her disappointment if not her disgust, and following a long silence she walks away, abandoning Capa with his drizzling pyramid of light and leaving Irwin to swig from his glass alone.

11

Ingrid receives her final summons from the studio. They're calling her back. She signed a contract and can't delay any longer. There are repeated telegrams, too, from Petter, urging her return.

Light rain soaks the streets and everywhere the green scent of the trees mixes with the dark sweet odour of wet earth. The city is damp and lit.

For dinner, we go to Maxim's. One last luxury. Afterwards we go to the clubs. Monseigneur first, then Jimmy's.

It's still raining when we leave Jimmy's. We feel the tiny pressure of it on our faces. We walk slowly, arm-in-arm in the mist and drizzle, listening to the sound of the wind like a river in the dark and our footsteps hollow on the cobbles. Tables remain on the pavement outside the cafés, dripping, cane chairs stacked on their metal tops. A barge glides by silently, lights dimmed, disappearing under the low curve of a bridge.

We saunter past the New York Herald building, its windows full of clocks. Each clock tells the time in a different part of the world. We work out that Ingrid will be nine hours behind in Los Angeles, so that when it's light here, it'll be mostly dark there and vice versa. Not to mention the thousands of miles of ocean and space in between.

The day dawns. Things start to separate out from their shadows.

In her hotel room, Ingrid's voice grows thin. 'Why are we doing this?'

I can't find an answer.

She begins removing her earrings. They each plink as she places them in a glass ashtray. 'If you ever get bored . . .'

'Why would I get bored?'

What she wants me to say, of course, is that I'll follow her. And the better part of me wants to agree with this, but the perverse part urges me to say nothing, to withhold any decision, to make no promises, to tell her that if she wants more, then maybe she'd better look elsewhere. But I don't say this either. I don't say anything.

She turns so that I see the back of her head in the mirror. 'I don't want to play games, Capa.' There's a silence. 'You want to run away like always?'

I try not to blink.

Something brims within her, spills into a wet smile. She's never seemed so beautiful. 'I'm scared,' she says.

'Of what?'

'You going off to another war.'

'I'm not going anywhere – for the moment anyway.'

'But you will, I know it.'

I shrug. 'I'm lucky, remember.'

'I'm serious. You've got to stop.'

It's true. Terrible though it is, however, it's still the only job I'd consider getting up for in the morning. Nothing compares to the sensation of being there, testing yourself against it. Nothing compares to the dreadful energy that floods your body. You become focused on what's happening and the fact that it really matters. It sounds nuts, I know, but everything else seems dull and unimportant, and it's hard to imagine that I won't keep on with it until either I die in my sleep or – more likely – in some hotspot, with an unpaid hotel bill, some cameras and a couple of fancy shirts. 'You don't think it's brave?'

'The brave thing would be to give it up.'

I laugh. 'Don't look at me like that.'

'I don't want you to die on me.'

'There's only one thing worse than death.'

'What's that?'

'Domesticity.'

She regards me for a moment. And without warning, she slaps

me hard across the face. A flat, angry smack, the sound of a belly-flop in water.

Startled, I feel the sting on my cheek, then a slow burning. High, the sound resounds for several seconds. The shape of each finger seems imprinted on my skin. The burning sensation penetrates deeper, quickens the heat inside me.

Her eyes glisten, borrowing a shine from the lamp. To prevent the tears from spilling, she lifts her chin.

I pull her towards me, needing her warmth. Her mouth still tastes of wine.

Then something happens that I don't expect. The salt of her tears, the perfume of her rained-on skin, the way her eyes darken when she's tired, mingle with the texture of the moment to generate something reckless in my head. 'All right.'

'What?'

A balance tips inside me. 'I'll come,' I say.

Her eyes look up, flared, incredulous.

I feel a pull inside like a line tugging me. 'I'll come to America. To be with you.'

I hear myself say it, having promised myself I would not. I want to disguise the words suddenly, to withdraw them. I want them to be light, but they sound to my own ears heavy and solemn.

'You will?' Her sobs become more widely spaced. She starts laughing as part of sniffing up her tears. Her eyes blink rapidly. 'Really?'

I can't look her full in the face.

Her mouth is stretched tight with the effort of containment. She dabs the inside of her wrist against her eyes.

'Really.' I say it so she believes it, and so that I believe it, too. I can't be sure that I don't say other things, or that I don't just suddenly take her in my arms and kiss her hard on the mouth.

'You're crazy,' she says.

'We've established that.'

'But you'll come?' Her eyes search mine for any hint of a retreat.

I can still feel the smart of her hand against my cheek, the sting of her fingers, delicious, and it's as if the warmth and goodness rise from her at this moment, condensing to cover us benignly in a cloud.

It's a hard thing to acknowledge that you need someone, to admit that the existence of another person is a condition of your happiness, that you need her presence to see you through. And I'm not sure I want to acknowledge it now. Try as I might, I can't make my thoughts come together so that they make any kind of sense. The only thing in this moment that seems right and proper is to tell her that I love her, and I don't know where the words come from, but I'm conscious of them distantly as though spoken by a ghost. It makes me feel good to hear them, to feel the sound of them vibrating in my mouth.

One hour later and still early in the morning, we leave her room for the final time.

Called from some remote floor, the lift arrives with its lights on. As the door slides shut, we fall through space. The floors of the hotel as we descend in the lift seem hollow, bottomless.

The taxi's motor is running outside. Ingrid's luggage has gone on ahead of her, organized by Joe.

She walks out in her headscarf and coat. The driver holds the door open. We both slide into the back, huddle close in the deep seats. The cab leaves the hotel with a fan of spray, swings into a new lightless space.

We sit together in the back of the cab, holding hands, our fingers intertwined, and don't let go until we get to the airport.

Joe is chatting amicably to an airline official, passport in hand. He looks relieved, even jubilant, to see Ingrid leaving at last. There's a spring in his step. He seems to have grown taller, more authoritative. He allows us a few minutes alone.

'So,' she says.

'Don't get sentimental on me.'

'Always the tough guy.'

'Why do you always assume that everyone is acting?'

'They usually are.'

I stroke her hair.

She touches a button on my shirt.

Then I remember. 'You never signed your photograph.'

She laughs. 'You'd only sell it.'

'Maybe I should.'

'You mean while I'm still box-office?'

I feel the effort in smiling.

Her hand drops slowly to her side. 'You know where I am, Capa.'

A man in airport livery tells her that the plane is boarding now. Ingrid knows she should go. She smiles bravely, on the verge of tears.

'I'll be waiting.'

'I'm already saving up.'

'Goodbye, Capa.'

I nod, moved by the solemnity of her attention and by the knowledge that things will never be the same again. I feel like crying myself.

⌒

The day has come, just as she knew it would. She experiences a flutter of panic. A feeling of dread grows heavy inside her. Too many things have happened in too short a time, and she can't begin to absorb them. All she knows is that she doesn't want to leave; she wants to turn around and go back so she can stay in Paris with Capa, but she knows this is impossible; she must face the fact that their time here together has come to an end.

In confronting this truth, she feels stricken with a kind of grief. And now here she is at the airport, saying goodbye. She's played the scene often enough, for God's sake, but for the first time in her life it seems horribly real. For a moment she has to fight to disentangle her own feelings from the reactions of characters she's rehearsed over the years. For an instant her screen self and real self contend, and she can almost see herself in close-up, filmed from the left side as always, part of her face in shadow cast by the brim of her hat; but the despair she feels is genuine and unrepresentable in any script.

With the airline officials in full view and Joe just a few feet away, she embraces Capa, and with her head less than an inch from his ear she says in a whisper that she doesn't want to leave, that she can't stand the thought of being away from him. Her words mingle with what is unspoken until she can no longer remember what has been said.

And though he gives her a hopeless, doting smile, there is no chance to say anything more before Joe touches her arm, takes hold of her elbow and lightly but purposefully gives her a push. It is enough. Without willing it or being forced, she finds herself turned, directed away from Capa as if compelled by some physical law.

It's as if already she's in another country. The sound of the plane is loud in her ears. The engines surge. Things start to rattle. There's a tremendous roar. Her stomach flips as the plane takes off, and she experiences a dragging sensation as though one half of her has been left behind.

She looks down through the scratched oval window at the ground below, at the buildings and boulevards touched with sun, at the river running across the city like a crack across a mirror.

He told her he loved her, and she said she loved him, too. She is sure of it. Still, she's aware of the fragility of this feeling and how short-lived it might be. In wishing to affirm her love, to sing its existence, in the blind wish and impulse to say yes, she's wary of the potential for any falling off. She's bothered by it, like an animal by its shadow, watches for it like the first drops of rain. When will he come? What if he finds someone else? The thought torments her.

Uplifted, dizzy, weightless in the sudden immense space of the sky, she's never felt so empty. Her insides sink. Only the rivets on the wings seem to hold things fast.

Below her, the world shrinks, and she with it. The air turns thin. The plane banks in a wide circle, continues to rise. The light is cool and shadowless. Everything that is big about the city grows abruptly very small.

12

I think of Ingrid, thousands of miles away in a warm rich city, standing under brilliant lights.

Every time I close my eyes, I see her face. So I close my eyes a lot. I talk to myself and pretend that she's listening. I write things down so that I won't forget to tell her. I think of funny things to make her laugh.

The bed seems empty and lifeless without her. The silence presses in. Through the window, the small white hole of the moon pulls everything into it. Dead light.

I needed to know what it was like and how I'd feel when she was far away, and now I know, it's killing me. I can't get her out of my mind.

I feel the need to reach out and hold her. I just want her here with me, and it doesn't seem right or fair that she's not. And when the streets grow silent and the air grows cold at night, I think of the heat she generates next to me, the hope and wonder she gives off. I long to see her, to touch her again.

I feel her absence inside me like a stone.

There's a dream I keep having.

It's about my father. We're in a department store. He's holding my hand. I'm four years old.

Everything's fine and I feel happy, and then suddenly it isn't and I'm not. I don't know when he let go of my hand, but already it seems like a lifetime ago. I look around and there's no sign of him. I'm lost, and though I can't yet put a name to the feeling, it seems terribly real.

Fear grips me. Panic sets in. I don't know what to do. I take a right, a left, another left, a right, redouble back in what I think is a square to find that I'm in a different part of the store. I'm completely disoriented.

I start to cry. A ring of faces surrounds me. I try my best to explain what has happened, but no one understands me, I'm crying so much. The words won't come out right.

Moments unroll.

Then beyond the circle of faces, I see him a few yards away. He's looking at me, arms folded, smiling.

Afterwards he repeats three things:

'I love you.'

And: 'I won't always be here.'

And: 'You have to be strong.'

When Petter quizzes her about Paris just before they go up to bed, she reacts angrily, dismisses his insinuations, complains that he wants to take away what little freedom she enjoys.

'Ingrid, is everything okay?'

She looks at her husband. His lips seem thin and bloodless. 'Why shouldn't it be?' she says.

He finishes pouring a glass of wine. 'There's nothing you want to tell me, then?'

Outside, spasms of rain tremble and break against the windows. The treetops stir wildly. The promised storm has come. Seeing this, Ingrid expects flashes of lightning to tear open the sky, to shock the trees into relief, followed by shapeless whoomphs of thunder. She waits for several seconds, tenses. Nothing happens.

'You think it's fine to go away for months, barely keep in touch, and because you bring back a suitcase full of presents, everything will be okay?'

'You didn't like yours?'

He doesn't blink. 'Do you ever keep things from me?'

'What is this?'

'I'm serious.'

Her tapping foot is the only clue to her inner agitation. After a silence, she tells him to turn out the lights when he comes up, and quickly leaves the room.

Upstairs Petter wears his reading glasses perched at the end of his nose. Glancing across, he sees the skin above his wife's night-dress both over and through his glasses, and is struck by the difference between the two. Seen with the naked eye, her skin appears a slightly reddened but otherwise undistinguished plane of flesh. Through the lenses of his spectacles, however, there's a graininess, a powdery texture that seems palpitating and alive.

He makes a show of setting down his book, removing his glasses and switching off his bedside light. He snuggles down into the covers, stretches his arm across her tummy.

'I'm sorry,' he says. There's no response. Ingrid continues to read. He tries again. 'I'm sorry.' She says nothing. And then, 'I love you.'

He begins to caress her stomach, the tops of her legs – nothing she could object to. After a minute, his hands widen in slow circles to touch the base of her breasts, her tidy triangle of hair. His movements are so gentle, he knows it would seem odd for her to protest. When he touches her more coarsely, though, she makes it plain that she's not interested. She's reading, she says. But he's not to be discouraged. He returns to those slow circles. He persists, knowing that there's an established routine between the two of them in their lovemaking, a slow inevitability. Still she resists his touch, and he senses her reluctance. Then he hears her gulp. She snaps a page over.

'No,' she says, slapping his hand. He carries on, more gently but just as insistently. 'I said no. I mean it.'

He ignores her and continues. He's reclaiming her, re-establishing his control, and wants her to know it.

Her legs twitch. It's some time now since she has turned a page. He senses the tension rise within her. He tries to swallow but his throat is dry.

Something animal gathers itself and overtakes them both.

It's brusque and a little brutal, and if it hurts her a bit, then fine, he thinks. There needs to be a little pain mixed in with the excitement. His heart races. He presses against her, though he notices she hardly participates at all. She averts her mouth from his kisses as if he has bad breath and trains her eyes on the ceiling, her mind seemingly elsewhere.

Eventually he senses her tremble violently to a climax, enjoys watching her eyes slide into that familiar whiteness like the snow.

Afterwards he watches her pee. 'Did you come?'

'Sort of.'

'What do you mean, sort of?'

'I sort of came.'

'Well, did you or didn't you?'

Her hair hangs down in front of her face. 'All right, no.'

'Thank you.'

'You see? Now you're angry.'

'I'm not angry,' he says.

In the morning, half-awake, Petter hears water from the shower drill into the bath. Unusually Ingrid is up before him. She's washing me off her, he thinks.

Before taking his own shower, he bends down and executes fifty press-ups on the bedroom floor, feels his heart thump. He finds himself wondering whether one day he will suffer a heart attack from over-exertion. He wonders at the same time whether, following his cardiac arrest, he will be found in an undignified position. He also has time to ponder how absurdly vain such reflections are.

Dressed, he goes downstairs. Pia is in the living room, playing with her new French dolls. Ingrid is in the kitchen, no longer mussed and crumply in her nightdress but smart and crisp-looking in a dark skirt and white top.

He watches her over breakfast, sees her cutting and buttering bread, absorbed in the task. Framed by the kitchen door, he stops to observe her. He hears the tick of two clocks, smells the odour of fresh bread, sees the gleam of the knife as it cuts and spreads. He's filled with admiration suddenly for this woman, captivated again by his wife. He has failed her, he thinks. He has not been devoted enough. He has concentrated too much on being a good doctor and her manager and not made it clear how much he cares for her. It is all his fault, he tells himself.

He imagines himself no longer here, gone away, dead perhaps. And he imagines, too, after he has vanished, Ingrid continuing as she is now, cutting the bread, carrying on as if nothing has happened, his absence making little visible difference to her. She seems so complete in her loveliness, he can't believe that she'd need him.

'That was nice, last night,' he says.

She shrugs above the plates and the noise of the radio.

He notices as she floats past, ignoring him, that she looks and smells marvellous. He realizes that she must always look and smell like this. Her smell attaches itself to everything – to the sink, its aluminium fixtures, to the pots and pans that hang from their hooks, to the walls. He wants to kick himself for not noticing this more often, for not paying sufficient attention. And he experiences a moment of fear at the thought that these features, this fragrance, might be given to – or stolen by – someone else.

He will be a better husband from now on, he vows. He promises himself that he'll do his best to improve things, spend less time at the hospital, spend more time with his wife, listen to her, encourage her, cherish and respect her.

Things will be okay, he thinks. Things will be okay.

13

It's December and snowy when I arrive in New York with a single bag, two cameras, and an increasingly dog-eared copy of *War and Peace*.

My hand hovers over the telephone in my hotel room. I can't resist the impulse. After several attempts, and still with a substantial time difference and distance in between, I finally manage via the operator to get through to her home.

'Are your eyes still blue, Miss Bergman?'

'Who is this?'

'What's your favourite song, Miss Bergman?'

'Capa? Is that you?'

'I came as soon as I could.'

'I thought you'd forgotten me.'

Her voice is faint with distance. She's just had a bath, she says, and now she's sitting on the edge of her bed.

I think of her with lovely fluffed-up hair, her cheeks and throat all rosy, her body warm inside her gown.

She says, 'There's no one else there with you?'

'Just my Leica under the bed.' There's a hiss and slight delay each time before her response. 'I want you to know that I've been good,' I tell her.

'I miss you.'

'You do? Really?'

'What do you think?' she says.

The cold in New York gives way to the heat in Los Angeles, where the sun puts such a sheen on things, they gleam unreally, adding a brilliance to the day. Everywhere there are palm trees, and pastel houses, with a sky so big and crystalline it seems the studio must have manufactured it. There are no power cuts or food shortages in this city. At night, the billboards glitter like dispatches from another world. The horizon hovers like a giant smile, fed with the energy that drives a million cars and sets another million kitchen gadgets whirring. The future seems spread before me, new-painted, glossy: the promised land.

I stay in a bungalow at the Garden of Allah. The name is a Californian fancy, part of a need to fill the wilderness. The cool white stucco of the Spanish-style houses disguises the hot social life that thrives just off the Sunset Strip. The rent is high, but the bungalow is furnished. There's a box hedge outside, and walls frothy with bougainvillea. At night, the scent of eucalyptus and jasmine mixes with the stink of the gingko trees beyond.

The first time Ingrid drives over, she parks some distance away. I meet her beyond the police patrol and the guard dogs employed to ward off intruders.

She's tanned, her hair a little longer. She's lost a few pounds, and looks terrific. It's great to see her, hold her hand again, hear her voice, that accent. Her perfume merges with the aroma of the night flowers, rich and strange.

Is she the same woman I met in Paris? Has she changed in any way?

It occurred to me before I arrived that I might be making a mistake. The wise thing might have been to turn around and go back to Paris. At least there, I know I'll feel at home. The wise thing might be to tell her we've had a wonderful time, that we shouldn't regret it for a second, but that it's unrealistic to think we can go on. Then I see how inexpressibly lovely she looks, and just one glance into her eyes, just one glimpse of her smile, is enough to tell me I'd be crazy not to stay.

We talk for hours, catching up, and she's thrilled to have found me work as a stills photographer on the set.

After an initial diffidence and a lengthy period of kissing, we renew our intimacy, twice.

Once more I feel that revelatory sense of freedom and well-being. Her skin, like sensitized paper, changes colour at the merest touch. And there on the bed our bodies become quick and hot and excited. Her body trembles like a radio turned down low, with a small vibration, a kind of purr. The sensation is so dark and sweet that I long to stay inside her, wanting the feeling to last for ever.

Still, I notice an impulse to cover herself afterwards. She seems unusually shy and guarded, folding her arms across her breasts, denting them.

'It's too risky, me coming here,' she says. 'I could be seen.'

'So where are we going to meet?'

She looks sideways as if she's heard a sound. 'I don't know yet. We'll have to be creative.'

I'm about to say something, but she sets off across the room.

'Watch this,' she says.

Without warning she pulls a wig from her bag, a platinum blonde mop that she tries on in front of the mirror. She fluffs it up, regards herself from a series of angles. 'What do you think?' she says.

I think it looks odd, comical.

She notices my frown and laughs.

'Is this really necessary?'

'I'm afraid it is. The press are everywhere in this town.' Her attention returns to her hair in the mirror.

'Can't you just be yourself?'

She doesn't answer. Instead she makes a few sly adjustments to the hang of the wig, straightening the strands on either side. Her hands remain poised around her head as if any moment she expects the mop to fall off. She holds the pose for a moment. 'How does it look?'

'You're enjoying this, aren't you?'

She catches my eye in the mirror, tilts her head. 'Does it look okay?'

'I can still see it's you.'

She lets the hair fall and walks away. She fishes a pair of dark glasses from her pocketbook, different from the pair she had in Paris – darker, more opaque and reflective, the rims lifting upwards, wing-like at the tips. She puts them on, checks them in the mirror before turning to me. Her arms drop to her sides. 'And now?' she says.

We sit in a corner of a restaurant in Westwood, at a discreet distance from the other guests. I watch Ingrid consume two scoops of vanilla ice-cream, with a double serving of hot fudge sauce.

'I'm not allowed to eat this.'

'Not allowed?'

'When we're filming, I'm restricted to cottage cheese and fruit.'

'That's crazy.'

'I have to keep the pounds off.'

'Don't listen to them.'

'They pay my wages.'

'If you're hungry, you should eat.'

'Then I wouldn't look so great.'

'You look great to me.'

She smiles, lifts her spoon towards me, taps me playfully on the nose. I wipe away the line of ice-cream. A sweet vanilla scent remains. A dimple appears in her right cheek. 'Once, I put on a stone.'

'Too many hot fudge sundaes?'

'And banana splits. I couldn't resist.'

'That's my Joan of Arc.'

'The studio was furious. They put me on a strict diet. No meat or potatoes, no chocolate or desserts.'

'What did Petter say?'

'They told him to put a lock on the refrigerator.'

'And did he?'

'He had no choice.'

'You're kidding.'

'We were about to shoot. The costumes were all sized. He was under a lot of pressure.'

'This seems normal to you?'

She shrugs.

I light a cigarette. 'Next it will be a chastity belt.'

'Over here,' she says, wagging her spoon at me, 'you need to understand, Petter controls everything – my schedule, my career. And what he doesn't control, the studio does.'

'And you let them?'

'They'd say they were protecting me.'

'You're a human being, not an industry. You let everyone drive you. All you do is work.'

'I hate not working.'

'So then you're happy?'

She shakes a cigarette from the crumpled pack on the table – another thing she knows she shouldn't do. 'I'm married to a man I don't love.'

'Have you tried telling him?'

Her legs begin a confidential jostling. 'It's easier to lie.'

'Why don't you leave him?'

She blows out a column of smoke. 'Are you offering me an alternative?'

Window light falls on one side of her face. Little wisps of hair glitter in a frizz, a kind of halo. She pushes her bowl away, catches the waiter's eye, asks for the check.

A little knife twists inside me. It occurs to me to ask, 'Do you still make love to him?'

She rummages for her purse, finds it. 'We have sex occasionally, if that's what you mean.'

'Isn't that the same?'

Her eyes darken. With a little snap of the clasp, she twists her purse shut. 'You want to know about our lovemaking?' She folds her arms on the table, leans forward. 'He keeps his eyes closed when he's fucking me. He turns his head to the wall. Then afterwards he looks at me as though he hates me, as though I got what I deserve.'

~

She's being slowly poisoned.

That's what it says in the script. Her head aches. She asks for the blinds to be drawn because the light hurts her eyes. Ingrid suspects the screenwriter added these details to suit Hitchcock, who hates being in direct sunlight.

She's playing a woman called Alicia Huberman, whose father, a Nazi spy, is convicted of treason against the United States.

Capa laughed when he first heard that.

She's also a woman *good at making friends with gentlemen*.

Capa laughed when he heard that, too.

Alicia's father's friends have repaired to Rio after the war, and she's persuaded by Devlin, an FBI agent played by Cary Grant, to infiltrate their group. At Devlin's bidding, but against her better judgement, Alicia allows herself to be seduced by the Nazi mastermind. To gain the group's full confidence, she even agrees to marry the man, though he is twice her age. Alicia, meanwhile, falls in love with Devlin. The feeling is mutual, but he's too fat-headed to declare his affections. So she lives in constant torment, sucked in by a kind of vertigo. She discovers that the cadre is amassing stocks of uranium ore, storing it in wine bottles. But her cover is blown and now her husband, together with his evil mother, is slowly poisoning her.

In *Spellbound*, she had to play a human glacier who melts in the presence of Gregory Peck. Now, in *Notorious*, she plays a woman of raw instinct and emotional need who must harden her heart – even if it kills her – to do her patriotic duty, to do what Cary Grant tells her is right.

The schedule is punishing. Each morning she wakes at 5 a.m.

The first thing she does is check to see that Pia is still sleeping soundly. The next thing she thinks about is Capa. Next she thinks about Alicia. And then she thinks about food.

She's permitted a breakfast of dry toast and grapefruit, and occasionally scrambled eggs. She's allowed one glass of orange juice and a cup of coffee, black. It's a regime the studio insists upon, and Petter is charged with enforcing it.

Arriving on the lot at 6 a.m., Ingrid experiences the kind of certainty and sureness she rarely knows outside. She enjoys the drive each morning through the studio gates – the spurt of the fountain in the courtyard, the tall white spider of the water tower, the smell of wood as new sets are constructed, the long aisles of numbered stage sets like a lesson in perspective. She's always on time, always courteous to the technicians, with a kind word for the make-up lady and a kiss for the boy who slips a sugar lump into her coffee first thing.

Depending on progress, they usually finish shooting around 7 p.m. and retire for drinks to Hitchcock's office on the lot.

Part of her likes the routine, thrives on it. She knows she should count herself lucky. Being here and making movies is the stuff of dreams, a fantasy fulfilled.

Why, then, does she feel so unhappy?

In one sense it's all very simple. She loves Capa; she no longer loves her husband. The position could be spelled out in a telegram. In another sense, though, she sees that the whole situation is monstrously complex. So, when considering her predicament, she finds herself stumbling over words, qualifying and correcting herself, still uncertain how she feels.

She faces the fact: her marriage is unravelling. When she looks in the mirror, it is another woman she sees.

She confesses it all to Hitchcock with such a look of anguish that he sends away his driver and pours himself another Scotch. Now in his mid-forties, though seeming older because of his weight, Hitchcock impresses her as wise, long-married, and a dispenser of common sense. At the same time, she's aware that he has a little crush on her, which she can never quite bring herself to discourage.

She refuses to deceive herself, she says. She no longer loves Petter and is finding it hard to conceal the fact. She's been prepared to take things minute by minute, she says, to proceed hour by hour. A person can manage for a long time like that. Maybe for ever.

Hitchcock allows a silence to develop. His face remains rosy, jovial, though his eyes hold a sorrow. He looks at her as if watching a perilous experiment unfold.

Now, she says, instead of intimacy, it is suffocation she feels. And there are occasions when she looks at him – when he's pouring a drink or tapping a pencil, or just lifting a fork to his mouth – that she loathes him, can't stand the man. His feet are cold in bed, she says. And he snores.

Hitchcock sinks the last inch of his whisky. Beads of perspiration line his brow.

The truth is, she says, she prefers men like her coffee, dark and bitter. To be consumed in a few quick swallows. Hot.

It is now that she tells him about Capa. Her blissful time in Paris; his arrival in Los Angeles; her need to keep their love a secret; her anguish that they are so frequently apart.

Hitchcock seems to have trouble breathing. His face is red from the whisky. He rises from his chair and moves to hug her. He says that he had no idea about any of this or how she was feeling, that she must be a saint to conceal all these difficulties, and heroic to soldier on. He calls her *my darling* and strokes her hair. He kisses her on the forehead, and she feels his weight press against her. The smell of his sweat and the whisky on his breath rise like a cloud around her. He says that he feels flattered by her faith in him, that he will always be there for her, and is delighted to have this intimate chat. He says she is doing a great job as Alicia and that work can be a great consolation.

She says he is a sweet man, like a father to her, and of all the people she knows, she is sure she can trust him with her secret.

157

Next day it's the most ambitious shot of the film. Everyone is there to watch.

Hitchcock has ordered the manufacture of a large gantry and small elevator to house the camera so that it can swoop seamlessly from a high ceiling with a wide panorama down past a chandelier to a marbled foyer where guests are mingling at a party, before moving in for a tight focus on Ingrid's hand in which she clutches a key.

Ingrid has to keep absolutely still except for a little twitching of her fingers so that the lens can reveal what she conceals.

Capa is so used to snapping away without anyone paying attention, he doesn't notice how silent it is once filming begins, so when he raises the Leica to his face, clicks and winds on in two swift movements, everyone glares in his direction.

Hitchcock calls 'Cut'. He looks at Ingrid, rather than directly addressing Capa. 'I'd be grateful if you could remain quiet on the set when we're shooting. Your camera may be tiny, Mr Capa, but it still makes an irritating noise.'

Hitchcock winks at Ingrid.

Ingrid winks at Capa.

Capa noiselessly apologizes, lets his hands fall to his sides. In the next take, she's conscious of him watching her as the camera swoops down towards her on the gantry. She doesn't find it at all hard to convey that little bit of panic beneath the poise.

At midnight, at a party on New Year's Eve with Petter, with the firecrackers going off outside, Ingrid retires to the bathroom, looks at herself in the mirror, and cries.

She tries to tell herself it's not her fault that all this has happened. She knows, though, of course, that it is. She has succumbed to temptations that ought to have been resisted, given in to the most primitive of impulses. With a little more strength and self-discipline, she considers, it could all have been avoided.

When they return home an hour later, she heads straight upstairs. She pushes open the door to Pia's bedroom and sees her daughter, her face white in the darkness, surrounded by her long-lashed dolls.

Ingrid approaches, adjusts her bedcovers, and the girl stirs, awake. Immediately Ingrid offers her a drink. Pia seizes both sides of the glass and insists with a seven-year-old's greediness on drinking down to the bottom. Finished, stupefied with milk, the young girl flops back onto her bed. She's getting heavy now, Ingrid recognizes. The girl has taken on a definite heft. In just a few months she has grown taller, and her legs are so long and lovely she doesn't know what to do with them.

She hears Pia smack her lips, and watches for a second as her daughter scratches her head in drowsy puzzlement. She listens for the familiar rhythm of her breathing, waits to see the up and down movement of her chest. Her sleeping peaceful face hovers like a little moon in the dark. Her cheeks are flushed, her hands clammy, her brow feverish with dreams.

Seeing her like this, she wants to be with her always, to protect her for ever, to keep things as they are. She resolves never to put her secure little world in jeopardy again. Certainly not for another man.

The next morning, however, when she wakes next to Petter on the first day of this new year, and before the maid returns from her few days away, she prematurely packs away the Christmas tree and greetings cards, clears up the litter of pine needles and stray bits of tinsel. She copies all her friends' telephone numbers and contacts into a new black leather address book, though when it comes to her own name and telephone number, she leaves the details blank.

14

Ingrid makes a deal with the girls on the switchboard at the studio. She gives them my name and tells them that, whenever I call, they should connect me directly. She tells them I'm her personal photographer and responsible for her publicity shots. The women on the switchboard relish this sisterly conspiracy and are always eager to put me through.

The shots I take are syndicated to newspapers and magazines world-wide. It's an easy job and a large market, and pays very well. I've never had so much money, and for so little risk or effort.

The only problem is, there's nothing else for me to do. I go to the odd screening, spend a little time in the cutting room, and hang around the set, hoping to catch a few minutes with Ingrid or even just a glimpse of her.

She works most days. It takes two hours each morning to put on her make-up so it can hold up under the Klieg lights. And then eight hours on the set to produce just two minutes of film. It doesn't seem much of a return for a day's work. The whole operation seems so ponderous and repetitive, and entirely without glamour, it's like living your life in slow motion.

When I'm not required on the set, which is most days, I head out to the track at Santa Anita, play tennis, walk along the beach or lounge around the pool drinking cocktails with strange names. All of which is great, of course, but I grow bored doing nothing, and after a time it's hard not to feel a bit empty like one of the town's vacant lots.

Then in the evening there are the parties.

Tonight the drive of David O. Selznick's mansion in Beverly Hills is packed with cars and jammed with vans from Los Angeles' florists and catering firms.

I hand my printed invitation to one of the heavies on the door, slick my hair back, and adjust my bowtie. The tuxedo feels too long in the arms, but it was the nearest fit in the rental shop. With a little tug on each of my cuffs, I slip inside.

I walk past a high-ceilinged library, an oblong screening room, and a ladies' room where the mink coats are piled high. I arrive finally at a set of French windows. Exotic plants are painted on the wall, their green tendrils extending like fingers towards the lights.

Two gold-coloured sofas seem to float on the marble floor and each supports a trio of expensively dressed young women, their legs all crossed the same way as if someone has been practising knots. Beyond the window, a large white marquee glimmers in the light from an oval swimming pool. The silhouettes of men and women mingle inside and move like shadows in a puppet show.

Cicadas rattle in the grass. Waiters circulate with pitchers of drinks and trays of ice. Bottles of Moët bob in iced water held in enormous tubs. Daiquiris are served in coconut pots with pink parasols.

The grass under my feet feels stiff and artificial, and the garden bristles with these spiky, vivid flowers that seem part of a futuristic film set.

Selznick himself is a tall man with owl-eyed glasses. He never stops talking or shaking hands, presiding like a minor deity over the stars.

Introduced to him by Ingrid, I ask what the O stands for in his middle name.

'It stands for nothing,' he says, and laughs.

He jokes with Ingrid about a film the studio is working on. 'The rough cut was four hours long.'

'Was it good?'

'It was terrible.'

'What did you do?'

'We cut it in half.'

'And?'

'Now it's only terrible for two.'

In the last couple of months, he has left his wife for the actress Jennifer Jones. Wracked with guilt over the affair, he's busy telling everyone how he's been several times to see a psychiatrist, paying double the usual fee. After listening carefully for a number of weeks, it seems the analyst agrees that in fact he's done the right thing and acted honourably in leaving his wife. So now he's going around cheerfully informing people that he had no option, that it was the only course open to him.

'It's all been scientifically proved,' he says. 'Better than a god-damn Gallup poll.'

Behind him the swimming pool shimmers, milky and inviting. Is there anything more beautiful than the blue of a swimming pool lit up at night? All that's needed to complete the scene are half a dozen bathing belles performing some Busby Berkeley number.

Producers and actresses shuffle and re-group. I recognize Miriam Hopkins, George Sanders, Lana Turner, Joseph Cotten, Hedy Lamarr. And Charles Boyer, who is so small that when he played Ingrid's husband in *Gaslight*, he had to stand on a box in order to kiss her lips.

Everywhere I look there are movie stars, half-familiar faces in small constellations. Guests circle like fireflies about the garden, with the moon tilted and pink as a grapefruit above.

It's at the parties that I get to meet and speak to Ingrid.

She stands nursing a wineglass in her hands, her legs crossed at the ankle. She's wearing a black evening dress and looks fabulous. Her white arms emerging from short black sleeves seem long and lovely. Her white gloves extend to the elbow. When she speaks to me, it is with a practised casualness, and she's careful not to let on. She puts a glass wall up, smiling sweetly and speaking out the side of her mouth with a kind of regal disregard. At least once a week she'll slip me a hastily scrawled note on a bit of lined paper asking me to meet her at a rented apartment or at Irwin's beach house in Malibu.

Petter is here tonight. It's the first time I've set eyes on him.

He's taller than I imagined, more convivial, drinks a lot and has an explosive laugh that echoes round the pool. He's a talented dancer, too, incredibly energetic, spinning out his partners with accustomed grace across the floor. He performs the jitterbug, rumba, and samba. But he perspires a lot and has to change his shirt at least twice during the next three hours.

We're introduced by Ingrid. She tells him how we ran across one another in Paris, that I was a famous war photographer – I notice the past tense – and that I'm looking for a position in Hollywood.

I could argue, qualify, correct her, but I don't.

She leaves us alone, gliding off to charm another knot of people, her hand raised in greeting as if she hasn't seen them for years.

Petter's handshake is intimidating, fierce. It's odd, I know, but it's only when I speak to him that at last I grasp the reality of his marriage to Ingrid. Until now, I've appreciated it as an idea, an abstract concept, but it's been hard to think of him as her husband in any meaningful way. And here he is, living, breathing, telling jokes. I surprise myself by finding his presence immediately offensive, the way he borrows his glow from Ingrid, the way he basks in an atmosphere of associated greatness. This is the man who sleeps next to her every night, who shares her bed, and who, as her manager, agent, as well as husband, owns and controls her like a piece of real estate. The thought touches a cold, hard place inside me.

'Tell me,' he says. 'You believe in Marxism?'

'You believe in the Virgin birth?'

'That's a dangerous question.'

'And yours isn't?'

In his one genuine aside, he bemoans the weakness of American beer, comparing it to piss. He winks, appealing to me as a fellow European.

'Don't drink it, then,' I say, not wanting to play along.

He looks at me, grins. 'I don't.'

The encounter disconcerts me in a way that I didn't expect it to. He's no monster or villain, but he exists, and that's enough. He moves off to curry favour with a producer, telling him loudly so everyone can hear how, in his opinion, Hollywood has mangled the theories of Sigmund Freud.

For once, I'm surprised but happy to see Joe. He looks more tanned and has grown a moustache since I last saw him in Paris.

'You look good,' I tell him.

'It took me ten years to get invited to parties like this, Capa. And you just walk straight in.'

'You sound bitter.'

'Damn right, I am.'

I laugh, offer him a cigarette.

He refuses, starts to smile, but something in the tension of his cheeks prevents him. 'You don't give up, do you?'

'You want to try and stop me?'

'That's what they pay me for.'

'Do they pay you enough?'

He gives me a dark look that has a glimmer of sympathy in it, as if to say I should count myself lucky – most people don't even get warned.

Someone taps him on the shoulder, whispers in his ear. He walks off without looking back.

I'm handed another glass of champagne. The music tinkles on, while the women flit like insects through the garden and the night. The party unfolds slowly. I measure three more drinks before I meet Ingrid again.

'Are you enjoying yourself?' she says.

'It's all right.'

'What did you think of Petter?'

'I liked him.'

'*You* don't have to live with him.'

'Neither do you.'

Her eyebrow lifts quizzically.

I say, 'At least he spoke to me.'

'Don't be like that.'

'Like what?'

'I said I'd phone you.'

'You said you probably would.'

'Well, I probably will.'

'You want me to hang around all day, waiting?'

I can see that already she feels compromised in talking to me again. Petter is dancing happily with the wife of one of the producers, a foxy red-head with a twitchy tail. Beyond him, I see Joe keeping an eye on me from the other side of the pool.

'Why don't you write a book?' she says.

'A book?'

'Or even a screenplay?'

'You're kidding.'

'In Hollywood, they pay four hundred dollars a week for that.'

'That's obscene.'

'Where else would you make that kind of money?'

'What would I write about?'

'I don't know. About war,' she says, and improvises in a voice that makes everything seem achievable. 'About what it can do to a man. How it can ennoble him, make him crazy, heroic . . .'

'I've never known war to ennoble anyone.'

She gives one of her earrings a little tug. 'Not even you?'

Inspired, I say, 'I know something I could write about.'

'Oh?'

'About how an obscure Hungarian Jew with a Leica round his neck in post-war Paris comes to love and be loved by the most beautiful woman in the world . . .'

Her mask drops for a second. 'Don't you dare!'

'I'm joking.'

She smiles tightly. 'I'm warning you.'

'You as well?'

'What?'

'Nothing,' I say. I stub out a cigarette with my foot on the lawn.

Joe is still watching from across the pool.

'It would bore me to write it up,' I say. 'The pictures are the point.'

'The point is you could be near me.'

'It doesn't feel real.'

'Haven't you had enough of reality?'

I light another cigarette. 'I don't like seeing you waste your talent.'

'Look who's talking.'

'Can't we go back to Europe?'

She sighs. It seems she's rehearsed this argument before. 'I'm in the picture business, and this is where they make movies.'

'Do you feel American?'

'I'm a resident alien.'

'What does that mean?'

'It means I pay ninety per cent income tax.'

'You want me to feel sorry for you?'

Selznick lopes over, tells her there's someone he wants her to meet. He steers Ingrid away as if rescuing her from a bore. And maybe he is.

I wander back inside the house, half angry with Ingrid, half angry with myself, cursing the studio, cursing Petter, my own impatience.

The young women on the gold sofas all have consorts now – three fat men with loud voices and outsize cigars – and I notice how the girls laugh and throw their heads back to reveal their throats whenever one of the guys makes a wisecrack. I notice, too, how the knots of their legs have loosened and come undone.

At least there's a poker game, in a room off the library.

I watch for a while, and then when someone retires, without warning there is Joe behind me. He steps forward and pulls back a chair, as if vouching for me. He even winks, and I wonder what he's up to. When I look up, John Huston smiles as he deals, one eye closed against the smoke that leaks from between his teeth.

He snaps the cards out so fast and hard, the edges must come close to ripping his fingers.

It's no limit, high stakes poker. The best kind.

To my surprise and delight, I manage to win the first two hands.

'Lucky son-of-a-bitch,' Huston says.

Holding his cigar with three fingers, he twists it in quick half-inches between his lips. The dark hair on his eyebrows is wrestled into a dense nest, a mess of insect feelers which seems to twitch as he inspects his cards.

When he learns who I am and what I do, he starts telling me about the games in London he enjoyed while waiting for D-Day, and the way they'd continue playing without flinching as the bombs went off around them – one bomb shattering the windows and spraying glass onto their table.

'I know,' I say. 'I was there.'

'Of course you were,' he says.

But the only thing that sprays over us tonight is the moonlight and the smell of exotic flowers, the blue of the pool and the music from a small orchestra performing popular numbers such as 'Prisoner of Love' and 'To Each His Own' into the small hours.

Each time someone new comes to the table, Huston introduces me with a flourish. 'You know the Normandy landings?' he growls. 'They only exist because this man recorded them.' And, 'If you ever go to war, make sure you take this guy with you.'

If this is his calculated way of disarming me, it seems lamentably successful. After my initial burst of luck, things no longer go my way. The pile of cash I started out with quickly dwindles to the zero of Selznick's middle initial and I hear but don't see Ingrid leave with Petter, his laugh like a scatter of stones on the drive.

The night ends as I sit with Joe, and we play that game where you take it in turns to burn holes with cigarettes in a napkin that holds a coin over a glass.

'It's good,' I tell him, 'that we're friends at last.'

He burns a small hole in the fabric of the handkerchief.

'If you go on,' he says, 'you'll destroy everything she's worked for.'

'She's unhappy.'

'You think she'll thank you for it?'

'It worked for Selznick, didn't it?'

'The studio has spent a lot of money placing that halo on her head. People won't take kindly to you decanonizing her.'

I laugh.

'I'm serious. She embodies decency for people.'

'That's quite a weight you're loading on her.'

'Nobody's imposing it. She created it herself.'

'You're saying I can't see her?'

'I'm saying you better watch yourself.'

I don't respond.

'It's in nobody's interests to change things.'

'Least of all yours.'

'Least of all hers.'

I burn one final hole clear through the white cotton of the napkin, and this time the nickel drops.

I meet William Goetz in his office after a liquid lunch at Romanoff's.

It's something Ingrid has set up. He's interested in publishing a book, he says, about the war as the basis for a screenplay.

Tall, wiry, smart, there's a tension that extends from his face to his braces. His handshake is firm, his eyes clear, his hair slicked back like a seal's.

Around him, pot plants lend a vaguely tropical atmosphere, an obscure lushness to his office, seeming to articulate a statement about the law of the jungle. He leans back in his big leather chair. Its upholstered buttons add to the impression of tautness in him.

He has faith in me, he says, his eyes narrowing confidentially. The leather chair creaks beneath him. The rubber plant behind him flourishes.

'You come highly recommended, Mr Capa.'

Something knowing in his manner makes me wary. 'That's good to hear,' I say.

The sun is in my eyes. He sees this and tips the blinds, but the wrong way. The light widens in an extravagant dazzle. My eyes wince at the brilliance. With a small clatter, he tugs the blinds down again. A crimp remains in one of them.

'So what do you think? You think you can do that?'

'When do you want it by?'

'I don't want it quick,' he says, throwing his weight forwards. 'I want it *good*.' He emphasizes the word like a suppressed threat.

I accept his offer of a cigarette.

He scrapes open a desk drawer, pulls out a long, thin manila envelope and slides it towards me. He gestures for me to take it.

'What is it?' I say, picking it up as if it might sting me.

'Why don't you open it?'

Inside is a wad of hundred-dollar bills. I try hard not to look impressed.

'An advance,' he says. 'To show good faith.'

'Yes.'

He leans back. His fingers form a pyramid that, for a moment, resembles absurdly the emblem on a dollar bill. Then, reaching behind him, he re-opens the blinds to signal that the interview has come to an end.

Beyond the window, the sun burns fiercely, making the asphalt wobble and shimmer as in a mirage.

～

Selznick refuses to deal with Petter any longer over Ingrid's contract. Her husband, he says, is ungrateful, stubborn, impossible to work with. And he's instructed his attorney to speak no further until Lindstrom gives some ground.

Ingrid likes to steer clear of negotiations and stay sweet with her producer. She leaves any talk of money to Petter and tries not to get involved. But this time it's hard to detach herself. She knows that Selznick, while bringing her from Sweden and helping to make her a star, has also hired her out to other studios at a vast profit, kept her out of work, prevented her from performing on the radio, never increased her salary while taking an ever larger slice of her income for himself. And now as if to spite her, and to needle Petter, he's bought the rights to the film of Joan of Arc – a role he knows she has coveted since girlhood – and given the part to his lover, Jennifer Jones. The news is a knife to Ingrid's heart.

She comes home and sees Petter sitting upright on the sofa, having just returned from the hospital, still with that lingering hint of antiseptic in the smell that surrounds him. She has to remind herself that she's married to this man.

When she raises it later, it's clear that he does not want to discuss the contract. 'Leave it with me,' he says.

'I have left it with you, and now see what happens.'

'You have to be tough with these people.'

'You have to be tactful.'

'They think you're a pushover if you don't play rough.'

'This isn't an arm-wrestling contest, Petter.'

'Look,' he says. 'We're in a strong position.'

She doesn't feel as if she's in a strong position. She feels she's perched on the edge of a cliff and that the slightest breeze might blow her off.

'Trust me,' he says.

She was eighteen and nine years younger than Petter when he first came to dinner as the guest of her cousin. And he seemed so grown up, so tall – a full six feet three inches. He could swim and ski, and even box. He lent her books. He took her out on Saturday nights to dinner and danced with her afterwards. And what a terrific dancer he was – so light-footed for a big man – and she so clunky and self-conscious; he made her feel like she was floating on air. On Sundays they drove out to the woods where they hiked and enjoyed a picnic, or else strolled along the harbour, and slowly they became inseparable until it was hard to consider herself apart from him. He seemed the answer to every question she'd ever posed. So when he asked her the single most important question, she answered him after only a second's hesitation.

She thinks of this now, and it seems it must have happened in another life. Whatever glue helped to fasten her and Petter together, she concludes that it has dried, its adhesive quality vanished, allowing them to drift like two limp bits of paper, apart.

In a fury of efficiency she tidies the house, changes the sheets on the bed, though the maid only changed them yesterday. It makes her feel better, and fits in with the crispness of the air outside, the lawn freshly cut and the apples in the bowl on the table downstairs.

Tonight, she knows, there is another party and she wants to surprise Capa, to impress him with her new dress, which she's had made specially.

She has a long bath, washes her hair, and puts on a favourite platinum necklace. It looks good above her neckline, she decides. And she puts on lipstick. She likes the glitter of it in the mirror. A vivid red strip.

When she emerges from the bedroom, she's wearing a black off-the-shoulder number and looks sensational. Her bare shoulders glisten.

'How do I look?' she asks Petter, thinking even he will be pleased.

'Overdressed,' he says.

15

I dial her home number.

No answer.

I hang up, dial again.

No answer.

I hang up, dial again later.

Petter answers.

I hang up.

Shit.

I sit outside with Irwin, smoking cigarettes and drinking Margaritas, watching the orange of a sunset wobble and sink into the waves.

'I have to admit, Capa, I'm surprised you made it out here.'

I smile.

'I suppose you're having fun?'

'It's better than being shot at.'

'Oh? I thought you liked that.' Ice cubes rattle as he swirls them round his glass. His eyes search mine. 'Is it how you imagined?'

'There's no metro,' I complain, 'and no sidewalks.'

'Where do you want to walk?'

'The light is a disaster for hangovers, the nearest store a mile away, while the restaurants are so awful you have to go to people's houses to be sure of a decent meal.'

There's a loaded silence.

'And Miss Bergman?'

'She works hard.'

'Ah-ha.' He throws his head back to release a gust of laughter. A cloud of cigarette smoke billows towards the sky. His laughter collapses into a cough. 'Well, don't say I didn't tell you.'

'I've taken her picture plenty of times.'

He takes a last swallow, gets up to refill our glasses. 'You'll need a bigger camera if you want to impress in this town.'

He's right, of course, but there's something smug about his tone that I resent, that hint of bitterness that surfaces the more he has to drink.

He says, 'You know what I read the other day?'

I can tell from his expression that he's lining up a wisecrack. 'What?'

'There's a direct relationship between the size of your dick and the space between your ears.'

'And you've got a big head, right?'

'It was a philosopher who said that.'

'Did he also say that behind every big dick is an even bigger asshole?'

He looks at me for a moment, unsmiling, judging me, then laughs furiously. He reaches for his glass, takes mine from my hand.

While he retreats inside, I look around at the palm trees, the smart new Plymouth behind the house, listen to the waves roll onto the beach and the boats jiggling in the distance.

Happiness may be enshrined in the constitution, but there's still something in this patchwork quilt of a Republic, with its prim liquor laws and promise of democracy, that's too neatly rectangular. The attempt to trap that fantastic blankness, to press all this emptiness into federal territory, to chop it into blocks and pin it into grids of numbered streets all seems a bit too easy, as if creating one vast convenience store. And for all the open space and big sky, I feel hemmed in here, with the desert on one side, the ocean on the other, and the San Andreas fault lurking beneath my feet.

I notice it is dark all of a sudden. The dark here happens very fast, flattening everything in shadow. At around six o'clock, the sky turns black, a bowl that empties suddenly. It's as if the sun just drops off a shelf.

Irwin emerges with two new Margaritas in misty glasses, mixed with lime juice and salt on the rim.

'It's good to see you, Capa.' He plonks himself down, takes longer than necessary to light a cigarette. There's a silence, filled with the warm wind, the shore lights, the silver of the surf. The smoke from his cigarette trails off into the night. 'You know all you have to do is let it be known you've slept with Ingrid Bergman and the women will come running.'

'You think?'

'It works for me.' He flicks me a glance to show that he's joking then explodes again with laughter.

A feeling of unease spreads through my body. I sip my Margarita. The salt stings my lips. I lean forward, start to say something, stop.

'What?'

I hesitate. 'Is it still okay if she comes here?'

He doesn't answer straightaway. 'Alone,' he says, 'or with you?'

A bit of ice slips between my lips. It's so cold, it makes my teeth throb and cracks loudly inside my mouth. 'I need $200,' I tell him.

'Why?'

'To replace the $200 you gave me yesterday.'

'What happened to that?'

I shrug.

'I can't keep doing this, Capa.'

'I know.'

'If you want to gamble, you've chosen the wrong town.' He looks at me for a moment, then carries on speaking. 'Don't try and compete with these people.'

'No?'

'Because you'll lose.'

He fishes out $200 from his wallet and counts it out slappingly into my hands.

I promise to give him the money back just as soon as I have it.

He tells me to get out, and not to bother coming back, though from the studious way he avoids my eye, I can see that he doesn't mean it.

Returning from Irwin's beach house, I take the coast road.

My eyes are glazed from all the Margaritas. I wind down the window to get some fresh air. The smell of sage penetrates the interior. Its scent is everywhere, and mixes with the leather smell of the seats. The car headlights slip and skim on the road surface, the signs and roadside grasses made vivid under the full beams.

I hate driving and haven't driven for years. But it's the only way to get around in this city, and the studio insists on giving me a big black 1941 Lincoln convertible in which to tank around. At least it's easy to steer on the freeway; it's as if you're travelling on rails. But then when you enter the city limits, the traffic darts at you from all angles.

There must have been a shower. The streets are damp and shining, and a thin drizzle persists, but still it feels muggy. I breathe in deeply, keep the window open. Raindrops touch my face, trickle slippingly down the windshield. Lights flicker across my fingers on the wheel.

After a time, the wipers begin to squeak. It has, I realize, stopped raining. My thoughts wander, bend towards Ingrid, and how unutterably lovely she is, how she has bewitched me. Why else do I find myself driving this black box at the edge of the world, but for this crazy impossible need to love this woman. I try to think what she might be doing now, and whether she is thinking about me.

At an intersection on Franklin Avenue, I'm not concentrating properly and fail to see the red light. I press my foot down hard on the brake to avoid the oncoming traffic. A map slides across the top of the dashboard. A couple of books in the back hit the door. Light widens like a fan of sparks at the side of my eyes, and though I'm not travelling that fast, I clip the side of another car.

The Lincoln emits a scream of resistance, jerks wildly, skids out of control. I register the change of key in the engine, the sudden high wild rasp of tyres, a sound torn like a shriek.

The car is deflected, spins off. Too late, I try to readjust and wrest the wheel back onto a line. Abruptly a dark upright shape appears in the centre of the windshield right in front of me, rigidly insists on its right to exist. I try to steer away but stubbornly it refuses to move. Fixed in the headlights, it sharpens into the stiff spike of a lamppost. And what startles me is the way it seems to leap forward at the last moment.

The slam happens in my head before it happens in reality. And then it comes. Sickeningly.

Wham!

There's a fat smack as the hood hits, followed by the terrifying high sound of smashing glass and the lower, deeper sound of crumpling metal, a screech as if a giant tin can were being ripped open. The glass shatters, fragments flying into my face and arms, nicking my skin.

The horn sounds a dreadful and perpetual blare that I have no power to stop. The radiator spurts like a geyser. Hot water fountains over the sidewalk, the cap falling a moment later with a hollow clunk on the roof. The streetlamp, now bent like a question mark, flares red and fizzles out.

I feel my heart jar. Everything splinters. A bubble enters my stomach, pops. In this instant all I can think of is Ingrid – what she'll say when she finds out.

In the seconds afterwards, I'm surprised to find a cigarette still in my hand. I can smell gasoline, hear a distant dripping. I switch off the ignition, stumble out as fast as I can. I hobble across the road. My right knee aches where it banged against the steering wheel. My skull feels fragile as a cup. The impact of the collision still rings within me, quickening like the rattle of a coin on a table top. My neck feels stiff and my collarbone hurts obscurely. Otherwise miraculously I seem to be all right.

Glass is scattered on the ground and crackles like sugar underfoot. I hear the metal of the car ticking, see its new, oddly distorted shape. The world outside the car seems to have changed shape, too, and for a moment everything seems weirdly out of focus.

The guy whose car I hit is out, and charging towards me. He's furious and shouting. I apologize as best I can, and pretend my English is not so good. He starts swearing at me. He obviously thinks I'm Spanish, and utters a couple of oaths that he thinks I'll understand. *'Lo siento,'* I say, as convincingly as I can: the words for 'sorry' in Spanish. It's the apology given by the workers on the lot when they're screamed at by the technicians.

The police arrive. The car is towed away. I'm taken to the station where I deny having had more than one drink. They say I stink of liquor. I explain that I have a bad cold, and begin sniffing as convincingly as I can. They ask to see my passport and visa. I don't have them on me. My mind races as I think what to do. They threaten me with a night in the cells. It's only after I give them Ingrid's name and number that the atmosphere changes and things are sorted out.

When she arrives, quite late at night after shooting, she's furious, though she puts on an act for the police and charms the officers at the desk. She thanks them profusely, commends them for their patience, gives them her autograph, writes personal messages for their wives and kids. They are, of course, enchanted.

'You can't give out my name like that,' she says to me once we're outside.

'I couldn't think what else to do.'

'Honestly, Capa. You could get me into trouble.'

'You're not angry with me, are you?'

'It's a good job Petter was on call tonight.'

'Are you angry with me?'

'Let's go.'

'Tell me you're not angry with me.'

'You've had too much to drink.'

From now on, she tells me, the studio will order limousines to take me where I want to go. I'm forbidden, she says, to drive in the city, consigned for the time being to the passenger seat.

That suits me just fine, I say.

I don't see her come in. But when I look up, without warning there she is at a table with Petter, wearing a black and white polka-dot dress. In profile she sits tall as always. The light bounces off her ring like spray. I'm here waiting for Irwin. We've arranged to have dinner and go to a game.

Lights burn and voices murmur. A ceiling fan whirrs above me. I sit staring at her so that, however remotely, she must feel me looking and sense my presence even if she can't return my gaze.

I see a sudden slight agitation of her hands. Her fingers flutter airily for a moment. She catches a glimpse of me, I'm sure. A few seconds later, she turns again. This time there's the frankness of a direct glance.

From this angle, I notice how the tip of her nose tugs downwards rhythmically in conversation. Candlelight flickers on the white tablecloth and shines flatteringly onto her face. She's lit as if for a portrait. Her eyes shine wetly, rich dark wells. She begins fingering her string of pearls.

It's unbearable seeing Petter with Ingrid, the two of them together enjoying the intimacy of man and wife: the proprietorial way he addresses her, the solicitous way he traps his hand over her glass, the manner in which he touches her shoulder. *Mine*, he's saying. *All mine*. Small acts of possession. There's something primitive and territorial about the whole thing, something distasteful about his display of ownership. The whole performance, it seems obvious, is designed to ward people off.

I realize with a pang that I'm jealous. I find the sight of his hand around her waist grotesque. The way she tolerates the gesture, too, seems obscene. I think of her in bed with him, sharing her body on occasions when she cannot reasonably resist. The thought makes me so agitated, involuntarily I shift the position of my chair.

I catch her eyes again. The oval of skin above her neckline flushes. A spot of rosiness enters her cheeks. Can it be the wine? Or has the pressure of my gaze burnt a hole in her cheek? She touches her earlobe, twists the ring on her finger. She's on fire; lit from within.

She has this habit, I notice, of reaching to her neck as if to pinch the collars of a shirt together. She keeps doing it, as though wary of exposing the flesh there. She reaches for her water glass and drinks. The ice cubes bump her upper lip.

After a few minutes, Ingrid gets up, wends her way towards the rest room. She floats past my table and flashes a tender heart-felt glance. The light seems to hover for a moment, scattering shadows across her arms. Her pearl necklace glimmers milkily above a crescent of freckles. The candle flame staggers a little, then recovers as she glides past.

Maybe I'm imagining it, but the rhythm of her walk seems to match exactly the music coming from a corner of the restaurant. A guitar and piano duo play subdued, lyrical versions of 'I Got It Bad (And That Ain't Good)' and 'You Rascal, You'.

I take a sip of martini. The olive glistens greenly on top. With the glass to my mouth, I glance across at Petter. He has his back to me, lighting a cigarette. Then I watch as he starts dismantling a packet of matches. The operation is performed with the same clinical attention he might devote to extracting a tooth or dissecting a patient's brain.

I stab my cigarette out in an ashtray, then on an impulse head for the rest room where I know Ingrid will be.

There are two toilet doors. No one is waiting. I knock on the women's door.

'Ingrid?' No answer. 'It's me.'

Inside I hear the toilet flush. The flush becomes muffled. 'Capa?'

'Let me in.'

There's a pause, followed by a long scratch as the bolt is slid across. Her face, in shadow, appears at the edge of the door. Her eyes dart around until she's certain no one can see us. 'Are you nuts?'

I step inside. Ingrid closes over the door, locks it. There's a faintly urinous smell, mixed with the bitter odour of cleaning products.

'What are you doing?'

'I've come to tell you something.'

'What?'

I give her the look of a dope. 'I love you.'

The floor repeats a pattern of blue and white square tiles. The blue leaps out, seems to tremble above it. A rimless mirror throws back an oddly angled version of the two of us.

I reach to kiss her.

She pulls away. Her eyes enlarge in protest. 'Not here.'

'Just let me kiss you. Please.'

She listens for anyone outside the door. No one. Just the faint strains of the guitar and the high squeak of a violin – thin strings that connect us to the web of the next room.

I move to kiss her again.

'You're out of your mind. We can't. Not in here.'

I touch her. The fabric of her dress is thin. The intimacy is illicit, thrilling.

'Have you taken leave of your senses?'

'Probably.'

'What if we get caught?'

'We won't, I promise.'

'How do you know?'

Something tips. Her closeness, the frustrations of the last few weeks, the sheer need I feel for her. This time when I kiss her, I feel the tension in her body dissolve. In a single fluid movement, I lift her dress up to her midriff, hungrily push her back.

'What are you trying to do to me?' She half falls, half plants herself on the toilet lid, her toes just touching the floor. Her shoes shake free, the heels falling with two sharp clicks onto the tiles below. The clicks operate like triggers.

I tug at her stocking tops, which unpeel like a second skin. The silk darkens, folded over, crackles as though about to spark.

In a tricky manipulation, my fingers fumble, discover a seam, then lose themselves in a rosy open moistness, a shapeless hot wet mouth.

Her breath snags for an instant. Her head slips sideways.

I sense something stretch within her. Her thighs flare, a net waiting to take me.

Her hands unbutton my flies. The angle is awkward, but I bend to make it happen.

My free hand gathers her hair into a thickness.

Her legs clamp me, making a triangle.

The music seems so remote now, it works to slow the world around us, while here inside these four small walls, time accelerates.

What starts as an agitation at the back of my knees shades into an ache and lingers as a sweetness as if my legs were injected with honey.

Her pearls click together distantly.

I feel my head swim.

Her hands push down against the lid beneath her so that her back arches and her wrists stiffen.

We work clumsily for what seems a couple of minutes before something within her brims. Every nerve strains hotly to complete the reaction that kicks off inside her. Her face stretches tight and her lips come unstuck from mine to issue a silent scream. Her limbs quicken in a final rhythm, shiver, then release me in a kind of sob.

Everything is suddenly blind sensation, followed by a sense of gentle endless falling like the rain. An obliterating sweetness. I want to possess the moment, to wrap myself around it, to give it weight.

Inches behind us, there comes a knock. The knock is rapid, becoming more urgent.

'Ingrid?'

A silence.

'Are you in there?'

It is Petter. He is just beyond the door. Ingrid freezes then leaps up as if she's just been stung by a bee.

'Ingrid?' he says again. 'Are you okay?'

Her voice comes out high and cracked. 'I'm fine,' she says. 'It's nothing. I had a stomach ache. I'll be with you in a minute.'

We both grow small, retreat into ourselves.

'Open the door,' he says, his voice laced with impatience.

'Just a minute,' she manages, her voice level again. But her eyes are filled with panic. She mouths to me, gesturing wildly, asking what we should do. Fear grips her. Wordlessly she curses me.

I tuck myself in. Blood thunders in my chest. Feelings of shame battle with the need for more practical action. I turn on the tap. It buys us a few seconds. He will think she's washing her hands.

In this time Ingrid fastens her stockings, slips on her shoes. I point behind her to the handle of the chain. She understands, yanks it.

Slowly the oval of water fills with bubbles and flushes with an enormous roar.

Ingrid straightens her dress, unmusses her hair, rinses her hands without looking at them. 'I'm coming,' she calls.

The tumult subsides and the toilet drains. The next logical thing is to open the door.

He's still there.

I'm trapped. There's no way out. The room is tiny, the window too small to squeeze through. The only chance I have is to hide behind the door. If someone else is waiting, I'm lost.

I flatten myself against the wall and signal to her to flick off the light. She understands and choreographs it perfectly.

The door opens and the light goes out, cancelling the pattern of tiles beneath my feet. The toilet drips and gurgles as it settles into silence. The smell of ammonia fills my nose.

'Darling, I was worried about you,' I hear Petter say.

'It's my stomach.'

'Ingrid, I had no idea. You should have said.'

'It's nothing.'

'Do you want to go home?'

'I'm all right now.'

'You seem hot. Do you have a temperature?'

'I'm fine. Really.'

They begin speaking in Swedish. Their voices recede, mingling with the soft jazz of the guitar and violin, the distant chatter and tinkle of the restaurant.

No one else has come in. I'm lucky. I'm saved. I sigh inwardly with relief. But just as I walk out, a woman approaches. Offended, she stops. Her glance takes in the fact that I've been in the women's toilet with the light switched off. She looks like the type who might make a fuss, call the manager and complain.

'I've fixed it,' I say quickly.

'I'm sorry?' she says, patrician, suspicious.

'The light. It should work now.' I switch it on, gesture with a screwing movement for the bulb. 'See?'

She looks baffled for an instant, then wary. The fat on her upper arm jiggles. Unsmiling, sceptical, she glances back at me as she enters the rest room. I hear her loudly bolt the door.

Returning to my table, I see Irwin. He has just arrived.

The olive still floats in my martini, swollen and diluted now by the melted ice. The wax on the candle has congealed around the base. It smells faintly of vanilla.

I feel hot and take off my jacket before sitting down. I know Ingrid can see me in the corner of her vision.

Irwin registers my drink half-empty, my extinguished cigarette. He hasn't seen her yet. He looks at me, puzzled.

I scratch my head.

'Where were you?' he says.

⁓

Even if in the brightness and bustle of the day she feels blameless, when she wakes in the night, sensations of guilt assail her. The feeling gnaws at her that what she's doing is wrong.

I must be crazy, she thinks.

She knows she has acted badly. Everyone will say so. She has no defence, other than a kind of amorous delirium that people will call selfish – which, of course, it is.

It's odd, because no one who knows her or who has worked with her would claim that she's irresponsible. In no other sphere would people accuse her of that.

What has happened, then? She's realized that she was dead inside, is what. And now some force has acted upon her, unhinged her, made her do things that are reckless and incredible. Something has entered and transfigured her, overtaken her with its power.

It is a benign force, she's convinced. So why fight it? Why oppose what is self-evidently good? And isn't it wrong to stay with Petter when she no longer loves him? Isn't she kidding herself if she thinks she's being good when in reality she's merely being a coward?

It's hopeless, she decides. This thing with Capa is compromising her. She will – must – give him up. It's best for everyone. No more telephone calls. No more secret notes or clandestine letters. Silence. Renunciation. It is the right thing to do, the good thing – the only true course open to her. Then she contemplates life without him. Dry, impoverished, but honest. And her whole being screams out, no.

Whatever happens, she considers, it's good to know that her heart is not so eroded. It's good to know that she's still capable of being stirred. But whereas in Paris it all seemed so exciting, enjoying the high gloss of romance, at home in Benedict Canyon, with Pia at school and Petter at the hospital, the reality of an affair leaves her feeling tawdry.

At least she has her work to sustain her. And some deep instinct steers her to preserve it. Of all the scattered parts of herself, this is what fulfils her, makes her happy. It is the same impulse, she supposes, that makes Capa want to take photographs, and draws on the same deep well of feeling.

'You don't think a woman can change?' is one of the lines she has to say to Cary Grant after her character untypically refuses a drink. It is in this moment that Alicia agrees to martyr herself for her country and for the love of a man she knows may well destroy her.

16

The advance from International Pictures is burning a hole in my pocket.

I wake up this morning to find the milk has turned to junket and there's nothing in the cupboard other than a packet of sugar, two cans of beans and some bread, already stale. Outside, fog condenses and drips from the trees, mist filling the valley like grey water filling a bowl.

Without warning an inner voice says, 'Put everything on horse number seven in the seventh race.'

I ignore it. The fog clears like a mirror outside.

Later in the morning, it comes again, more insistently. 'Put everything on horse number seven in the seventh race.'

Once more, I ignore the voice. But it continues unabated up until lunch. It's like an itch, an irritant that won't go away. With more emphasis this time, the inner voice says, 'Put everything on horse number seven in the seventh race.'

I know I shouldn't pay any heed. It's the kind of advice that madmen, religious fanatics, killers listen to. But I succumb.

In the afternoon, I go to the race-track at Santa Anita and place my bet. I put everything on horse number seven in the seventh race.

The inner voice congratulates me. 'You did the right thing. Well done,' it says. 'You won't regret it. You'll see.'

The race starts.

Horse number seven lies third after the first circuit. He appears comfortable, strong and relaxed, moving easily up the field.

The inner voice says, 'Trust me.'

And on the second circuit, well placed, he begins his charge. Things are looking good. My fists are clenched, urging him on.

He starts to edge it, moves ahead by a nose. Things are looking very good. But another horse, a grey, makes a late kick and steals it.

My heart freezes. The voice is silent.

'Shit,' I say.

Two dark-suited men in hats sit up, interested, when they see Ingrid enter the restaurant. She nudges me subtly. 'Watch out.'

I look around.

'Reporters,' she says, smiling determinedly into the middle distance.

'How do you know?'

'I can spot them a mile away.'

'You want to leave?'

'If we go now, it'll look as though we've got something to hide.' She calls over the maître d'.

I try not to look at the reporters.

'A table, somewhere in the centre,' she says.

'Are you sure?' I whisper.

Ingrid follows the maître d', striding confidently, almost ostentatiously towards the table. She holds her head high, making no effort to conceal who she is. We sit down.

I say, 'You think we'll get away with this?'

She allows a napkin to be flattened on her lap. The two newshounds who sat up like hyenas when we walked in look bored again. Her tactic seems to work. She convinces them that there's no story, nothing out of the ordinary, nothing remarkable going on here.

She lights her own cigarette. 'I still feel as if I'm doing something wrong.'

'That's silly.'

'Having to creep around guiltily – it makes me uneasy.' She looks round as if certain someone will overhear.

'I thought you found it exciting.'

'I did.'

'You don't any more?'

She says nothing, blows smoke in a column from her lower lip.

'I don't mind if people know the truth,' I tell her.

'I'm sure you don't,' she says.

All those handsome leading men with their mansions, parties and fast cars, I consider, and instead she chooses a gypsy newspaperman. Who would ever guess? Who would suspect a schmuck like me?

But it's as if she's been spooked. She takes a long swallow of wine. In returning her glass to its sticky circle, she misjudges the angle slightly, placing it too close to the edge of the table. She pushes it back across the surface, running it through a small bubble of damp.

'The way you handled them was impressive,' I tell her.

She's not interested in compliments. Her face remains impassive. Her eyes slide towards me. 'I remember once,' she says, 'I had trouble with a scene. I couldn't get the emotion right. I didn't believe in the character. So I said to the director, "It's no good, I can't do it." And you know what?'

I shrug.

'He took me aside, sat me down and in a calm voice said, "If you can't do it, fake it. Just fake it." So I did, and it all made sense.'

'Is that what you're doing with me?' I say. 'Faking it?'

She consults the menu. I start laughing. She ignores me at first. 'What's so funny?' she says.

'Nothing.'

Sunlight pours through the window, throwing slats of shadow on the floor. Cars glide past outside.

I long to hold her in my arms, to say her name over and over, to look her in the eye and tell her that I love her, that everything is okay. I want to touch things because they belong to her, but I can't, because she's married and I'm here in this restaurant with two reporters watching, in this city where she works, in this world where she stands as a paragon of virtue. That's why I'm laughing.

So instead, jokingly I cock my thumb, make my fingers into the shape of a gun, point it towards my temple and pretend to pull the trigger. I purse my lips, then blow to signal an explosion. My eyes rise heavenwards.

She doesn't laugh.

∽

She tries to imagine the facts stacked in the balance pans. Impossible to measure, impossible to quantify the hurt and heartache involved. She changes her mind a thousand times. Her imagination is feverish with different scenarios. She can't see a clear way ahead. It is a non-choice, a leap into the abyss, a knife slipped into her whatever she decides.

More than once, in that instant when she wakes in the morning and turns to the empty space next to her in the bed, instinctively it is Capa she expects to see and not Petter. She looks about her in astonishment. She doesn't recognize the room, doesn't understand where she is for several seconds.

She is shocked to find that she distrusts herself, her ability to know what she wants, to understand who she is. I'm a bad person, she thinks. I've done selfish things. She can't stand lying, hates being deceitful, loathes hypocrisy, and yet when she sees herself in the mirror, she wants to scream, 'Look at me!' She's confused at the happiness she feels when she thinks of Capa, and she thinks of him all the time. She feels proud of him, though she has no right to. And she feels the pain of excitement this intimacy affords. She feels closer to him than any man. Being with Capa, holding his hand, sleeping with him, feels the most natural thing in the world.

Why must she always be the responsible one? She's been responsible all her life, she considers. Isn't it time she enjoyed herself a little, had some fun for a change? Is it asking too much to spend some time with the man she loves?

She knows very well that it is.

It strikes her as ironic, the way every camera angle, each sound cue, every word of dialogue is established beforehand, fixed in the script. Her working day is a model of order and predictability, and mocks the confusion of her private life.

The studio has prepared five alternative endings to the film. She's read all of them and it's yet to be decided which one the producers will choose, but she's clear in her own mind which one she prefers and has made her feelings known. If only she could ask one of the writers to resolve her personal problems, too. Maybe Ben Hecht could develop a few plot lines to show how she might navigate a way out of this mess.

She finds it impossible keeping it all to herself. She's desperate to confess, to tell Petter everything, to put an end to all the lies and excuses, the daily deceptions. It seems wrong, her living here with him now in what she calls her home. Already she feels that she belongs elsewhere.

What would be his reaction if she were to leave? Violent? Incredulous? Suicidal, perhaps? She doubts the latter. Compassionate? That's not him, either. She sorts through the possible range of his responses. Would he fight? Would he want immediate separation, divorce? And what about Pia? Would he want custody? He loves her. Whatever were to happen, she knows it would be spiteful and messy. The thought appals her, makes her want to cry.

The longer she leaves it, the more she worries that she might not have the strength to see it through. She understands suddenly why people join the Foreign Legion, why they jump from bridges, why they board planes with just some hand luggage, a few dollars in their pockets and are never seen again.

And now she learns from Joe that there are rumours, whispers at the studio. People are talking, muttering darkly. Capa, she hears, is indiscreet.

The walls are closing in. She decides that she must act, however painful the consequences. She's seized by the need to do something, to resolve the situation once and for all. Only fools leave things to fate, she decides. She's not going to wait for the operation of some remote destiny. She has a chance to change her life, to make it better, and she will. The opportunity may never come again.

Standing before the bedroom mirror, she practises a solemn expression. 'I'm leaving you.' She repeats, 'I'm leaving you.' As she tests the words in her mouth, her face grows stern, her voice deepening with conviction. 'I'm leaving you.'

But as with all words repeated often enough, they seem nonsensical after a while and lose their relation to the world. Her throat grows tight and dry. She despairs of ever telling him. She feels it curled inside her, folded like a secret.

She gathers herself sufficiently to go downstairs.

'I'm going for a drive,' she shouts from the kitchen, retrieving the car keys from a drawer.

'What?' Petter says, above the noise of the radio.

'I'm going for a drive,' she says, not waiting for an answer, though she hears his distant question, 'Where?'

∽

I see the rushes at the studio.

Ingrid's face fills the screen, her two great shining eyes like wounds I want to heal. There's something magical about the way her features are transformed on the big screen. The artistry lies in the way she underplays the scenes. That nuanced wrinkle of the lip, the infinitesimal twitch in her cheek, the barely detectable flare of her iris – each inflection conveying more than any larger, dramatic gesture.

She inhabits her role as Alicia so deeply, her character seems completely real. She manages to draw the audience in so that immediately you're on her side. And when in close-up she turns on that searching gaze, that misty, questing look, you feel as if you'd die for her, just as in the movie she's prepared to die for love. I'm reminded again how beautiful she is, what a glow she gives off. Her beauty is like a thing apart. And when the stills are developed, the production team are thrilled. She looks gorgeous, framed like a painting, and I savour the sensation of her face lighting up breakfast tables all over America as people open their magazines.

Luckily for me, though, she now has two days off.

She waits until Petter leaves for the hospital and Pia goes to school. Then she takes her Oldsmobile from the garage, heads up the sweeping drive of her stone and redwood one-storey house and turns into Benedict Canyon, where we've agreed she'll pick me up.

I get in quickly as she pulls over. A headscarf tightly frames her face. Her eyes are unfathomable behind dark glasses.

She drives, as she would every day, down Sunset Boulevard. But instead of heading east to the studio, she makes a right turn and speeds along Sunset to its end. Then we head north on the Pacific Highway towards Malibu.

I have the keys to Irwin's beach house stowed safely in my pocket.

Once we're clear of the city limits, Ingrid releases her head-scarf. We wind down the windows, and like bolts of foam the breeze from the ocean shoots through our hair.

Within minutes, the Pacific glints off to our left. The sun is shining, the sky cloudless, but there's something wrong, I can tell. Ingrid seems sullen, unusually subdued.

I look at her in the rear-view mirror. 'Are you missing work?'

'No.'

'What, then?'

'Nothing.' She straightens her arms on the steering wheel as if pushing herself back. There's silence for several seconds. 'A journalist spoke to me yesterday.'

'Oh?'

'He said you've been boasting to everyone.'

'Boasting?'

'You know, showing off.'

'About what?'

'That I'm your mistress.'

I laugh, catch her face in the mirror.

Her eyes remain stubbornly on the road. 'Why would he say that?'

I shrug, wipe my hands on top of my knees.

'Do you talk about us?'

'No.' My voice sounds thin in my own ears.

'You talk to Irwin.'

'We talk about all kinds of things.'

'About us?'

'He's just sore because I took some money off him in a game.'

'What about others?'

'I might have let it slip once or twice.'

'Jesus, Capa.' Ingrid bangs her hand on the steering wheel, causing a small swerve.

'I tell them it's a secret.'

'I don't believe this. Are you mad? Why do you tell them anything?'

'They're friends. Wouldn't you?'

'No. Never.'

'You told Hitchcock.'

'That's different.'

'Is it?'

Unflustered. 'I trust him.'

We've already had this argument. I decide not to raise again the way Hitchcock had Ingrid play a scene with Cary Grant nibbling her ear, kissing her lips and paddling in her neck for three uninterrupted minutes. Nor do I complain about the way he had the camera move in for an endless series of takes. Blah-blah (kiss) blah-blah (kiss) blah-blah (kiss), each kiss lasting no more than three seconds in order to get past the censor, while Hitchcock dribbled over his triple chin onto his tie. Nor do I mention the way he leered at her afterwards – his way, I guess, of getting back at me for his own failure to get inside her pants.

Ingrid's anger is transferred to her foot. She presses down hard on the pedal. The car is travelling fast now. Her hair snarls wildly in the wind.

'All right, I'm sorry. I shouldn't have said anything.'

'No,' she says. 'You shouldn't.'

'I keep forgetting how ambitious you are.'

The car shakes with the sudden increase in speed. The steering wheel judders. The trees either side of the highway grow blurred, hurtling by.

'Things are different here. You have to understand that. We have to be careful.'

I stare straight ahead. 'You're ashamed of me. Is that it?'

'I don't want you ruining my career.'

'You've been talking to Joe again.'

The needle on the speedometer quivers around eighty-five. The wheels emit a high whistle. The whole car vibrates from the strain.

'Do you ever look at the tabloids?' The road disappears quickly under the car, slips away like a river in spate. There must be a hundred bugs spattered on the windshield. Their blood makes little red flecks on the glass. 'Have you ever heard of Hedda Hopper, Sheilah Graham?'

'I've heard of them.'

'Do you realize what they're capable of? They serve up your life with the morning coffee.'

'I said I'm sorry.'

'The studios sell dreams,' she says. 'They don't deal in damaged goods.'

She overtakes a car on a sweeping bend. For a few moments, she's on the wrong side of the road. Blind, a second car careers around the corner. She accelerates into the narrow gap. The Oldsmobile almost tips over as she takes the curve.

I close my eyes, expecting a crash, but somehow the balance of the moment holds. The car squeezes through, then straightens. The prolonged hoot of a horn becomes lost in a cloud of dust behind us.

'Are you crazy?' I say. If I were Cary Grant right now, this is where I'd take the wheel. 'A car crash with another man in the passenger seat? What would that do for your reputation?'

Her arms stiffen. 'I have a lot to lose.'

'And I don't, I suppose?'

'No,' she says. 'You don't.'

I goad her. 'Is that as fast as you can go?'

In the silence that follows she lowers her head. 'Have you told anyone else?'

I don't answer.

'Who *have* you told?'

'No one you know.'

'Who?' she insists.

'You really want to know?'

'Tell me, for God's sake!'

Grudgingly. 'My mother.'

Ingrid looks across at me for an instant, the sting gone out of her. She eases off the pedal. The world catches up with us, comes back slowly into focus. Her tone remains harsh, unyielding. 'What did she say?'

'She said she thought I could do better.'

She shakes her head. 'You're such a bastard,' she says. 'You know that?' But she's smiling now. She starts banging the wheel, then hitting me playfully with her right hand, laughing, her hair flying free.

'Hey,' I say. 'I told her I was willing to give you a chance.'

At the beach, Ingrid runs full pelt across the sand and dives without flinching into the sparkling water of the Pacific. Her head bobs up like a seal's twenty feet away. She shakes the wet from her head.

The hills are tan with purply stains, as if someone has spilt wine on them. The sand is ribbed beneath my feet. My shadow wobbles on the bottom as I wade in. I stretch out star-like on my back. And with my eyes closed, the skin behind my lids turns red.

We float, holding hands, allowing the breeze to twist us in gentle circles. Then, salty and warm, we swim out further.

I kiss her, push back her hair. Her limbs are slick, her body elongated like a Modigliani in the water.

We swim, buoyed not just by the water, but by something light inside us – an invisible gas: happiness. We laugh, and for a few minutes don't care about anything or anyone else – not Petter, not Joe, nor the press – and suddenly everything is very funny as I send a long thin fountain of foam upwards from my mouth.

Back at the beach house, we draw the blinds, lock the door, and with the sound of the waves beyond the window and the smell of the ocean still in our noses, on the fresh white sheets of the bed we make love.

Later, a dribble of water seeps warmly from my ear onto the pillow. I tilt my head, put my little finger into my ear, and wiggle it.

∽

Adultery has a colour, red. And a taste, dark and sweet. It is a heavy thing, this loving, she decides. The feeling weighs upon her like an atmosphere double the gravity of the earth.

In Hollywood, she finds there is too little time to consider relationships with other men. Of course she's aware of her co-stars – Humphrey Bogart, Spencer Tracy, Gary Cooper, Gregory Peck – those fantastically handsome actors with their rock-like jaws and spicy aftershave, the swirling energy of their sex like a cloud that surrounds her. How could she not be? But she feels immune to their charms and able to deflect their attentions.

Then in Paris, something unanticipated happened. She realized just how incidental a relationship she had with her own life, and how she craved more. She wanted to open herself up to fresh experiences, to educate herself sensually. It was like discovering a new dimension or set of colours in which to depict her life. And her mind was swept clean by the kind of love she didn't think existed.

Back in Los Angeles, however, her situation seems little short of calamitous. Her life has reached an impasse, a violent crisis, an abyss from which she wonders if it's possible to escape.

She repeats the mantra that she loves her husband and adores her daughter; she's connected to them by essential threads. The ties are deep-rooted and, in the case of Pia, indissoluble. But now this man, this Capa, has come along and turned her world upside down, made her insides feel all kinked.

When she returns late from the studio after another gruelling day that started very early in the morning, with costume fittings, make-up tests, hair styling, she finds Pia is still up.

Ingrid says, 'You're not in bed?'

'She hasn't seen you for days,' Petter says.

It's true, of course. She leaves before her daughter wakes up in the morning and returns home long after she has gone to sleep. She can't remember the last time she picked her up from school.

Pia runs up to her, having waited several hours for this moment. It's not often she's allowed to stay up for such a treat. She's been drinking hot chocolate and her lips are smeared a milky brown. In a rush of tenderness she buries her face into the folds of her mother's white dress.

If Ingrid had thought to drop down on one knee to receive her, to bend to the girl's eye-level, it might have been avoided. But it all happens too fast, and when the girl comes away, a dark stain has transferred itself from Pia's mouth onto the cloth. Tired from working all day, feeling anguished by her love for Capa, frustrated at the negotiations on her contract and bewildered by her own inability to see a way through, the fog of confusion mixes thickly in her brain and in a reflex she immediately regrets, Ingrid slaps her daughter across the face.

In the vaulted living room, the sound echoes sharply and is slow to fade.

'My God,' Petter says.

The girl recoils, horrified, and runs crying to her room.

Ingrid herself starts to cry, clenching her fists as if she wants to squeeze herself dry of tears. In a fit of self-loathing she throws down her pocketbook.

Petter goes to see Pia, pausing on the stairs to hurl a judgemental look at his wife.

Ingrid feels ashamed, and experiences a sudden hatred for her life, for what she has become. It seems as if, after all the hard work she has put in today, everything is spoiled.

She leaves her pocketbook on the floor and slowly makes her way to her bedroom. The house with its vaulted beams seems suddenly cavernous, like an old railway station that makes her feel small and cold and desperately sad. Did that really just happen? She can hardly believe it. She wants to apologize to Pia, but will wait until Petter is gone from her room so she can talk to her daughter alone.

She tries to rehearse what she might say, to find some words of comfort, some justification for her behaviour, but she knows there is none and that what she did is unforgivable.

A numbness comes over her; a little buzz starts inside her head as if she has drunk too much.

She grows composed enough to notice a brown moth by the window. Papery, weightless, it clings to the wall and remains motionless. She watches it for what seems like several minutes. She makes a conscious decision to empty her head of everything else, to concentrate on the moth. She waves her hand at it. It remains perfectly still. She blows on it, but it doesn't budge. She wonders if it might be dead. But if dead, she considers, how can it cling to the wall like that?

Her attention switches. She's conscious of Petter still talking to Pia. She hears his reassuring voice, if not the words he is saying. She hears her daughter still sniffling, but calmer now. Even though they are in the next room, they seem a world away.

With her finger she begins to draw shapes in the condensation. The glass is cold. It squeaks a little. She presses the finger to her cheek.

Everything around her in this instant seems especially vivid:

the feathery branches of the redwoods elastic in the wind, the sky dark but crisp with stars, and the tight weave of the carpet beneath her feet, the green appearing to leap out.

She opens the window, admitting a cool blast of air. She breathes in deeply, filling her lungs. Then something else catches her eye.

Two dark smudges move in the distance, beyond the drive. She registers the fact that two reporters – who else could they be in those gabardines and homburg hats? – are waiting across the road.

A sensation of dread overtakes her. The pull of negative spaces. She feels as if she's falling. The tops of the trees become blurry, the sky darkens visibly. The carpet rises to meet her. She tugs the window shut again.

In the renewed silence, she feels the warmth creep back into the room, sees the trees retreat to a safe distance, the tide in the carpet ebb.

She removes her shoes like a penitent and makes her way to her daughter's room.

The next evening she meets Capa at a brick-walled restaurant out of town. She takes in the din of voices, the clash of cutlery, the subdued music. The chatter around them ceases for a minute as they take their seats. Gradually the buzz resumes, but at a higher pitch and with sly glances fired in their direction from the surrounding tables.

'I'm starving,' he says.

'We can't stay here.'

'You want to go to Hamburger Heaven?'

'No.'

'Schrafft's?'

'It's not that.'

'What, then?'

'You see those two?'

'Where?'

'At the table opposite.'

'Where?'

'Don't look.'

'You recognize them?'

'I don't want to take any chances.'

'Honestly. Let's eat.'

'We can't stay here.'

'You're not hungry?'

'Come on. Let's go.'

'You're over-reacting.'

'I don't think so.'

'I thought you said the best thing to do was just to ignore them?'

'We should leave.'

'You're making a mistake.'

'I can't do this,' she says.

17

She hugs me from behind. I feel her breasts press through her sweater against my back. Her fingers come together around my waist. She puts her lips to my neck, adopts a spoilt, babyish tone. 'Can I ask you something?'

My tongue feels dusted with something heavy. 'Sure.'

'Why won't you let me get close to you?'

'Are you kidding? I can't get near you most of the time.'

'You know what I mean.'

I turn and kiss her on the lips. 'How close do you want me to get?'

Her hair curls under my chin, touches my throat. It tickles a little, and I'm aware of a mingled feminine scent of shampoo and perfume. But there's something suffocating about it suddenly, and her questions all up close.

'I need you to love me.'

'And I need to defend myself.'

She recoils. 'Against what?'

I sit down with a thump on the sofa, fiddle with my watch.

She plants herself down next to me, tucks her legs up under her, leaves her two shoes next to each other on the floor. Wearily she picks up a script bound by three brass tacks, and begins reading.

I notice how lovely she is, her lips tensed in concentration as she learns her lines, the way she puts her hand to her mouth, then flips a page. I feel guilty suddenly for being so mean. She looks so sad and serious, and I've looked forward to seeing her all week.

Needing to be forgiven, I point at the script. 'What is it?'

It is her turn to be sullen. She lifts the cover so I can see. *Arch of Triumph*. The brass tacks shine. She lets it fall to her lap, flips another page where the lines are printed at a slight angle.

'Any good?'

She shrugs, rejects the offer of a cigarette.

'What's it about?'

There's a few seconds' delay before she answers. 'Passion versus duty.'

'Oh?'

'Things are fine until he refuses to marry her.'

'Is that so?'

'Even *you* would think he's stupid,' she says, without looking up.

She tucks her hair behind both ears to reveal two hoop earrings, gypsyish. I want to nibble them for a second, to taste the metal in my mouth.

'If he married her, he'd have a passport and be able to stay in France.'

'Does she love him?' I lean across, rest my head on her lap so that she has to adjust her position.

'Yes.'

'So what happens?'

'Do you care?'

'I'm intrigued.'

'He's deported.'

'What does she do?'

'She has an affair with a new lover, who then shoots her in a rage.'

My unshaved jaw makes a crackling noise against her top. I see her red lips in granular close-up, her chin with its microscopic down of hair. 'She's obviously unstable.'

She turns a page, moves her legs away from some vague ache. The fabric in her sweater changes its sheen around her breasts. 'She's passionate.'

'Unstable,' I say.

After all the battles and the snow, the bullets in the throat and the reek of burnt explosives, finally I finish *War and Peace*. There's a marvellous scene towards the end where Pierre meets Natasha again. Aside from one small encounter in a passing carriage, he has not set eyes upon her for many years. His wife is dead now, so finally he is free, and she too is alone.

She has grown old and pale and thin. The shape of her face has altered, her eyes gone watery with age, and at first he does not recognize her. The woman he longed for and loved in secret, this woman who stirred him so that he could think of nothing else – here she is at last. And it's tragic because he does not know her, cannot see who she is, until abruptly he recognizes a look in her eyes, a familiar glimmer that revives a distant memory, triggers a remote echo in his brain. He realizes it is her, Natasha, the woman he adores, and he experiences a flash of joy that transforms him, that reawakens his yearning and literally makes him glow.

It is an extraordinary moment. Reading it makes me want to cry, for Pierre, for Natasha, for Ingrid, for me, for everyone – and for all the time that is lost between people who love each other and find themselves apart. Now it's all over, with the last few pages read, I'm sitting in the tub and I want to blubber. I feel this terrible sense of grief, a desperate sense of emptiness. It's over-whelming, as though people I know have died. The feeling persists within me, lingers like a splinter.

As for my own life, the war is a distant echo. No one's heard of me here. My name means nothing. Would anyone other than Ingrid notice if I were to pack my bags and leave?

And another thing: I've written virtually nothing of the book commissioned by International Pictures. When William Goetz telephones, I tell him that it's going well, and when he asks how close I am to finishing a first draft, I tell him that I don't want to rush it, that I want to give him something good. He seems happy, though he's keen to see a few chapters. I tell him I'll tidy up the opening section and send it over, when in fact all I have is a stack of blank paper and a few scribbled notes.

I decide it's time to get down to work. It's not Goetz I want to impress, though; it's Ingrid. I need to show her I can be self-disciplined. I need to prove to her that I can produce something worthy, something she can point to and be proud of.

I sit alone in Irwin's beach house, with its view of the ocean, take out a pen and start to write. I write many pages, read each one over and throw it away. The writing seems flat, lacking the vividness and immediacy of the pictures, missing the straightforward urgency and intimacy of being there. I took the photographs so I wouldn't have to say anything, knowing that when people saw them, there would be nothing left to say. And now here I am trying to recapture what I thought I'd caught already. The whole thing seems ridiculous. So I just sit for a time, measuring the silence, waiting for the words to come.

Slowly the moments untangle. I'm able to put things together bit by bit like a complicated mosaic, images dissolving and re-forming, quickening like bits of mercury so that faces swarm together and seem to merge into one. Walls fall away, melt into dead spaces, lit with ghosts. The carbonized remains of a man being handed down from the cockpit of a bomber. The feet of Italian children poking out from their small coffins. A soldier struck by a shell while tucking into his C-rations, his body ripped open so that it's impossible to distinguish between the beans in his stomach and the beans blown from the tin. They are still there, ready to haunt me. Like a secret army, they invade me, colonize my body, lie in wait, ready to attack.

I understand suddenly why I can't allow myself to feel too much, to become sensitive again, because to do so would be to expose myself, to grow mad with compassion, to become vulnerable to all the terror and the dread. And so I retreat into numbness, into drunkenness, to deaden the senses, to plug the emptiness, to stay alive.

Hours pass. Days and nights and months flow around me. The darkness presses fold upon fold. I remember a warm night with Gerda on a beach in northern Spain. The stars, I recall, seemed magnified, enlarged beyond anything I'd seen before, flickering like bits of phosphorescence, so that even now recollecting it, I begin to feel dizzy. It was the last time we were together and able to relax and talk about things other than the war. The last time, though we could not know it, we were able to sit down and enjoy each other's company. The next day, we pushed south towards Madrid. I feel sad and nostalgic to think of that night when we laughed to see the stars so big and trembly. And I grieve again for the time that has passed, for the people that have gone, shocked into consciousness of the darkness, the waves outside and the bits of light we cling to.

And then this morning after just a few hours' sleep, I feel a tug on the bed. The mattress slides sideways, given a small heave. Accompanying it is a tinkle. The light fixture jiggles visibly.

I jump up. In this instant the ceiling seems to move closer, the floor threatens to open into a void. A feeling of nausea rises within me and is gone.

It is all over in a matter of seconds; less, perhaps. I wonder if I've imagined it, but no. It is a small earthquake, I discover afterwards.

I don't know why I'm surprised. Tremors are frequent in this part of the world, and I've experienced bigger quakes before, but for some reason, this one unsettles me. I feel shaken by it, displaced, as if the world has been thrown out of focus, as though the floor has been pulled from under my feet.

This is what happens.

At eleven o'clock at night, I watch from outside her home in Benedict Canyon. The hall light goes out, followed by the light in the living room. A moment later a bedroom light snaps on, illuminating the leaves of a walnut tree next to the window. Shadows grow solid. The grass shines waxily. Thick branches spill over the fence.

A few quick seconds later, something alters shape in the darkness. I see it in the corner of my vision. The curtains twitch in her bedroom, and straightaway she's there. Her face at the window, pale as the moon. A ghost.

For a painful instant I hardly dare to breathe. Everything remains incredibly still. Then she spots me.

Another minute and I'm at the door, with Ingrid peering over the chain. She looks startled. So must I, I realize.

'What are you doing here?'

I see that her instinct is to close the door. Before she has a chance, I put out a hand. 'No,' I say. 'Please.' Bedraggled, red-eyed from lack of sleep, unshaven, I know I must appear like some desperate animal pawing at her door. 'I have to speak to you.'

'Are you nuts?'

I don't answer. I wasn't expecting this. I look away, see a spider-web in the hedge, the ponderous heads of flowers.

'What do you think you're doing?'

'I want to check that you're okay. After the quake.'

'Capa?'

'I wanted to see you. Is that so bad?'

I half expect her to turn away, but instead she stands there motionless. Her eyes stare straight ahead. The chain like a little mouth trembles between us.

She whispers, 'Have you been drinking?'

The truth is, I've been drinking solidly since this morning. When I think of Ingrid, I want to drink. And when I drink, I think of her – so what the hell am I supposed to do? She can smell it on me, probably, see my eyes shining.

'I don't get it. When I'm with you, you keep me at arm's length, then when I'm not, you follow me like a lost puppy.'

I realize how pathetic I must seem. Leaves scrape against the gravel in the drive. A single car slides past on the road outside. My heart thumps so hard, I can feel the roar inside my skull.

An impulse passes through me the way a finger cuts through a candle flame. I reach across to kiss her.

She leans back, puts a finger to her lips, points inside to where her husband and daughter lie in bed, asleep.

The chain remains intact between us. For a moment or two, nothing seems to make sense.

'Go home, Capa.' Her head tilts, impatient. She hugs her arms against the cold.

I try to win a smile.

She blows a kiss and closes the door, leaving me inhaling her scent in the darkness, alone.

I stand for several seconds watching her shrink, become shapeless, disappear behind the frosted glass. And as she diminishes, in a mirrored gesture I feel myself retreat.

The light snaps out in the hallway.

I walk back, wrapped in the silence of the night, the warmth of whisky, hopeful, unconsoled.

Early March. A dark afternoon. The darkness spreads like a stain over the beach and the ocean beyond.

I look out the window. Ingrid stands next to me.

'All right,' I say. 'What would you tell Petter?'

'The truth.'

'Which is?'

She studies her fingers. 'That I've met someone. That I'm sorry, that I ask his forgiveness, that I've tried to conquer my feelings . . .'

'You have?'

'That I don't wish to cause any hurt, but I've decided to leave him, that I've found a person I want to be with, and I hope he understands.'

I lean back, impressed. 'You've got it all worked out, haven't you?'

She laughs, shakes her head. 'I wish.'

'You think he'd fight?'

'No one likes to be humiliated. Least of all, Petter.'

'Is it worth it?'

'I'd be free.'

As if shifting my position will break the silence, I scratch my head with both hands. 'I don't want to live in your shadow.'

'So you'd just go off again?'

'You could come with me.'

'Like Gerda, you mean?'

I'm aware of the ocean boiling outside, the wind shaking the trees. I can't think of anything to say.

She's back at me again. 'Well, maybe I will.'

'What?'

'Come with you.'

'Don't be absurd.'

'What's so funny?'

'What would you do without your cocktail dresses, your nylons and high heels?' Two flies buzz near the ceiling. The sound is thin and insistent. The buzzing has an edge to it, touching off a feeling of hysteria in each of us. 'You're a movie star, for God's sake.'

'And you're a gambler and a drunk.'

I stare at the space between my feet.

'What the hell is wrong with you?'

'I have nothing to lose, remember.'

'You have me!' she says.

Her anger expands, then diffuses like cigarette smoke. 'I just have this horrible feeling that one day I'll pick up *Collier's* or *Picture Post* and there'll be this piece about you being killed somewhere in some pointless conflict.'

'I hope I don't detract from your notices.'

'You want to play court jester for ever?'

The wind outside rattles the windows. I pour a large whisky, take a good swallow.

'Look at you. It's embarrassing. Every day you're drinking before lunch.'

'I'd drink before breakfast if I could get up early enough.'

'Maybe you could hold your booze in the war, but here you're just a drunk,' she says. 'Everyone says so.'

'Is that right?'

'Yes, everyone.'

The air in the room grows heavy, the walls seem in the wrong place, and the light enlarges until my eyes begin to burn. I don't say anything for a minute, just clench and unclench my hands. I can feel her gaze upon me, unrelenting, measuring my intentions, hear the shush of the ocean outside. Finally, I say, 'I need some money.'

'What happened to the money I gave you?'

'I lost it.' The two flies batter against the lampshade. I can't meet her eye.

'How come you always have money to gamble but never any to settle down?'

I start to make a joke.

Her voice narrows to a funnel, down which she pours her scorn. 'The drinking and the gambling may not be your fault. The world has done that to you. I put up with that, even understand it. But your frivolity – that's what you bring to the world. And you know something? It drives me mad.'

'You're the one who won't take me seriously.'

Her voice grows shrill. 'You don't take yourself seriously.'

As if sensing the vibration rising in each of us, the two flies grow quiet.

Something snaps within me. 'How would *you* feel after ten years of shit?'

'I wouldn't spend ten years doing what you did.'

'No,' I say. 'You wouldn't.'

Things happen. It's never just one moment, I know, but there's always a tipping point. Day after day, little accumulations of hurt build up and you don't notice until one morning you get out of bed and your heart cracks open with the pressure.

The heat rises in my head, screams for release. Charged, an impulse shoots through me. I pick up a glass from the table and throw it against the wall. Hurled, it smashes with a fat crack. A hollow tinkle follows, a scattering of fragments as splinters hit the floor. A stain from the liquor forms a dark spot on the wall.

There's silence for several seconds, then an odd thing occurs. It's as if the action of smashing the glass causes something to shatter within me, too. I shiver for an instant. Everything seems blurred. I feel the muscles in my cheeks go taut. My stomach feels queasy, my hands grow mottled. A tide of nausea rises from my gut. There are tensions and pressures in my face that make the skin there crumple. Something fragile like a membrane breaks. I feel this collapsing inwards and before I know it, I'm crying like a baby. The tears leak from me and I can't make them stop. Real sobs, torn from me, so that my whole body becomes involved. The first flood dwindles to a subdued but steady stream of weeping. Everything seems to be breaking apart, becoming detached, flying off at all angles.

Ingrid seems startled, open-mouthed. She's never seen me like this. And it's as if she knows that in this moment, if she doesn't hold me tight, I might shatter like a vase into a thousand fragments. Quick to respond, she embraces me.

I cling to the warmth she releases, the scent of her skin.

We must stay like that for several minutes, just rocking gently to and fro. Then she takes hold of my face in her hands, kisses me for one prolonged moment on the brow, and orders me to go to bed and get some sleep.

'You have every right to hate me,' I say.

'I could never hate you, Capa.'

Everything is very quiet now. I watch, numb, recovering, as she cleans up the mess, scrubbing with puritan vigour the stain from the wall and sweeping up the smashed glass.

She's efficient and brisk, though part of me wonders whether she's clearing up for me or removing any trace of herself.

She looks at her watch. 'I have to go now.'

'Yes.'

She smiles the slight smile of someone enduring pain.

The seconds stretch. A silence opens up between us, grows heavy. She gives a little wave, then she is gone.

I hear the door click like a trap being sprung. A few quick

footsteps, a car starting remotely, then nothing. The last sound of her mingles with the empty generalized noise of the ocean and the wind outside.

Once she's left, I can't think what to do. I can't sleep, I can't read, and I don't want to drink. I just sit and breathe as the window grows dusty and listen to the cars pass on the road outside: shh shh shh shh.

I take out the harmonica from my pocket, look at it, feel its reassuring weight. A consolation. I run my lips along its pores and blow softly, without quite making a noise.

⌒

Petter goes out of his way to be kind, to compensate for any coldness, to atone for any arrogance he might have shown. With the self-discipline and determination that characterize his approach to everything in life, he resolves, again, to be a better person. A better husband, better father, doctor. He vows to perform small charitable acts that make a difference but are not vulgar in the Hollywood fund-raising way. And today he does something wonderful.

He asks one of his patients with a tumour on the brain if she wants anything special.

The lady says what she'd really like is an ice-cream in a cone.

So straightaway Petter jumps in the car and drives out of the hospital until he finds a drugstore that sells ice-cream in cones and brings one back to her. He has to hold it upright while he drives one-handed back to the ward and rushes it to her bed, all the time swabbing with a handkerchief as the ice-cream melts and dribbles around his fingers.

He doesn't tell anyone about this because that would be bragging and would detract from the simple act of kindness. But the woman appreciates it very much, and it makes Petter feel virtuous, reaffirming the image of himself as a fundamentally good man.

Back home that evening, he's brushing his teeth at the same time as Pia. Their toothbrushes shush in unison, the sound of his brushing a tone lower than hers. They share a look and a smile in the mirror – a smile that acknowledges that they are father and daughter, that brushing their teeth together is an intimate act, and the minty flavour and clean smell become a part of that.

Pia asks, 'Why was mummy crying last night?'

'Because she's sad,' Petter says.

'Do you still love mummy?'

'Yes, of course. Very much.'

'Does she love you?'

'I think so, yes.' He's been dreading this. He must restrain himself, not grow emotional. He hates himself at this moment. 'Though sometimes people don't love each other enough.'

'How much is enough?'

'That's difficult to say.'

'To infinity?' The girl stretches wide her arms.

Petter smiles. 'That would be good.' His next utterance is inspired. 'That's how much we both love you.'

'Why is mummy never home?'

He feels the acid in his stomach rise to his throat and contend with the freshness of his breath. 'You'll have to ask her that.'

The taste of toothpaste still lingers in his mouth. His throat feels dry. This is terrible, he thinks.

Pia ponders for a moment, twists her lips sideways in thought. 'Daddy?'

'Yes, sweetheart?'

'Would you be sad if mummy died?'

꙳

Technicians at the studio restore some early home movies that Ingrid's father made when she was a child.

She sits in the small projection room alone, watching the images unfold in drizzly black and white on a single reel. The first film, lasting just one minute, reveals her on her first birthday in a park with her parents on a sunny August day. She's wearing a white dress and is kissed by her mother, who is kneeling. Her mother stands and must then take the camera, for it is her father who next walks into shot. He's in his best suit, his hat at a dandy-ish angle so that you can only see half his face, and he's swinging a cane. He, too, kneels and kisses Ingrid.

The next film records moments on her second birthday. There she is again in a pretty white dress, more frilly this time. She puts both arms around her mother's neck and kisses her broad forehead as she bends low. The angle switches for the shot that follows. With almost comic formality for a two-year-old, Ingrid shakes her mother's hand and curtsies, something she has obviously practised for the camera. She doesn't look into the lens.

The final film, taken when she was three, shows her no longer in a white dress but in a dark coat and scarf, even though it is a summer's day. She's carrying flowers, a bunch of lilies, along a path. She's in a churchyard. She passes several gravestones before stopping and placing the flowers on her mother's grave.

The whole sequence of three films lasts less than five minutes. The reel slaps to an end. The lights come on.

She'd like to pretend to herself that she remembers these moments, but she doesn't. They are all a blank. This is all she knows of her mother, a woman with a kind smile who kneels to kiss her in a park on a summer's day in Stockholm before the end of the First World War.

Ingrid sits there motionless, unblinking, absorbing the images one by one. She asks the projectionist to run the reel again, which he does another five times.

She feels a deep sense of sadness but doesn't cry. She tries hard not to be sentimental. Her immediate thought, though, is that she wants Pia to see these films; she wants her daughter to see her grandmother so that she can know something of her, so that she can recognize where she came from, no matter how unsatisfactory and inadequate this glimpse of the past might be.

She also wants to draw a line from that girl in a white dress on her first birthday to the girl in a dark coat at the age of three. And she wants to extend the trajectory of that line until it reaches herself sitting here and now in this room, looking backwards, fascinated, a little frightened, belatedly grieving, and hopelessly confused.

'You seem distant,' Petter says, at dinner in the kitchen of their home.

Ingrid regards herself in the mirror above the table, inspects the puffiness under her eyes. She pulls her face sideways, grimaces so that all her teeth show. 'I feel ugly.'

'Try smiling for a change.'

Her eyes remain fixed on the mirror rather than looking at him. 'I don't want to lie to you.'

'Okay,' he says.

The thought floats free like one of the bubbles in her glass of water. 'I feel capable of bad things.'

He stops eating for a moment. 'Is there anything you want to tell me?'

She plays with the food on her plate. 'You resent me doing anything for myself.'

'You're inventing this.'

'You always put me down,' she says. 'In front of other people, too.'

'This is text-book paranoia.'

'Would you even care if I left?'

He puts down his knife and fork, wipes his mouth with a napkin. 'Are you telling me you want to leave?'

'No.'

'Then why bring it up?'

'Just a feeling that we're not getting on, and haven't been for a while.'

'Since when?'

'Since I can remember.'

'So what are you saying?'

Her shoulders slump, her knife remains at an angle as if aimed at him. 'I'm telling you how I feel.'

'It's late. You'll feel differently in the morning.'

'I've felt this way for months.'

He resumes eating, stripping his lamb cutlet precisely with his knife. 'It's never enough is it? I negotiate a new film for you, free of Selznick. You get twenty-five per cent net profit. You get to work with Charles Boyer again. What more do you want?'

A silence opens up around them. She lifts her thin gold necklace to her mouth, nibbles on it. 'I hate my life.'

'You're very capable, you know that?'

'Meaning?'

'You manage incredibly well.' He ignores the shake of her head, ceases eating for a moment. 'Can I ask you something?'

She sees his eyes and what lies behind them so that she has to look away.

He pours himself more wine, remains composed, obstinate, logical. 'Have you been unfaithful?'

'You think I hide things from you?'

'I don't know. Do you?'

A clock on the wall notches a second. 'No.'

He examines her face like a magistrate. Pia calls from the living room. She's thirsty.

'Just a minute, sweetness,' Ingrid shouts.

'Is there someone else?' he says.

She puts a finger to her lips to quiet him, afraid that Pia might hear. She moves to the refrigerator to get some milk, performing the task with deliberate slowness to buy herself some time.

Her mind is racing. Her hand trembles as she fills the glass. Some of the milk dribbles onto the table. She attempts to steady herself.

When she returns from the living room, she sees that Petter's face has hardened. She can tell by the look in his eye that he wants to say something hurtful, something unanswerable, something that will hit the mark.

There's a moment in which he seems to consider, leans forward. 'You know the trouble with you?'

'What is it this time?'

'You have no passion,' he says.

The cruelty, she decides, is in the control with which he says it. In this instant she despises him.

She says nothing, though she remembers a time before they were married when she was desperate to sleep with him, and he said no, insisting she save herself and remain a virgin until the wedding night. At the time, she thought this was noble and romantic, and she relished the sacredness of it, but since then she's come to understand that this was not so much honourable as cold and controlling. She almost flings this at him now.

His face is tough, unforgiving. 'You have no passion,' he says.

Abruptly from the living room comes a thud and then a yell. It is Pia. She has tripped and hurt herself. The milk has spilt across the floor.

Ingrid and Petter look at each other, register the fact. For a second they share the complicity of caring parents and recognize it in themselves. They both rush into the living room.

When they reach her, there's a competition suddenly for the child's affection. Petter gets there first, but Pia makes it clear that it is her mother she wants. The girl holds out her arms towards Ingrid, ignoring her father, pressing her head into her mother's chest.

Ingrid hugs her daughter with a desperate possessiveness. Already she feels she's attempting to form a circle from which Petter is excluded. And though she might be wrong, she imagines in the last few hours and days that he has grown afraid of her, afraid of her power to wound, conscious of her ability to injure him.

Now when she comes back into the kitchen, he seems conciliatory, sheepish. He even risks, 'I love you.'

The need to defend herself, to protect Pia, mixes with a retaliatory impulse inside her head. 'What's that got to do with anything?' she says.

18

The days are warm, the nights are clear. Beyond the window, a full moon. Blood orange over the city.

I unspool a roll of film and it curls like a wood shaving around my finger. I set the perforations over the sprockets and wind it on with my thumb until I feel it grow taut. I close the back of the camera, hear a reassuring click and wind on, waiting for that little tug of resistance as on a fishing line when something bites.

I mix vodka, tomato juice and Worcester sauce, drop in two ice-cubes, notice the way they bob and float. Lovely.

The telephone rings.

It's Ingrid.

The filming is over. *Notorious* is in the can.

'Did you get the ending you wanted?'

'You'll have to judge for yourself.'

'I will.'

'So?'

'So.'

We've already made an unspoken agreement not to talk about what happened the other night. I recognize it as a weakness. It is a lapse, that's all, and though the spot on the wall remains like the aftertaste of a bad dream, I want her to understand that it won't happen again.

A dead place comes back to life inside me. It's a stinking shame, I tell her, that we can't be together like a normal couple.

'Since when have you wanted to be normal, Capa?' A small silence follows. 'What are you doing for Easter?'

'It's not a big Jewish holiday.'

Ingrid laughs. Then she says something, but I don't quite catch it.

'Can I what?'

'Can you ski?' she says.

The image of her teeth mixes for an instant with the crisp whiteness of the hills, a winter moon, the blankness of a new canvas. Snow.

Ingrid and Petter have organized two weeks skiing in Sun Valley, Idaho. With a nanny engaged to take care of Pia and her husband still finishing off at the hospital, Ingrid manages to come early, so we can have a few days together, alone.

We wake to the whiteness of sheets and curdled sunlight. Out-doors the landscape sparkles with a brilliance that makes us wince. A marvellous transparency inhabits everything: the clarity of blue March days. The world is dazzling, glassy.

The snow has come late this year, then come in a rush, making some of the slopes treacherous. But the smell of pines and the blue of the sky, like an upturned bowl, make it good.

Ingrid is tanned and looks invigorated. Her cheeks glow and seem to widen her smile, her hair made wild by the wind and the sun. There's an energy about her that she can't suppress, a vitality that shines. Life simply spills from her, through the light in her eyes, the heat in her cheeks, her laugh like a shot of oxygen.

We have lessons each morning. The main trick, I learn, is to lean forwards rather than hang back; to sit lightly the way a jockey does, to maintain a low centre of gravity. I'm told to bend my knees and swivel more, leaning my weight into each turn, and to give myself to the descent, accepting it. It helps that the snow is soft and powdery, so that when you fall there's no hard landing, just a mouthful of wet freshness that turns to water on your tongue.

I love the hiss and shush of it, the burning in the lungs as you hurtle down, the snow's crispness smoking. It's so quiet, the smallest noise becomes audible – the flap of a bird's wings, a ledge of ice slipping from a tree. The sound of snow crunched underfoot is loud as a radish in your mouth.

In the morning, the air takes on a thick solidity. Big wet flakes swarm against the window. Sleet hurries against the glass. At night we feel sealed in here, with the snow gently falling and our bodies dissolving in the warm darkness. Then when it clears, the sky slides back like a planetarium, and the stars seem round and fat like fruit.

Petter arrives and everything changes. I move back into a separate chalet. The days of lovemaking, warmth and togetherness come to an end.

When I bump into him in the lodge, Ingrid passes it off as a coincidence. But she needn't fear. He barely recognizes me. I'm like one of the many extras on the set, one of the dozens of Hollywood hangers-on and bit-part players that he must meet each week.

'I know you from somewhere,' he says.

I make the action of clicking a camera.

'Oh, I remember, you're that photographer fellow.'

What goads me most, I suppose, is that he doesn't even seem to consider me worthy of suspicion. His wife together with someone like me? The notion must seem so preposterous, the idea so laughable and absurd, that the possibility never enters his head.

His eyes move on as though I don't exist for him.

Two days later, Ingrid hits a mogul at a bad angle and goes over awkwardly on her skis. I see it happen. Her sticks trailing, she tumbles clumsily and fails to get up straightaway. It's obvious that she's hurt. She lies there for several seconds, then gathers herself slowly as if picking up bits of glass.

Petter has already gone up ahead. He's way beyond us on the higher trails, a diminishing speck, a dark spot on the slopes.

I snowplough to a halt a few feet from her, take a couple of wide sideways steps. The impact of the spill has loosened the bindings on her boots.

'Ouch,' she says, as she tries to move, and then again, 'Ouch!' more emphatically this time.

She's clutching her right foot, wincing. Aside from the dab of red that is her lips, her face is drained of colour.

I slap her jacket free of powder and carefully snap the bindings back on.

Tears spring to her eyes. 'I felt something rip,' she says. She struggles to put any weight on her foot.

'It's all right,' I tell her, and give her my hand.

She removes her glove. Her fingers are warm and pink in mine.

One of the instructors swishes over in a series of effortless crescents. With his help, she clings to my supporting arm.

Back inside the chalet, Ingrid lowers herself into a chair, removes her boot and manoeuvres her leg up onto the table. Angry little red capillaries already snarl the skin around her ankle bone.

My fingertips sting with the cold. The frost on the window-panes sparkles. Beyond the window, the clouds are motionless as though snagged in the tops of the trees.

'A drink?' I offer.

'No thanks.'

'I'll get you some brandy.'

'It won't do any good.'

'It won't do any harm either.' I pour two cups. The brandy bites, with an aftertaste of sweetness and heat. Sulky, beautiful, she takes a long sip.

I sit down. The thickness of the salopettes makes it difficult to cross my legs. 'What's the matter?' I ask. It's not just the ankle. Something else is bothering her, I can tell.

She doesn't look at me, just nurses her drink in both hands, balancing it on her midriff. Her eyes focus on something remote beyond the window. Her foot, raised on the table, operates like a thumb held up for perspective. She moves it minutely, flinches, anticipating the pain.

Her voice is different suddenly, lower in tone. 'I don't want to become dead to you, Capa.'

'What are you talking about?' Emptied of brandy, the cup feels cold in my hand.

The world outside the window grows wobbly, though whether it's a flaw in the glass making things wavy or things inside me shaking, I'm not entirely sure.

'I feel,' she says, 'that if I didn't make an effort, if I didn't go out of my way to try and make this work, I'm not convinced you'd do much about it.'

'I don't give up that easily.'

'You'd fight for me?'

'I've been fighting all my life.'

'That's not the same,' she says.

I start to argue.

'Capa, I'm not going to chase you any more.'

'What are you saying?'

'I want someone who's crazy about me, someone who can't live without me.'

'You mean like Petter?'

I wonder if in the last few nights she has reconciled with her husband. Is that it? Is this her way of telling me that she no longer loves me? Or is she just being provocative?

The light through the window glistens. Beyond, the landscape is an answering blankness. She sits there in her ski jacket, her hair snarled, her hurt little foot all vulnerable on the table, her eyes shiny from the drink.

'It doesn't have to end badly,' she says.

I catch a glimpse of my face in a mirror on the wall. The skin around my eyes looks flaky, my face unshaven, my cheeks hectic from the cold. Seeing myself like this revives a feeling of inadequacy, seems to confirm my unworthiness. 'I thought you preferred happy endings.'

'Don't underestimate me,' she says. There's no mistaking the challenge in her voice.

Maybe she's testing me, I consider, giving me a kind of ultimatum. I glance down at the varnished floorboards, see the scratches made by thousands of feet.

'I want to tell you a story,' she says. 'About a man and a woman.'

'Is this one of your movies?'

She stares into her empty cup. 'They both love each other, only she's married to somebody else.'

'Right.'

'The woman gets sick. But the man is afraid to ask after her, because the husband is suspicious and doesn't like him anyway. He still comes by occasionally and watches the house from a distance, but there's no longer any contact between them. And he makes no attempt to go inside.' It's as if she's in a trance, I think, her voice steady, her eyes fixed on some distant point. 'Days go by, months even, without them seeing each other. Finally he summons the courage to ask someone how she is. And you know what?'

'What?'

'She's dead.' She gives the syllable a solemn weight.

'How?'

'No one suspected how serious it was. She declined rapidly, and by the time the doctors arrived it was too late. So she's dead. The man is devastated. He feels terrible, guilty because he didn't write or telephone. And now there's nothing he can do. She's gone, and he'll never see her again.'

I wait for her to continue the story, but she takes a sip of brandy, stops.

'That's very sad,' I say.

'It's a true story.'

'Have I heard it before?'

'I didn't say it was new.'

'Why are you telling me this?'

'Because . . .' She inches her foot away from some ache on the table.

'You're not sick are you?'

Her eyes make an unvoiced appeal. 'You don't need me, Capa.'

'That's not true.'

'I'm stronger than you think,' she says.

I'm about to answer when, following two sharp knocks, the doctor comes in, play-acting an exaggerated shiver. Bits of powdery snow blow in with him. Behind him, a rectangle of whiteness fills the door. He stamps his boots clean, apologizes for not arriving sooner. Straightaway he removes his gloves and bends to examine her ankle. With the look of a man testing the ripeness of an avocado, he begins manipulating her foot.

'Does that hurt?'

'Yes,' she says, trying to smile.

Ingrid watches me over the doctor's shoulder, betrays nothing of the pain she must feel.

A few minutes later, Petter rushes in. Lovingly he holds Ingrid's hand and whispers reassuringly to her. He helps set the ankle in a bandage. Medically expert and attentive, he is quick to take control, performing his duties as both husband and doctor.

He doesn't look at me. It's as if I'm invisible to him.

I regard the scene as though I were framing a photograph – a portrait of man and wife, a contented couple, with me in the corner of the picture like a flaw.

～

Ingrid sits upright on her bed, her ankle thickly strapped. The room is warm, her nostrils tickled by the smell of woodsmoke. Alone for the moment, she looks around her at the elegant sparseness of the chalet. The plants on the sill, she sees, are touched with wilt. She becomes mesmerized for a few seconds by the gauzy shadows of leaves as they shuffle themselves on a shapeless moonlit patch on the wall.

At night before sleeping, she likes to read. But lately she finds that she can no longer lose herself in a book. She fails to be entertained or distracted by the characters. For the moment, her own adventures seem more pressing. She is too eager to participate in her own life to be diverted by figures that exist only in print.

She pictures her house in Benedict Canyon, its rooms laid out as in an architectural drawing. And she tries to remember what the place looked like empty when they first moved in. The image disconcerts her in its shapelessness and vacancy, makes her cling to the covers like a woman nearly drowned.

Just imagine having to start over again. The prospect terrifies her, fills her with dread, sends her compass point spinning.

She thinks of her family, the space of their home together – the fruit in the bowls, the books on the shelves, the lamp with its circle of warmth. And she experiences a sudden blind need to touch and feel, to remember each of the things, to make a space for them in her head, so that when they're no longer there they can be recalled and she can name them and continue to own them remotely, even though materially they may have gone.

She remembers for a moment her old childhood home, the way she kissed the four walls of her bedroom in a kind of blessing the day she and her father finally moved out. She recalls the grainy texture of the plaster against her lips, the unexpected coldness of the bare patches exposed behind the pictures and the mirrors. She remembers being startled by the way the room looked, stripped of all her things. It was so strange, as if she'd never lived there, this house where she'd grown up and learnt to speak, to read and to dream – every trace of her existence, all the nights she'd slept there, suddenly gone. And with the same sense of foreboding, she thinks of the known spaces of her current home with Petter: the furniture accumulated over the years, the shape of the tables, the longer oblongs of the bookshelves downstairs.

As the seconds tick by and the darkness expands, though, something shifts within her. She finds herself excited by the chance to begin afresh, the opportunity to construct something new. For a minute she even considers which of the many books

225

she'd take with her if she did decide to go, contemplates which ones she'd leave behind.

⌒

In today's ski lesson, the instructor tells me to loosen up, to bend my knees and swivel more, leaning my weight into each turn. Don't resist the fall, he says again. Accept it.

Later, on the slopes, I notice that Petter, when he turns, keeps his legs very straight. He doesn't crouch enough. I happen to stand next to him for a moment at the top of one of the runs. He brings his skis round sharply.

I tell him that maybe he should bend his knees more. I say it instinctively because it's something that I'm conscious of and have been told to notice. I don't say it to annoy him particularly. At least this is not my aim.

Like Ingrid, Petter is an experienced skier, much more accomplished than I am, and he doesn't take kindly to me giving him advice. It irritates him, I can tell. He just shrugs, looks away and, if anything, stands even straighter. In his eyes, it's clear I'm just an upstart, a nonentity, someone he can afford to ignore.

Ordinarily I wouldn't care, but his last patronizing glance makes something inside me trip. Helplessly offensive, I tell him that his wife looks thin and tired. He looks at me, suddenly alert.

'She needs to extend her vacation,' I say. A plume of breath issues from my mouth, wholly at odds with the number of words spoken.

He regards me as if I'm witless, insolent. 'What business is it of yours?'

The diabolical impulse is still in me. 'She looked much better in Paris.' After a moment he begins to realize what I might be saying. I swallow a smile. 'We saw a lot of each other there.'

There follows a silent clatter of calculation, an invisible whirl of information inside his head as he absorbs what I've just told him. The clatter ceases. An answer pings in his eyes. He looks at me and knows suddenly, his suspicions urgently confirmed. He understands everything. It all makes sense.

It's as if you can see events replay themselves inside his mind. Odd recollections come: half gleams and flashes. A thousand-piece puzzle resolves itself, all the bits fitting instantly. It must be apparent to him now. Those moments, half-remembered, when he glimpsed us together at parties, drinking and laughing. The flaw in the corner of the photograph revealed at last.

His mouth falls open. He puts his fist to his chest as if forcing down a tough piece of meat.

He's probably cursing himself for not realizing sooner. Why did he not see it coming? It seems impossible that he missed it. But how, he must be telling himself, could he ever have guessed? The male population of the world all itching to seduce her and she chooses this chancer, this gypsy with a couple of cameras dangling around his neck. All those leading men he suspected, those suave and moneyed stars, with their peach-melba voices, their hydroplanes and vintage cars, and after all it was none of them. Instead it was me, Capa, with my Contax, my cheap cigarettes and sideways smile.

Even now he must be denying it, telling himself it can't possibly be true. One look into my eyes, though, and the dark knowledge he sees there is enough to persuade him. You can see it stretch his face, this sudden understanding, see it widen inside him.

Petter is neither obtuse nor stupid. Gone is his frivolity. The air around us grows dense and heavy. The suddenly charged atmosphere can have only one cause. He directs an intense, quizzical gaze at me. I feel his big-eyed, unwavering stare pin me like a butterfly on a plate of glass, and though he tries bravely to contain it, his whole face fills with fury. There is silence for several seconds, filled with the wind and the scattered brilliance of sunlight on the slopes.

Like a crack ramifying through a crystal, the telephone cuts through the silence in my room.

227

'He knows,' Ingrid says.

My heart turns over. 'How?'

'Does it matter?'

'What did you tell him?'

'He interrogated me.'

'How did he react?'

'How do you think?'

❧

Ingrid picks up a tangerine from a bowl on the table next to her. She digs her thumbnail into its spongy top, creating a fine spray. A sharp citrus smell fills the room.

Petter stands over her, where she sits in a broad wine-coloured chair, her ankle still heavily strapped. The veins in her lids are purple from crying. Motionless, pale, her eyes stare dead ahead. There is something strange in the air between them, something deep and unfathomable. There's a smell in the room, too, a familiar odour, though for the moment she fails to place it.

Petter's expression is one of false cheer. His eyes are lit. It is clear that he's been drinking. There's a cruelty beneath his bonhomie. The sinews are busily twisting in him, tightening like wires.

'I didn't think you liked scandal, Ingrid.'

Her one good foot taps agitatedly. 'I don't want a scene.'

His eyes are full of resentful energy. 'You play enough of them.' Again that smile, but beneath it the knowledge of the torturer – the persistent viciousness, the clinical sensitivity to the limits of human skin.

Her chin lifts in profile. 'You're pathetic,' she says.

'You want me to be brave, is that it? You want me to face things?'

'You're drunk.'

'Probably.'

'Pathetic,' she says.

'You're in love with him?'

Yes, she considers, that's the explanation; that accounts for everything. It's so simple. Just hearing him utter these words seems to crystallize it for her, sets it straight in her head. She's almost grateful to Petter for clarifying it like this.

His steel-framed glasses glint in the light. 'You admit it, then?'

Her heart thumps. Emotions chase themselves across her face. 'At least he thinks I'm passionate.'

His voice grows small. Something is broken. 'Why?' As if torn from him, the energy seems suddenly gone from his body.

She looks off to one side. Spiders of light in her lashes attach themselves stickily to her sight. 'It's not something I planned, Petter.'

His fists clench, an aggressive reflex tenses his arms.

She stiffens, feels his eyes upon her. 'What are you going to do?'

'You obviously can't stand me being here.'

Ingrid is careful not to exaggerate, not to deploy the distortions and half-truths that emerge routinely in a quarrel, that are part of the essential arsenal of a row. She wants her words to be measured, her feelings clear, precise. 'I didn't say that.'

'You didn't have to.'

She twists the ring on her finger, feels its weight and power, the tight circle of pain it describes. Her voice grows husky, her hair makes a tent around her face. 'I'm sorry, Petter.'

'Why couldn't you just be honest with me and say you wanted an affair?'

'It's not really the kind of thing you say, is it?'

'Why couldn't you tell me the truth, damn it?'

'I suppose I was scared.'

'Of what?'

She feels around carefully for the right words. 'I thought it might make a difference.'

'And has it?'

She sees a lampshade tilted at an odd angle and wants desperately to straighten it.

'Just tell me it's nothing, and I'll believe you.' There's a pained silence. 'Do you want me to beg? Is that it? Do you want me to get down on my knees, and beg?'

'Stop it, Petter.'

He grabs her hand, taking a certain pleasure in hurting her. She permits the gesture, looks away for a moment as if thinking of something else, then just as abruptly snatches back her hand, folding her fingers together in her lap.

'Can you tell me it's been worth it, at least?'

Her voice contracts to a whisper. 'I need more.'

'And you think he'll give it to you?'

'He might.'

The question emerges as a half-laugh. 'He might?'

Her voice is so thin, it sounds disembodied. 'It's all I've got.'

'You've got me!'

Ingrid battles silently with herself for several seconds. She doesn't want to be cruel, but he's forcing her into it. 'Suppose I don't want you.'

This ignites a fury in Petter. A look of concentrated rage transforms his face. An implacable energy takes over, a masculine talent for destructiveness. Hard and hungry like sex, there's a ferocity in his body.

The room grows unsteady. She imagines a vase knocked from the mantelpiece, a chair overturned, the light fixture swaying. Blood thunders inside her chest. Her eyes averted for a moment, she tenses, braced for a blow that does not come.

Petter walks towards the window, paces back again.

Seeing his eyes, the light drained from them suddenly, she wants to take back her words. She has gone too far. She doesn't want to hurt him.

'What about Pia?' he insists. 'Have you thought about her?'

'She'll blame me,' she says.

'No,' he says, shaking his head for emphasis. 'She'll blame herself.'

Ingrid lifts her big eyes, shining. Her heart falls through the silence.

And it dawns on her suddenly what that smell is in the room. It's the smell of a family decaying – the smell of a husband and wife fighting, with their daughter asleep elsewhere. The smell of fundamental human corruption. It floods the space around her, inundates every surface, fills the room with a dark sweetness that makes her want to gag.

She rises clumsily from her chair, trying not to put too much weight on her damaged ankle. And then without warning, as she limps past Petter in the doorway, she does something neither of them expects: on an impulse she reaches up to kiss him.

He catches a familiar whiff of her perfume, the scent of her hair. Her face becomes blurry at such close range. But the moment, full of tenderness and regret, is over far too quickly. He wants to slow it down, to repeat it, to prepare himself properly. He wants to seize hold of her in this instant, to recover her somehow. Instead she averts her face and pulls away. It's over in a second. He's left with his arms open, beckoning, empty. A shiver runs the length of his body and emerges with an involuntary stamp of his foot.

More quickly than he anticipates, she moves away, leaves the room, closing the door behind her with a gentleness that fails to meet the slam inside his mind.

So, he reflects, it has happened at last. What did he expect, marrying a beautiful actress on the verge of becoming a movie star? Did he really believe that he'd be enough for her, that he could keep her for himself? He always knew this moment would come, always dreaded it. Not that he feels more prepared because of it, or that it makes it any easier now it has arrived.

She doesn't seem remorseful, doesn't ask for forgiveness, he notices. She hasn't expressed any regret or said she's sorry. Why? Because obviously deep down she feels that she's done nothing wrong, that there's nothing to be sorry for. She's been led astray, he considers. She's been tainted. She would never have initiated something like this.

Can't she see that when she accuses him of meanness with money, he is only trying to protect her from the excesses of Hollywood? And when she accuses him of being possessive, doesn't she understand that the liberties he permits, the freedoms he grants, are beyond what most other husbands would tolerate? For God's sake, in the last three years she must have cooked him all of three meals, and then wasn't it just spaghetti?

He recognizes, with the clinical detachment he exercises every day in his job, that he might seem short-tempered, even emotionally cold at times, and he realizes, too, that living in a foreign land far away from his native Sweden might quicken any natural feelings of intolerance in him.

It's not the way he likes to see himself, or the way he thinks others tend to see him either. He has always regarded himself as chivalrous and dignified. His good manners and formal courtesy make him appealing in a clean and wholesome Nordic way. Women like to dance with him at parties, while men, seeing little threat in this hardworking and likeable hospital doctor, are more than happy for him to partner their wives out on the floor. After all, isn't he married to Ingrid Bergman? What more could any man want?

He feels humiliated by his inability to keep her and to manage her feelings, by his failure to make her happy. The knowledge of this impotence twists in him until his insides seem ready to snap.

He has a sudden urge to step out onto the balcony, to get some fresh air, to clear his head, even though it's freezing cold outside.

Closing the door behind him, he stands there for some time, listening to the hum of a distant car, to late-night revellers returning from the hotel bar and casino. He sees the stars in the sky, the moon like a hook, and knows that tonight he will not sleep.

He tries not to be resentful, yet feelings of bitterness consume him. Grotesque images of his wife and her lover torture, gnaw at him. He has never before considered himself a victim. Now, though, a whole new vista opens up: a perspective of the lost, the desolate, the vanquished. How could he have missed it? All these people with their melancholy destinies, and he among them suddenly.

The one consolation he has is that Ingrid no longer seems to be the same person. She's changed. The old Ingrid loved him, shared his life, his bed. The new Ingrid belongs to someone else. The two are different people, he considers. It's as if the woman he married has died, and now he must mourn her going.

After a while he begins to piece together a version of their falling out, to arrive at an account that makes sense. The more he rehearses it, the more he believes it to be the only true version of events. He will entertain no other, can see no other. Without escaping blame entirely, he dignifies himself as the victim. Capa becomes a kind of evil genius, wilfully manipulating his wife. Ingrid, meanwhile, emerges as weak and vulnerable, ultimately corruptible and capable of treachery. It's what he can cope with. It is a start.

Standing out in the cold on the balcony, contemplating this, he finds himself oddly enchanted for a moment by the distances and silence. He breathes deeply, filling his lungs, sucking in the air until the space inside him seems to match the space outside and he closes his eyes, imagining that he might just float away. He's able to escape for just a few seconds, get a fresh sense of perspective, before he feels again an immense emptiness descend, feels the hollow within him enlarge, the silence widen inside him like a crack along a wall.

⌒

The lights of the casino dye the snow red and blue. Cigarette smoke hovers like a fog along the ceiling. A piano plays in the background, 'I'm Confessin' That I Love You'.

Straightaway, I win a substantial amount of money. And then again. Each time I win, I double my stake.

A fairground atmosphere surrounds me. There's the sense of an event. I am the toast of the table. Eager to be entertained, and detecting my recklessness, people buy me drinks.

Then something shifts. Three times I put ten dollars on red. Black comes up on each occasion. I stake a hundred dollars, again on red. A fourth time, the croupier announces black. Each time I lose, I double the bet on red. Eight times in a row, black turns up.

'Unbelievable,' says a woman next to me.

When you're winning, you develop this little edge, a special touch, an aura of invincibility. You're driven and just go with it. Losing becomes unthinkable, everything falls your way, and there's this sensation that you're no longer in control. It takes you over. Then of course, things begin to go wrong, and all of a sudden nothing runs for you. You lose the touch. The charm vanishes. The light no longer shines on you and the money just disappears. Pouf!

It's crazy, I'm thinking, as the croupier rakes in the chips. Someone really should stop me. It should be someone's responsibility in this world to take me by the shoulder, to lead me away and say, 'Enough'. Mine, probably. But no one does, and I can't help myself.

At first I don't see Ingrid come in, and I don't know how long she's been standing there, but long enough probably to clock what's going on. When I catch sight of her, I smile. But as she sidles over, she shoots me a look of barely disguised distaste.

She refuses a cigarette, moves forwards stiffly. I see the strapping on her ankle. She must have risked aggravating the injury to get down here.

'What are you doing? Are you mad?' she says.

'At myself, maybe.'

She stands behind me, as if claiming me. She puts her hand on my shoulder and allows it to rest there as a plea for me to leave. 'You could lose everything.'

'What difference would it make?' I look at her but she doesn't answer. 'I'll just have to work harder.'

And I realize that this is what being a gambler means: enjoying winning, but not minding too much when you lose – or perhaps not minding enough.

The ceiling seems to lower. Lights swarm. Mirrors tweak everything into another possible world.

I try to concentrate. The motion of the roulette wheel blurs, seems to run backwards like the wheels of a car or a movie unspooling, and for an instant it feels as if time has been reversed.

There's a momentum to losing, I recognize, a heedlessness that propels you, as when you're skiing fast downhill. It has its own internal logic. All you can hear is the spin of the wheel, the rattle and clatter, the high hum and chance of it. It's hypnotic watching the ball drift and click above the rush of numbers, and you're drawn in as though by a vortex. A piano plays in the background, innocuous enough, and with the slick little pile of chips that is lovely to run your fingers through, the money never seems quite real. So, subtly you're seduced, lured into it. And when you lose, you face it the same way you face the rain and the snow, relishing that feeling of being at the mercy of something bigger than you.

I've lost twelve hundred dollars already. I have a thousand left in the world.

Ingrid urges me to leave now, before it is too late, but there's the desire as in everything to go to the limit.

I feel a strange kind of power.

The croupier's French accent is terrible. '*Faites vos jeux.*'

A familiar inner voice whispers, *Bet it all on red*. An unseen hand prompts me.

In the tobacco haze, Petter's face appears like a goad.

I tell the croupier to put it all on red.

'*Les jeux sont faits.*'

Ingrid looks grave-faced. Petter walks over, stands right next to her, attaches his arm to hers. He sees me, smiles.

One thousand dollars, everything I have, is stacked in two wobbly columns of chips on the red.

I feel closed-in, assaulted by the world's hard corners. Everything seems to teeter on the brink like a drop of water at the edge of a tap, the whole room reflected in it.

'*Rien ne va plus.*'

The croupier spins the wheel and avoids my glance. The ivory ball skitters and hits the chrome ridges. I feel an icy calm descend. A chill enters my kidneys.

The hum of the wheel merges with the hum inside my head. For an instant, everything in the casino seems to spin. The sensation of vertigo quickens, and for a hallucinatory moment Ingrid's features seem superimposed over the bowl. I drink to make everything steady. The inner voice says not to worry, this is it.

The ball clicks more softly along the notches, then settles. The wheel begins to slow.

I feel my hand move upwards as if tugged by a string.

'*Vingt-deux. Noir.* Twenty-two. Black,' the croupier announces.

People reach for their drinks. I feel a couple of consolatory slaps on my back.

I smile, take it in, bow theatrically like a matador, inviting an ironic round of applause.

When I look round, Petter has vanished.

'Happy now?' Ingrid says.

She turns and walks away.

My stake of a thousand dollars is raked from the table. Next to the red, the black becomes a hole through which I fall into a larger darkness, an irresistible plunge into nothingness.

I feel absolutely no pain at all.

Stepping out into the starless blackness and the snow, I feel curiously light, afflicted with a kind of dizziness. Though the cold and wind press through me, my nerves are so numb anyway that I hardly feel a thing.

I wander back to the chalet. The beam of my flashlight skids against the walls, jiggles its zero on the snow. When I point the torch up into the sky, it reflects nothing back, just blackness. Blackness and silence. The dark seems an extension of myself.

Back at the lodge, the doorman – an ex-serviceman probably fallen on hard times – stands in the cold between the inner and outer doors.

I stop, rummage in my pockets, find a couple of notes I didn't know I had, and pass them over. He thanks me, half-salutes.

I reach my room and collapse on the bed. I am more tired than I realize. I feel an ache behind my eyes as if I've just drunk very cold water. And as though a cloud or vapour steals over me, my insides slip, a sort of letting go. I feel myself drift, then sink, and though I do not expect to after all that has happened, I sleep like a baby for a full eight hours.

The final morning sees a heavy fall of snow. It accumulates quickly, building in bright banks, burying cars in the town and generating drifts beyond. The weight of it oppresses the roofs. The hills fill as if picking up static. Visibility is down to a hundred yards.

The ploughs are out early and the cable car still operates. For those of us who leave tomorrow, it's our last chance to be out on the slopes. The funicular arrives with a few crisp inches on it.

My skis are waxed and my boots secured. I go higher than I've been all week.

At first the going is sluggish, and I have to drive with my poles to make any sort of progress. There are a few soft spots where I almost sink in to my hips, but once I get started, I soon gather speed.

Though the storm eddies densely, I can still make out the mountain's white shadow, the grey shapeless trees. The snow pecks at my eyes and nose, clings for a second before melting. Flakes snag in my lashes and tremble there. A quick watery taste trickles into my mouth.

Underneath the top snow, the ice has a glassy smoothness. I hunker down as the ground dips, holding the poles horizontally under my arms. My knees are clamped together and I'm conscious of picking up speed. The wind tugs at my jacket. The skin of my cheeks is pressed back. It's like freewheeling on a bicycle or sledding with my brother on the slopes above Budapest – that flood of oxygen into the lungs, that heart-in-the-mouth excitement.

The whiteness and silence pour past. The snow seethes around me. I feel this little kick inside. A hurried shush is followed by nothing as my skis leave the ground. It's the same feeling I had when I jumped into the Danube from the Elizabeth Bridge, when I chased and clung to the back of a streetcar, the head of a gang of boys.

Energized by a new lightness, I seem to be flying. I feel giddy for an instant, weightless, all but lifted into the air.

Something happens. The equilibrium shifts. It's as if a switch is pulled. Suddenly the current reverses within me. The awfulness of the storm mixes with the heartache of the last couple of days. Blind anger – at myself, mostly, at the world, at Petter – drives me on.

The world tilts. I feel cheated, incomplete.

The moment I learnt of Gerda's death, something dark entered me, the sense of loss like a hole. I always swore I'd never let another woman get close; I couldn't stand to. And all I know is that each new relationship has seemed a dilution of the original energy and ecstasy of that love. Then Ingrid came along and it's as if slowly my faith was renewed, only for everything now to come undone. I can't believe what a fool I've been.

I wonder for an instant whether, if I can go still faster, it might be possible to get ahead of time, to rewind it, and for a second the space seems to warp around me.

My skis hit the ground with a thump. I let out a long wordless howl that trails in a cloud behind me. The vibration shudders up my legs until my whole body is shaking. I want to hurt someone suddenly and I don't care if it is me.

As if willed, as though I'd projected it from within, a hole opens up in front of me. Brilliantly revealed for an instant is a massive crevasse, a sheer precipice like a white mouth that swallows everything ahead of it.

A lightning calculation takes place in my brain. The angle of descent is vertical. There's nothing to deflect me, and I'm going so fast now, have built up such a momentum, that I'm not going to be able to stop in time.

A blue light seems to illuminate the snow. I see my body as from above, the clouds lifted like a lid – my fingers limp, my mouth a dark triangle, my mind an empty room. The snow closes over me, a white sheet drawn across my face.

There's a long moment of falling as in a dream. I think of Ingrid, all the things I long to say to her, all the things left unsaid. Then I feel my insides swerve.

Something hits me hard and without warning from the side. The impact slams inside my head. I feel myself hurled off at an angle. I fall awkwardly, my skis flying off, the poles released like spears from my hand. I tumble headlong for several seconds, snow exploding in a powder like glass.

The world around me comes to a stop. At rest, my insides feel as if they're still being flung on. My face is motionless, cold against the snow, my fingers numb inside their gloves.

It takes a second before my brain reconnects with my body, before I re-establish where I am. The wind stings my eyes. Everything is in negative. The universe shrinks to a vivid point of pain.

What struck me? Did I hit a tree, unseen in the blizzard? Did another skier cross my path? Was I pushed by some benign hand?

Above me, the sky slides back into place.

Bewildered I look up, squinting. And amid the swarm of snowflakes, resolving from the blue-white shadows, I make out a grey form, a tall figure, ghostly in the gloom. The shadow of a man.

He must have seen me careering towards the edge, swung across at speed and by some miracle of collision knocked me clear. He stands over me, his wind-burnt face expressionless, sticks pressed like totems in the snow. A hat covers his head; goggles hide his eyes.

Slowly I reach out a hand.

He remains upright, solemn, gigantic for a moment. His breath forms a shapeless cloud in front of him. A badge on his jacket catches the light and flashes. He stabs the snow with both poles and with a fierce push he is off, sending a spray of powder over my boots. Within seconds, he's beyond me.

I watch his figure recede, grow small in the distance – a furious blur, a crazed dot, a smudge on the otherwise immaculate whiteness.

My bag is packed. I'm waiting for a taxi. Through the window, there are wet shadows and orange spots like rust where the snow has been. Slivers of ice linger. Stretched tight against the glass, they extend to a feeling of tautness in me. Outside someone drives a shovel in a series of low gravelly slurps. The sound scrapes across the floor of my mind.

There's a knock on the door.

It's Ingrid.

Her eyes are moist, her lips bloodless. She flattens herself against the wall, her hands behind her back.

Neither of us speaks.

Bits of ice melt, drops of water falling from the gutter and smashing like atoms onto a metal drum below. Beyond the rooftops, the sun holds a steady golden chord. Like the snow, Ingrid becomes part of the hushed glory.

Slowly her eyes take in the single packed bag on the floor, the room emptied of my things. She looks at me, says something. At the same time, loudly, a crow squawks outside. Clearing her throat, she tries again. 'So,' she says. 'You got lucky again.'

I don't feel lucky.

The thin, high sound of a car arrives below. Neither of us smiles. 'He left you alone?'

She looks down at the floor, nods, painfully lovely. I move

towards her, put my hand to her cheek. It is hot. In the mirror a few lilies duplicate themselves. The reflection of a clock hand advances the wrong way round.

'He wants you back?'

She laughs bitterly. 'He wants me to suffer.'

'Don't be a martyr.'

'You have no idea how obstinate he can be.' She picks up one of the fallen petals, feels its softness, touched with wilt. 'He says he'd never let me see Pia again.'

'He's bluffing.'

'You don't know him.'

'And me?'

She says nothing.

'He wants to beat me up. Is that it?'

'He leaves that kind of thing to his lawyer.'

Slices of sunlight slide around the room. Slabs of shadow follow.

She folds her arms across her chest. Petter is prepared, she says, to give her time to think things through, time to make a decision, to come to a judgement as to what's best for everyone.

I understand immediately what he means by this. He's relying upon her weighing up the financial consequences of separation and divorce, the emotional upheaval for Pia, the social stigma Ingrid will endure, the incalculable harm to her career, knowing that she'll come to the conclusion that it's not worth it after all.

But what about the cry of pain within her, I want to say, the pull of love, the feeling that her inner life needs completion? 'Can you be happy with him?'

'Does it matter?'

'More than anything, I would have thought.'

'Not everyone can be happy.'

'Maybe some people need it more.'

Her eyes darken as if dipped in shadow. 'Maybe some deserve it more.'

I reach forward, so slowly that it can't frighten her, and cup the back of her neck with my hand. Her skin is warm. I motion her to lean back and settle her head against my palm, which she does for a few seconds. The gesture has something baptismal about it, something solemn and sacred. For a moment, I hold her skull as if it's the most precious thing in the world. I take in her scent, feel the tiny pulse in her neck. And as she allows her face to slide from my fingers I feel her lips – not quite accidentally – brush my palm.

Her voice, low and coarsened by crying, seems to travel a vast distance. 'I would have followed you anywhere. You know that.'

'You still can.'

'I don't want to be your mistress.'

Desire twists in me. I want to sink into her coolness. One last wild chance. I summon up everything in me and offer it to her in a smile. 'Then marry me.' The words sound right in my ears, as if I'd rehearsed them.

Her eyes sweep my face with a mixture of amusement and disapproval. 'Why?' she asks.

'I love you.'

'No other reason?'

'What other reason is there?'

Her face dissolves, her mouth becomes blurry.

Having started inside me, the feeling won't let go. 'We could get a house, with a big bed and a large fire, books and wine and cigarettes. We'd have champagne glasses next to the bath, and the house will always be there so we can meet up when we've been away.'

'Why are you saying this now?'

Because, I think, it's only now that I've come to understand that life has a point to it when she's around. When everyone else has gone, when the dark descends at night and the streets grow quiet, when I'm up in my room and my mind is empty, she alone stays in my thoughts. I realize that she gives me a reason for getting up in the morning, for being alive.

'It's too late,' she says.

'Is that what he told you?'

'You're asking too much.'

'I won't fail you.'

There are two, perhaps three seconds before she says, 'Capa, you already have.' Her speaking my name possesses an act of finality.

'You're still afraid?'

She doesn't answer.

The surge of love I feel inside has nowhere left to go. 'I guess you have everything you need, then.'

'And nothing I want,' she says.

There's a silence. The look in her eyes seems far away. Nothing moves, except for my hands, a little tug of the fingers as though trying to pull her back towards me.

'You'll call me?'

'Soon.'

'You mean later?'

'I mean soon.'

The space around her starts to re-arrange itself, subtly adjusting to the fact of my absence.

'You know,' I say, 'it's only now I feel ready to love again.' And as I say it, I recognize that this is true. But my words, having tested the emptiness, come back with nothing. Already she seems beyond me, any claim I had on her gone.

She tries to smile but her face is tense with sadness.

Is she asking me to forgive her? If so, there's nothing to forgive.

I feel no anger. Instead I feel lost, like that time as a boy playing hide-and-seek when I hid so long my friends forgot to come and find me.

A lamp next to the bed makes a low buzzing sound. The noise hovers with the energy of a conscience.

'Where will you go?' she says.

I look across at my Contax on the table. Its dark lens looks in this instant like a hole.

'Oh, Capa.'

I close my eyes and everything is red suddenly. My heart lurches. An ache opens up in my gut. I feel a sense of endless falling like the snow.

∽

A hotel porter knocks on the door of Ingrid's room. She's lying on the bed, reading a script. It's late. She's just made herself comfortable, and now this knocking.

Petter is still in the bathroom. 'Get that, will you?' he says.

With visible reluctance, Ingrid sets the typescript down, pulls herself up from the bed and makes her way to the door, just as there's a second, more determined knock.

A young man wearing a small round hat at an angle nods. 'A delivery for you, Miss Bergman.'

Ingrid takes possession of a package and remembers just in time to tip the porter, retrieving a dollar bill from her purse on the dresser.

'Here,' she says.

'Thank you,' he says, and retires, closing the door behind him.

The package is addressed to her. Intrigued, she opens it and pulls out a long rectangular box from inside. A shoe box.

Her stomach clenches. She removes the lid, sets aside the layers of tissue paper to reveal a pair of beautiful red shoes.

There is no name, just a note that says simply, 'Sorry they're not perfect.'

Ingrid experiences a painful sweetness, feels the tears held inside her head.

'What is it?' Petter calls from the bathroom.

'Nothing,' she says.

Ingrid wakes with a sensation of falling.

When she opens her eyes, she's surprised to see the windows on the other side of the room to where she remembered them. She appears to occupy a different place, twisted, unfamiliar.

She can't sleep at night or get up in the morning. She can't bear the daylight so she turns her face to the wall. Everything seems heavy. A band of tightness spreads across her chest. She finds it hard to breathe, starts wheezing like an asthmatic, needing to gulp little cups of air. It seems impossible that Capa has gone.

Worse still, she finds that as the days and months go by, she starts to forget what he looks like. She tries to conjure his features, the colour of his eyes and hair, the shape of his face. This is terrible. She can't remember. Her body has forgotten him. All that's left is a blur, like an image seen through crazed glass.

She turns over on the bed, presses her face into the pillow and keeps it there for a long time. She inhales through her nose and mouth and prays for the faint, achingly sweet scent of him somehow to rise from the fabric. But although she breathes in deeply, all that comes is an echo, the memory of his smell, a vanished magic; and to remember it is to feel it again, to name it, to know that it is lost.

What happens, she wonders, to all the love that's left now that he's gone? Does it remain inside her? Will it leak away without her noticing? Will it ever come back?

Everything she knows about love, she learnt from Capa, and now he has taught her everything about loss. The great humming nullity of it, like a void. First the shock of love like cold water, and now this sorrow.

She thinks of the months and years to come without him. Grief like a fifth season grips the earth around her. She feels it, a solid physical thing, palpable as a landscape where people like the trees retreat into themselves and rain is squeezed from a thin grey sky.

As long as he was with her, she never thought she could die. Or if she did, then somehow it would be all right, and she wouldn't be afraid because he'd be there to hold her hand.

She recalls a conversation they had just before he left.

'Promise me something,' he said.

'What?'

'That if anything happens, you'll forget me.'

'How can I promise that?'

'Not for my sake.'

'Whose then?'

She remembers it took him several seconds to reply.

'For the sake of being alive.'

19

It's extraordinary, but some days I can be walking down the road – the sun will be shining, I'll be feeling happy – when without warning, I'll think of her and immediately start to feel rotten. And it's not because the place is terrible, it's the fact that she's not here with me.

We sit in a café on the boulevard Saint-Michel. Her hair is tied up and she wears no lipstick. The light and shadows compose her into something wonderful. The radio plays 'Exactly Like You'. Outside, the sugar in the leaves turns the trees a vivid colour. Pollen drifts diagonally – tiny white bits of fluff gliding like little parachutes across the window. Ingrid holds a spoon in her hand. The smell of vanilla rises from her bowl.

We haven't met or spoken for months, but still I recognize every gesture, every pore of her skin, the tiny changes of colour in her eyes like the bands of light in water.

Then we're in her room.

We don't eat or sleep.

Behind her the sky warms from grey to pink, graduating finally to light blue. We sit on the floor arm-in-arm, surrounded by empty bottles, flutes half full of flat champagne.

We've made love several times already. She looks beautiful, sad and tired.

I tell her I love her, and that she has nothing in the world to fear.

I hear her whisper, and though I can barely make out the words, I know she's repeating the sweetest things.

Then while I'm in the bathroom, the telephone rings.

When I come out, a towel wrapped around my waist, something has changed. Her eyes have grown hard and dark, her face closed, out of reach. Her skin gives off a nameless scent.

Something flowery, but coarse too, fills the room. Already she's dressed and ready to leave, wearing her scarf and dark glasses.

I start to say something.

She finds my hand, holds it. 'Don't spoil it,' she says.

The blue light from the window forms an oblong on the floor. I hold her for a moment. My hands leave damp patches on her jacket. She gives me one last regretful over-the-shoulder look, a final glance, remote and soundless. It's as though we're swimming under water, smiling through masks. And abruptly our love becomes a rumour, an obscure adventure, a mystery, no longer real.

I see her open the door, descend the staircase. I hear myself call her name, but it's as if she can't hear me or doesn't want to, and she puts one foot in front of the other and suddenly I know that I have to let her go, that it's the right thing, the necessary thing, and I watch as she walks towards the shadows, becoming part of them, moving away from me, shrinking like a light sunk under the waves.

She's gone for good this time. I know that she won't come back. And while she's tucked up warm in bed with her husband or whoever, I know I'll be thousands of miles away, hurrying up some gangplank to cover another war.

I recognize the sorrow of lost spaces, of possibilities gone. Things might have turned out differently, but they didn't.

Still, I tell myself, the earth will keep on turning, the sun will continue to rise, and I console myself for a moment with the fact that we achieved a kind of splendour; we made each other laugh.

Something of her continues on inside me – a trace, shadowy, unfathomable, and at the end of everything what more can anyone ask for than a love that makes you believe in it, that makes you feel bigger than yourself, that makes you happy and alive for a time?

Beyond the window, the light begins to quicken. The trees sway, full of colour and movement.

The sun emerges like a gift.

*

My bag is packed, my two cameras ready, but something feels wrong.

One thing you realize after covering wars for all these years – they are all the same. In war, there are no distinctions. A good man stinks as much as a bad man when he's dead.

Something else you realize: you have to take a position. Whether it's a murderous Mexican election or the bombardment of China by the Japanese, you need to feel as if you're on the right side, that you're doing something good, otherwise it's pointless and you can't stand what goes on. But then you grow used to the routine and, without realizing, you become a part of it, so that nothing matters except the need to survive. And if by some miracle you manage to make it through, the odd thing is you long to go back again because that's all you know, that's what's familiar, that's the way you live your life and everything else seems trivial.

I used to think that the world was perfectible. I used to think that the perfect girl existed, too.

And here I am now on my way to Vietnam.

How did that happen?

Something clicks. An ugly conjunction like a thunderhead. Everything aligns, slots right into place.

Life's photographer in Hanoi is sick. I happen to be free.

My mother tells me not to go. My brother tells me not to go. Irwin advises me against it. 'Christ,' he says. 'Haven't you had enough?' But my wallet is empty, my debts piling up, and the largesse of my friends has reached its limit.

An inner voice reassures me, urges me on. 'It's all right. You're doing the right thing. You've done it a hundred times before.'

The magazine offers me a lot of money, while the editor tells me I can come back whenever I want.

And the truth is, the only thing I know is taking photographs. I should also know one other thing: risking your life can become a bad habit.

I feel like an insect trapped inside a bathtub, the slippery sides unclimbable, the water beginning to pour.

In my one recurring dream, I don't know where I am. It could be any of the haunted corners of the globe. But always there's a flash, and it's as if a furnace door opens or the mouth of hell itself. The noise shatters my eardrums, followed by a wind that stings my eyes. I try to breathe, but can't. For a moment I seem to be floating and everything happens very slowly, but when I come down it is with a crash. The pain is incredible. My head hurts like crazy and my heart knocks inside my ears. Debris lies scattered all over. A fine rain of soot covers everything. There's a terrible stench of burnt flesh and the sound of gunfire explodes upwards like a flock of crows.

I wake up safe.

Next to me is my bag with its flashbulbs, bedroll and two last letters. I've never felt less debonair.

I grab my camera, load a new film, set the lens to infinity, and click.

The sun blazes, the heat barbarous, the air humid and thick like glass. The feathery edges of a small cloud twist and dissolve into the deep blue sky. There's a smudge of black smoke on the horizon. The fields reek on either side, the rot of vegetation assaulting my nostrils, clinging to my skin. To the right of the rutted road runs a stream. Further off, puddles glint like mirrors, blinding me.

I'm sitting in the back of a jeep, itchy in my fatigues and perspiring heavily. My Contax and my Nikon hang around my neck. The ride from Doai Than to Thanh Ne is bumpy, the driver going too fast for the terrain. There's a jolt as we hit a pot-hole and disconcertingly in the next few minutes the engine starts to rattle. The gears clank. There's clearly something wrong. The jeep putters and grinds to a halt on the thin dirt road, with dark fumes churning from the exhaust. A truck loaded with infantry steers round us, the driver in mockery beeping his horn.

The heat grows more intense. My throat feels parched. Insects hiss like a lit fuse. The Vietnamese driver and his colleague jump out. They have the hood up and are looking at the engine, speaking rapidly in Vietnamese. They point and gesture hotly, and it's hard to tell whether they're having an animated debate or a full-blown argument.

I watch a scrawny ox drop one turd after another in the field next to us. It stinks. I smell it straightaway in the sun. Flies swarm, settle in a black cloud, start a thick buzzing. The ox lopes off, swishing its tail, oblivious of the war and the slaughter going on around it.

I check the time. Two o'clock. The hottest part of the day.

Restless, impatient, I jump down to take a piss and relieve myself against a tree. The seethe of insects continues like static on the radio. I watch for a minute as the men work on the engine. I light a cigarette. In slow, loud French, I say, 'Listen, I'm just going up the road a little.' I point to where the road curves to the left. I make a circular sign to indicate that I'll walk around and that they can pick me up later.

Preoccupied, the driver and his colleague look up and seem to register what I'm saying. They nod briefly and return to their business under the hood.

In chainmail and full medieval armour, Ingrid stands alone on stage in front of the curtain, receiving a rapturous ovation. She bows repeatedly, taking in the applause as flowers are thrown singly and in bunches onto the apron of the stage. The metal of her breastplate gleams under the lights.

Minutes later in the dressing room, the director pops a champagne cork, and glasses are filled until they spill.

The room is crammed with a dozen people, all celebrating the success of the play. Ingrid removes the heavy web of chainmail from her arms and legs, but leaves the breastplate on. Gratefully she takes a drink of champagne, feels the liquid ripple coldly down her throat.

Her fellow actors and crew raise their glasses in a toast. Shyly she acknowledges the salute.

'Have you seen the reviews?' the director says.

Still charged with emotion, Ingrid shakes her head.

He hands her a copy of *Collier's*. The review of her performance is unqualified in its adulation, a rehearsal of the superlatives. There is her photograph in left three-quarter profile, with the headline in big letters: 'Joan of Arc Resurrected'.

Her eye picks out words like 'stupendous', 'marvellous', 'stunning' and 'compelling' before wandering to the next page. There she sees an advertisement for Alfred Hitchcock's new film, *Rear Window*, starring James Stewart and Grace Kelly, and below that a picture of Robert Capa, with an accompanying article: 'War Photographer Dies'. The photograph shows Capa with a happy-go-lucky smile, expressive eyebrows and a cigarette clamped cockily to the side of his mouth.

I walk up the road a bit. The sound of gunfire comes from every direction: artillery rounds behind me; small arms fire pinging in the woods some distance off to the left; shells and mortars pounding a village about a mile ahead.

I climb down into the gully between the road and the long grass, and start across the field, avoiding the largest puddles.

That's me in the middle distance taking shots of the soldiers as they trudge along the soggy path between two fields. There I am, moving back a little, trying to get a better angle. Away from the road, the metallic hiss of the insects increases. The shadows are short, the sun directly overhead. My boots are covered in mud.

Meanwhile at the jeep, the two men continue to debate the best way to fix the engine, their heads bent low under the hood, their hands now black with oil.

Without warning, beyond them there's a vivid flash followed by an explosion in the field to the left. The earth rises in a wall. The vibration shakes the jeep and almost causes the hood to fall.

In the same instant, stunned by the blast, the driver and his colleague duck their heads. The smoke from the explosion comes from roughly the position I was standing in just a few moments ago. But the density of the smoke and its blackness make it hard for them to see.

Soldiers from the road take cover in the gully. One or two start moving warily towards the spot. There are seconds of confusion, panic.

I can't remember what happens next.

The world lurches. A curve of terror forms in my belly. Fear burns in my throat. And abruptly I find myself lying twisted, stricken, listening to my own impaired breathing, inhaling the air in thin sips. I want to gulp great mouthfuls, to take rejuvenating scoops of oxygen, but for some reason that seems impossible. I feel something denser than water pressing relentlessly against my chest.

Oh, God.

I try to speak but it's as if my words have been scrambled or as if I'm talking underwater. I try to get up but my legs seem non-existent, my mouth open, the wind breaking against my face, strangely warm.

My head whirls like a parachute released, open and endlessly falling. And it's as if the ground with its ribbons of road and stripes of field rushes suddenly up to hit me, bang.

Ingrid's face freezes. Her whole body stiffens. Her hand shoots to her mouth.

The sound around her ceases. She scans the article, stares at the photograph. The image of Capa dissolves as if the emulsion has run and become liquefied. Her eyes quickly fill with tears.

She hasn't seen him for several years now. In between, she has left Petter, pursued an affair with an Italian director, whose love blew into her life and whose passion exploded over her like a volcano, leaving her family and her career smothered in a film of hot ash.

She has suffered the full righteous fury of the studio, the moral opprobrium of the public and felt the weight of the heavens fall upon her head. Suffice to say, it hasn't been easy. At times she feels as if she's been living on the lip of an abyss, the edges of the precipice melting. She's still clinging on and feels the steepness of the slide inside her now.

Capa has remained supportive in his letters and generous in his presents, while still leading his rootless, zigzagging life, sustained by some original spark that pushes him on. She has always been grateful for his influence. And now she can't believe that this man who was so full of courage and adventure, who brimmed with joy and optimism, this man who meant so much to her, can possibly be dead.

With remarkable self-control, she puts down the magazine next to a single-stemmed white rose on the dresser.

The director sees her, senses something is wrong.

'Excuse me,' she says.

'Ingrid? Is everything okay?' The director exchanges puzzled glances with other members of the cast and crew. He skims through the review, finds nothing offensive, shrugs, and looks towards the door just in time to see her disappear. The others turn to him. 'It's been a long night,' he says.

I have stood on a mine. That much is obvious.

My cameras are smashed. I can feel the remains of one of them still fused to my hand. My left leg itches like mad. The taste of blood enters my mouth.

My head tells my hand to move, but nothing happens. It won't budge. The connection is gone.

Shit.

I try to swallow. The blood bubbles inside my throat. I make an effort to turn my head. Nothing. Only my eyes move occasionally, and then the space around me moves with them.

I hear myself say, 'No,' quietly as in a prayer and everything grows silent. I feel the breath sucked out of me as if by a pump.

Next to me lies a mangled harmonica, just a few feet away but out of reach.

I feel my eyes close slowly, open again.

Something thick runs from one of my nostrils. I try to sniff it up, but can't. It's too painful. And the pain increases so that it feels like a knife is sliding behind my eyes.

I'm still aware vaguely, in a kind of hallucinatory stupor, of where I am: in a field, with the sun blazing above and black flies starting to buzz in mad circles around me.

A white-hot light shoots through the roots of my hair. The pain is unbelievable. My head is an inferno. My insides are on fire.

This isn't good, I realize. In fact, this is very bad.

I sense something massive and implacable push at me, rip me open from within.

Not now, I think.

Ingrid makes her way through the dark back of the stage as though through a small labyrinth, still feeling the oppressive weight of half her armour.

She makes a silent effort to remain calm, but her legs start shaking. Her heart hammers. She feels the throb inside her head.

Everything around her grows cold and dark. She staggers over suppressed gulps, feels her cheeks now hot with tears.

The truth hits her. The world has an edge and Capa has fallen off it.

Impressions rush in on her, converge in a single spot at the centre of her chest. Her throat swells so that she can hardly swallow.

She remembers the smell of him in her bed, the way he made it warm and musky, lending it a sweet heaviness; she remembers the wet shine of his eyes and how he'd stretch there next to her so that she could touch the whole length of his body; she recalls how he found everything funny – not because it was, particularly, but because the sense of merriment he felt couldn't help but spill – and now something in her revolts at the thought that he could have gone from the world. Her whole being shouts out, 'No!'

And yet part of her feels ashamed. What right does she have to feel this grief? She had the chance to save him from himself, didn't she, to prevent him going away again? She had the power to rescue him. And she let him go. Let him go in order to protect herself.

She realizes something else: she always thought this moment would come, always feared it was inevitable. It seems obvious now, looking back, that things were going to turn out this way. He went to a place she couldn't go, somewhere she couldn't follow, and while she tried hard to imagine a world in which they might be together for ever, she always came up against this area of darkness, a space she could not live inside.

Her legs unsteady, she emerges onto the stage. The theatre is empty. She stands for a few seconds, lost in the silence, contemplating the red plush seats, the litter of used tickets, the hanging branches of lights.

Without warning, a man emerges from the shadows brandishing a camera.

In moving forwards to meet the moment, I feel the wind rush from some dark mouth like the future hungrily sucking me in.

My blood is using up the redness of the world. It feels like there's a needle in my chest when I breathe. At first I try to resist the pain. Then I give myself up to the hurt that surges through my body. And slowly comes a remote floaty sensation. My brain shuffles pictures, generating an inner mingled hum.

My fingers open like a starfish and return slowly to a limp leaf curl.

I enter a vast nameless space, shadowless, beyond perspective, where it's impossible to know what is up or down.

It's a moment of exceptional balance.

Everything grows hushed as at an eclipse.

I think of Ingrid. It is her image that enters my head, and though there have been other women and several years in between, I can't forget her because I know it was my one chance to get out of this mess, to avoid all this horror, and I blew it.

I can't let go of the memory of her face because it is the most beautiful thing I've ever seen, and it makes me happy to think of it even though I'm lost. And while I'm startled by the vastness and the silence, things don't seem quite so terrible in this instant, just still and quiet and blind.

At the last possible second, the world goes stretchy. A dream-like distension, moving from colour to black and white.

The moment composes itself.

The darkness possesses me, inhabits and takes hold of me, grows without me knowing until I find myself consumed.

My eyes like a doll's are lifeless, misted like the skin of a plum.

It's as though someone has opened the back of a camera in sunlight and all the images have whited-out.

Past and future dissolve until there's only the present, this instant, now. And slowly in this crumpled moment, emptied of the vibrations of life, I feel absorbed like a liquid, embraced like a lover, a whisper of dust, still warm.

'Miss Bergman?'

Ingrid looks up, startled as the photographer takes a shot of her standing alone on the stage.

The flash blinds her for a second then fades, leaving Ingrid's face frozen in the afterglow. There follows another explosion of light as he gets right up close.

'Thank you, Miss Bergman,' he says.

And as he retreats, with the spots of light still staining her eyes like glimmers in a cave, there's something about his jaunty walk, his rapid manner, his roguish charm and streetwise liveliness that makes her want to call him back. But by the time she's registered the fact, he's gone, vanished as if by magic at the back of the theatre, slipped through the door beyond.

She feels herself grow pale, which is strange because her face has always enjoyed high colour. It's part of her shyness, her lid-fluttering diffidence – that sudden rush of blood through the capillaries to the thin surface of her skin. What she would do for that now, to enjoy that hectic element in her veins again and feel her face quicken with a hot prickly flush. At this moment, it is heat she needs.

All she can think of is Capa, the fact that he's gone. She wants to hold him, shake him back to life, tell him how glad he made her, how happy she felt just being with him. And while she knows that it's too late and there are too many moments to recover, still something of him lingers in the dark, a recreated sweetness that mingles with the warm scents of the June evening beyond.

Live intelligently, he once told her.

She stands motionless, a mockery of heroism in her medieval breastplate and ridiculously fringed hair. She thinks about what he said, and in this instant a gust of love runs through her. She holds her breath for what seems longer than is possible while her ice-blue eyes grow clear again and the lights strike unexpected rainbows on the stage.

Alfred Hitchcock slyly dramatized the relationship between Robert Capa and Ingrid Bergman in his film Rear Window, *released in 1954.*

That same year, covering the beginnings of the war in Vietnam, Capa stepped on a landmine and was killed. He was 40.

Ingrid left Petter Lindstrom for Italian director Roberto Rossellini. The resulting scandal forced her to leave America. Though it yielded three children, including the actress Isabella Rossellini, the marriage failed. Ingrid made a successful Hollywood comeback in 1956, went on to secure two further Academy Awards, and married once more. She died on her 67th birthday after a final glass of champagne.

Acknowledgements

Books that proved especially useful in researching the novel include Robert Capa's memoir of the Second World War, *Slightly Out of Focus* and Ingrid Bergman's autobiography, *My Story*, written with Alan Burgess. In addition, biographies of Capa by Richard Whelan and Alex Kershaw, and of Bergman by Charlotte Chandler, Laurence Leamer, Donald Spoto and David Thomson helped to establish the essential facts within which the fiction is framed.

Thanks to my agent, Caroline Davidson, for her wise counsel and endless patience, and to Victoria Kwee, Laura Macdougall and Isobel Ramsden for their many helpful suggestions. Thanks to Venetia Butterfield at Viking for her initial faith and subsequent encouragement, and to Elspeth Sinclair for her impeccable editing. Thanks to Katy Ricks and Sevenoaks School for the award of a Taylor Fellowship, which helped give me time to write. And thanks ultimately to Ruth, Saul and Ethan for their love and unstinting support.